The Children Must Dance
Penguin Books

Tony Maniaty was born in Brisbane in 1949, the son of a Greek migrant. He grew up in a succession of corner stores, and joined the Australian Broadcasting Commission at eighteen. As a journalist, he has worked for ABC News and Radio Australia, the BBC and other organisations in Australia and Britain. In 1975, he covered political events in East Timor. With a grant from the Australia Council, he gave up full-time journalism in 1981 to concentrate on fiction writing. His short stories and photographs have appeared in a number of magazines. *The Children Must Dance* is his first novel. He is working on a second novel, set mainly in Greece.

THE CHILDREN MUST DANCE

Tony Maniaty

PENGUIN BOOKS
Published with the assistance of the
Literature Board of the Australia Council

Penguin Books Australia Ltd,
487 Maroondah Highway, P.O. Box 257
Ringwood, Victoria, 3134, Australia
Penguin Books Ltd,
Harmondsworth, Middlesex, England
Penguin Books,
40 West 23rd Street, New York, N.Y. 10010, U.S.A.
Penguin Books Canada Ltd,
2801 John Street, Markham, Ontario, Canada
Penguin Books (N.Z.) Ltd
182–190 Wairau Road, Auckland 10, New Zealand

First published by Penguin Books Australia, 1984

Copyright © Tony Maniaty, 1984

Typeset in Italia by
Dudley E. King, Melbourne

Made and printed in Australia by
Dominion Press–Hedges & Bell

CIP

Maniaty, Tony, 1949– .
The children must dance.

ISBN 0 14 007089 3.

I. Title.

A823'.3

CONTENTS

The island of Inhumas is not real, and the places, people and events described on it are also invented. Any similarity with persons living or dead is purely coincidental.

ACKNOWLEDGEMENTS

This novel was written with the generous assistance of the Literature Board of the Australia Council. With thanks also to Ed Douglas, for help and inspiration; to Rose Creswell, my agent, who nursed the project with undying faith; and Carla Taines, for her invaluable editing and advice; and to Angela Kerley, who was there from the start.

The following works are cited in the text:
The Malay Archipelago: The Land of the Orang-utan and the Bird of Paradise by Alfred Russel Wallace, MacMillan & Co., London, 1872; *A Naturalist's Wanderings in the Eastern Archipelago, a Narrative of Travel and Exploration from 1878 to 1883* by Henry O. Forbes, Sampson Low, Marston, Searle & Rivington, London, 1885; *Natural Theology; or, the evidences of the existence and attributes of the Deity, collected from the appearances of nature* by William Paley, Faulder, London, 1803; *The Mysterious Island* by Jules Verne, Sampson Low, London, 1894.

Lavender Bay, 1984

For my parents;
and for Goinxet Bonepart, who knew well in advance
how short his golden life would be.

The boy banged the side of the fuel drum to see if any had been stolen overnight, but he wasn't brimming with curiosity. It was a revolutionary job, like the rest. A seagull winged overhead in the empty sky, and behind it a light aircraft circled the town. The year was 1975, and the war was over. The dead on both sides were buried, under the black shade of bougainvillea outbursts by the sea. The survivors had tried to put the Livre fighters under white clusters, and the Fragas beneath the orange and red. But the August sun had beaten them: the decomposing flesh had to be tossed in and mixed, and now it was impossible to tell which side they had fought on. The sea had kept its secrets too, swallowing brothers and strangers alike. And we, the living, had tried to forget and couldn't; and now the trouble was growing again. Dead or alive, they would not rest: just as we had not rested, and finally won. The war, war! The vibration off the rusty drum got halfway up Eduardo's arm and dissolved. But the dull noise told him it was full of something.

BOOK ONE: THE TOWN

Have you seen? I have not seen.
Do you know? I do not know.
Have you heard? I have not heard.

ONE

'He couldn't wait?'

'No, no. He had to get back by dark.'

'To Darwin?' the boy asked.

'Yes.'

'Was it the same pilot?' He paused, at the question. 'Did he bring the senhor professor here?'

Ranse nodded. 'Probably. But you weren't old enough, were you? That was seven years ago.'

The boy said he was twenty-four, but looked much younger. He lifted the wooden pole, high up. 'Over there he lived, in the hills.'

Dust stirred in the treeline – the vehicle, coming to get him – but he could see enough to imagine where Goddard might have lived, and worked. Up behind the algal coast, where the country was strung off a spine of volcanic residue; or perhaps further down, where the spare vegetation tangled at the foothills with thicker brush and vines. The foliage loosened then with tropical hints; and sprouted suddenly from the colonial remnants of Novo Viseu, setting the odd floral blowup against dusty stucco buildings, cream and yellow and finally mustard with age. *Was this Goddard's world?* On approach he'd seen the pylons of grubby, unfinished wharves; a few government structures patched back to service; the delinquent outlines of the Tropicala Hotel for foreigners. And through the whole town, the broken alley-ways and discomfort of recent fighting and war. The descending aircraft was barely moving too, and its sole passenger – the nephew of senhor professor no less – felt exhausted inside it. *Or was it that awkward time of the after-noon, that time of the year?* Some of the people below were shuffling and pulling buffalo, but hardly mobile. Only one had looked up to wave, and was facing him now.

'What's your job?' he asked.

'Security,' the boy said. 'What about you?'

'Fruit. Papaya, mainly.'

He stalled, tapping his stick on the runway. 'Do you know about coffee?'

'Not much. Why?'

'We need a coffee export, that's all.'

'You mean expert?'

'Yes,' the boy paused. 'The priests taught me. You know any Portuguese?'

Ranse rocked his heels, waiting. 'Não.'

On the other side of town, the face of the last governor stared through the broken glass, and Thermudo da Cunha observed it closely. The eyes sank into dark flesh and the uncomfortably thin mouth was pulled into a smile, but held back equally by a lumpy chin. *Even then they should have guessed.* A portrait of uncertainty, the Minister for Information of the Democratic Republic of Inhumas thought as he stepped back a little. *Taken only four, five years ago.* And did the rulers of Lisbon know in advance they were going to lose, were the unfocused eyes trying to show it? Or perhaps conceal it: as the Empire of four indestructible centuries had obscured its own demise for so long that its sudden collapse was almost incidental, in passing. Da Cunha gulped down his drink – the frame was splintered now, after all – and lifted the needle from the scratchy record. *Stardust, revolution.* All he knew was the Governador wouldn't accept reality for an answer, quite common among bureau-crats; or confront it for a fight, unusual for a soldier. But had left the turmoil to them – a politican in the end – to the Fragas and Livres, to thrash it out. And the side which fights against hypo-crisy and personal ambition always wins, of course. *Bullshit, stardust, naturalmente, of course.* He poured another drink, and looked out to sea: a long way from anywhere, it was. *All I know is: the Fragas are left this troubled island, an abandoned*

6

gift. Given to us, more or less. And half our brothers are dead and the true people of Inhumas are left where they started, with prehistoric trunks and a determined lean not to Left or Right but to the sea: like those pandanus palms out there. And new-comers to our evolving history will enter, he thought, on a dubious rise. Because he could hear the plane buzzing over-head, like a miserable fly. He kicked the dog at his feet.

'Come on,' he said. It was time to meet the stranger, the suicide man.

'This is him now,' the boy said.

The grubby jeep ambled up the runway, and the driver pumped the brakes a couple of times and halted. He gave a single wave. Three soldiers in the back lolled out with rifles and waterpacks and confronted the wilderness of the airfield. They set off singing for the perimeter, or talking to themselves. The driver got out.

'I'm da Cunha,' he called, 'from the Central Committee.'

Ranse walked over, followed reluctantly by the boy.

'Call me Thermudo, please.'

'Nicholas Ranse. How do you do?'

'Information.'

'What?'

They both paused. Ranse was confused and tired, da Cunha not. He looked at the Australian with caution, or curiosity per-haps.

'You've come about Senhor Goddard?'

'Yes. My uncle.'

'Nearly three weeks ago it happened. He shot himself.'

Ranse nodded. 'The embassy in Bangkok told me. I was out on a project.'

'Now's a better time to come, anyway.'

'Yes.'

Da Cunha walked around the jeep, pushed down the loose bonnet, and came back. 'If we can help.'

'Thanks.' He turned to the clear sky, hardly a trace of blue in it. Beneath it sat a new nation, and he could have been its first tourist.

'The light was going on him. The pilot.'

'Too bad,' said da Cunha. 'I wanted to send some brochures back to Australia. But then I suppose he loves his own country more.'

'He loves his plane, that's all.'

'Maybe,' he said. 'I'm the Minister for Information, anyway.'

'I see. Can we go to the town?'

'Of course, to the hotel. Please get in.'

As they drove off, the fuel boy threw his stick into the long grass edging the tarmac and adopted a handstand: a reaction to a very private thought, a pose.

The year was starched by heat, but they swam on a road ground smoother than any spice. Ahead the town was layered carelessly from the flat with its rows of Chinese shops in ambuscade, to a fading cross on the hospital up the slope. A swat of clay roofing here and there, a bent cathedral cross – hit by cyclones, or fighting – and all this against the diminishing scale of the Tagua Mountains, with fine edges of smoke rising from scattered fires where the natives were burning off. Ranse looked about, at a familiar but alien landscape. *If it's not Asia, where are these people from and where are they going?* Their platform had floated across Oceania, absorbing all the physical cultures it could find: the birdlife and outrageous plants, miniature kangaroos and tropical frictions wherever they existed. But resting now off the northern hints of Australia's enormous bodyweight and leather gums. And only the toughest eucalypts cling to granite cracks here, he thought, on this side of the Shark Nest Sea that separates them from us. Everything about it was slightly different, and empty. The air itself, not even yesterday's air from Asia coming down to stifle them; but so dry it smelled of nothing. Except the vague emotional vacuum he found himself in. His nostrils gave up, and eyelids lowered to a blur. Did it really belong to his earlier days, or was the discomfort born simply from the bandaged rhythms of the jeep? The epidural landscape would always surface, from time to time. And now da Cunha was driving somewhere to test him against the heat fatigue of getting there: simply that, or what?

On a swelling tide of dust, he listened.

'Sooner or later,' da Cunha was saying, 'the worm sticks his head out, or the weeds expose themselves through the ground. You know that's it, with traitors. And then you kill them before the weed grows, because it spreads sideways into the schools and villages. But that's not why you're here, is it?'

'No,' he said.

I've come to find a dead man, he might have whispered.

'Well?'

'Perhaps it is.'

Da Cunha nodded, steering the jeep around a stray buffalo. 'What I'm talking about is a very old fight. It goes back into history, a long time. My ancestors fought for this land.'

Ranse surveyed the bleakness of it. 'They must have been very excitable people.'

'Oh, always. And now we are.'

'Who did they fight?'

'Each other,' da Cunha offered. 'And nearly everyone, sooner or later. My own father fought the authorities, of course. He traded monkey hides. They were very popular in Europe, before the war.'

'I've never seen one.'

'Never?'

'Only on monkeys.'

'You've been to Europe?'

Ranse gave a nod. 'Tell me about your father.'

'Por exemplo. He suffered a heart attack, his wagon was blocking the road. The governor was coming and they knew he hated the authorities. So they shot him, dead.'

'That's quite an example.'

'Just there,' da Cunha clutched at his chest. 'A gentle man, very kind. I was studying in Lisbon, but I'm told there were more monkeys at the grave than people.' He grinned. 'They say he traded their skins but never killed one. Can you believe it?'

Ranse smiled back, uncertainly. 'We're all monkeys, I guess.'

Da Cunha was encouraged. 'What about your father?'

'He died. When I was young.'

'And the professor, he looked after you?'

'More or less.'

After the next explosion of dust, da Cunha steered to another topic. 'I'm doing broadcasts, too. Believe me, no lies.'

A stopwatch hung from his neck, and he shook it.

He had been through Asia, shifting north to find what Australia couldn't give. And from Bangkok had flown to this, the Uncle's paradise, and would return soon enough. There was no language he couldn't speak coming out of Thailand's steamy bowl of cultures. *Ranse looked at his shoes. 'Não,' he whispered.* His body dragged along now, still bound mentally for Chiang Mai: the platforms jammed with Thais going north and nowhere; away from whatever with sauté rice, Singha beer, hot peppers of sex, miles of slowly sinking slums, the kids in putrid klongs, trains away on a hot September night, the wind blowing long hair over his shaven face. He knew Bang Sue Junction and kids riding rusty bikes, playing tennis on the tracks: how could you do that? Where the pregnant mother pauses for rest, smiling sorrow, endless boxcar blues, express to Chiang Mai the man said but he should have guessed. And always wondering: do they love me, love me not, those Thai orchids with three petals and a scarlet pistil on fire; and never waiting for cruel answers, escaping the Bangkok bars and heading north for fresh air and higher mysteries of life. Quitting the grimy days, no class in Bangers. And none here, judging by men in threes: sitting around the hotel sipping beers. He'd never been to this country before.

Ranse carried his own bag through the beer garden, stepping over strands of dead party lights. An old man was hanging them from the branches, but there were no tourists in sight. Only the locals. And dangling from a mango tree, a monkey: playing with itself among the dark, shiny leaves. 'It runs in the family,' the ghost of da Cunha's father could be heard calling from above.

Just another game, but he hadn't come for fun or escape. Ranse shut the door but the catch wouldn't work, and leaned on it. At last inside the Number One room. With its enamelled lampshade and crusty shutters overlooking the Nameless Ocean which he couldn't see, because they were shut. It didn't matter, the sea was full of submarine life and dangers. Be there afterwards, but first to sleep. To gather strength, to face the bitter unexpected end of filial love as it was once. *Lift the crab pot, Nicky!* On the flight over, a dream he'd forgotten about. *I'm going down in the river mud, Uncle Sam. Grab a hand, help me!* As it was, before the fates took over; the way they always did. But he wouldn't rush or push them this time, or force his luck into dark unequal corners.

Ranse stepped forward and emptied his pockets on the way, shooting for the bed. He could afford to sleep.

These are complex times, millions are lost in tides of treason and discontent. Aren't you glad you got away, weren't all the others stupid for staying on? Of course I can't talk – in Thailand hoping for hope, and making a few mistakes. But looking at things with my own fallible eyes at last. Or did you think I'd be eternally blinded by human kindness, or what passed for it years ago? The nephew supported by a crippling mentor, wasn't that it? No, no? I see a frown – the oldest surviving turtle, all that grit and swallowing sand and you love it, Mighty Naturalist, soaking up your atmospheric regeneration and the stench of leaves. I'm half drunk all right. Why would I disturb your island constitution, by visiting? What could I say to a tower of positive thinking, or is it the Mental Giant you're supposed to be? The others thought you had designs – but I know better. You're just trapped Sam, and getting old and bored in the sun. Will I send this, my first scrap in five years? You'd probably use it for shit-paper, or worse – evidence for the locals. How are the testy Portuguese treating you – or coping, more to the point? But who cares, I'll leave them to it. And get back to the swelling jungles Sam, where I belong. Dribbling by day but the nights are sealed on tight lips and thighs. Oh yes – I'm into it. Open the bottle, Nicky Mouse! A couple of smiling shots for you.

In a mirror the day's growth hid little, did nothing but raise more questions. Deeper and darker the brown eyes fell – the unmistakable eyes of Nicholas Ranse – until they caught sight of the dangling bulb and were exposed to it. *Oh, that was some letter all right. Rising from the Ocean of Badmouth and Regrets, a single tissue of wounds infected by a year's handling. And never sent. Waiting for much more than a stamp, it was.* He scraped over the jugular and slipped a few hairs off those blood vessels near the ears, which were faintly protruding. But the lines of a strong jaw, and a reasonably happy man were also there. Only transient too. You could take away that balance, or have it snatched from you and there'd be blood all over the floor. And that was no way to treat a new blade. It didn't matter with Goddard of course, who hadn't shaved for thirty years. *And now the Brisbane photos were ruined, caught in last year's flood with the humble flotsam of other faces and lives.* Under the tangle of confusion and hair, what was the Old Man really like? Whether good or awful, Ranse hadn't seen behind the mask; and now it was rotting like old Agfa paper, and gone.

TWO

'Same again, Gecko. Twice.'

The barman produced two bottles and opened them clumsily. Ranse looked around, waiting. The tired hand of Portugal had come and gone, leaving a half circle of cedar with fake portholes and maroon walls. A gallery of mirrors stressed the blunder, and caught the reflection of the stranger at his side.

'Dutch stuff,' said the Englishman.

'Thanks. Nicholas Ranse.'

'I'm Aggett. You look like you haven't slept for a week.'

'I just woke up.'

The barman smiled and held a glass to the light, and started to hum. It wasn't quite *Waltzing Matilda,* but a vague rendition of gum leaves on ice.

AGGETT   Clever of Gecko to notice. (Grins) The gecko on the wall knows all, they say. Especially when it gets dark.

RANSE   They prefer the sun.

AGGETT   Probably. But I think he prefers it in here. (Tapping his ear) Isn't that right, amigo? (Turns) So what are you about? I hear Goddard's name mentioned.

RANSE   (Nods) Getting his notes, books, things like that. Cleaning up, I suppose. Couple of days and I'll get back.

AGGETT   (Lighting a cigarette) To find out what happened.

RANSE	Perhaps. That's pretty clear.
AGGETT	So they say. Suicidio.
RANSE	The police?
AGGETT	Just the army. No police here, they're still working that one out. I was upcountry when it happened. (Looks at barman, still polishing the same glass) He was your uncle, right? (No answer) We never met.
RANSE	That's all right. I hardly knew him either.
AGGETT	You don't sound too upset.
RANSE	(Shrugs) Still trying to figure out why he did it. A gun of all things.
AGGETT	(Emptying his bottle, slowly) The place is full of mysteries, though fairly straightforward ones. I think Goddard got left behind, that's all.
RANSE	Or the past caught up with him.
AGGETT	Oh. Why did he leave? (Cheerfully) I thought Australia was *la dolce vita*. That's what the Maltese say, in their own way.
RANSE	A few rough years, I suppose. It's not all sunshine and beer. If that's what you're after.
AGGETT	So why live there?
RANSE	I don't, anymore. (Sipping) Bangkok. I bought an apartment, Nang Linchi Road. (Looking up) A furnished box, really.

He'd have to leave quickly before he blamed his deranged uncle for this. Goddard was a curse. But as quickly he recalled the name of the man on the bamboo stool; or his notorious retreat to Malta at least. The jungles heaving with napalm and George Aggett – on friendly terms with half the leaders of Asia, important enough to be shunned by the rest – snapped by his own Fleet Street pruning vines in the sun. And here he was, a little rougher in the flesh. Aggett's face rose from a double chin to flat cheeks where nothing emotional seemed to happen. Only the spectacles were buffed up like crystal, and every time he grinned the settings around the jewelled eyes drew in and lines were sketched in all directions. He might have been forty or fifty, or even sixty in a harder light; and impeccably close to the edge, like a well-spoken tramp. It wouldn't take much to bridge the gap, he thought.

AGGETT You're a naturalist too?

RANSE A botanist by training. Formerly CSIRO.

AGGETT What's that, SPIES?

RANSE (Vaguely amused) Commonwealth scientific outfit. Mostly research.

AGGETT Sounds respectable enough. Doing what?

RANSE Fruit. (Pauses) Storage problems, things like that. Not as exciting as your game.

AGGETT You know?

RANSE I read newspapers too.

AGGETT That's a bad habit, like writing the stuff. It burns you up.

RANSE (Slightly brighter) Beats specialising in papaws.

AGGETT That's what you do? (Looks back at the barman, breaks into laughter) Listen, a cocktail party. The socialite approaches the officer and asks him, what do you do? (Drawls) I'm a naval surgeon, ma'am. (Gasps) My, how you doctors *do* specialise!

Gecko nodded along. 'Very funny fella,' he said, putting the glass down at last. It was still coated with something. He opened two more beers without asking, and spilled one on Ranse's elbow.

AGGETT Such animals exist?

RANSE (Unsure) Specialists? You should know.

AGGETT (Looks over his glasses) These days it's everything. The rot started with Vietnam, of course. Asia's crawling with kids who've tasted the spotlight. And they won't go home.

RANSE I was called up. (Examines the beer label) They deferred me.

AGGETT Lucky man. (Lightly) Parents famous?

RANSE They don't exist.

AGGETT Oh, too bad. Flat feet, a broken heart?

RANSE (Smiling cautiously) I was never impetuous.

	University, of course.
AGGETT	It's over now, anyway. Save it for the next one. All the misery and complexity and boredom of it, in the end. (Looks away)
RANSE	Why did you come here?
AGGETT	(Vaguely) Me?
RANSE	Yes.
AGGETT	Who knows? I too was shaken from my rest. For safety, perhaps. (Digs into pocket and unfolds sheet of paper) Listen. *Malta's only seismograph was out of order today and no one knew whether an earthquake had struck the island of Gozo.* That's where I live.
RANSE	Could only be true.
AGGETT	It should be, I wrote it. (Drinks his beer) Malta got a bit slow, that's all. I'm not a generalist at heart. *The man who's ready for anything by virtue of his specialisation in nothing.* Nice line, not mine.
RANSE	(Warming) Verne had a character, a reporter who *learned everything so he could speak of everything.* I like that too.
AGGETT	(Suddenly tiring of it) Come on, they're serving next door.

The dining room, overdone with glass and lace. A fleet of tables moored under the windy ceiling fans. The rattan from outside merging into mock European slipping with age. Pride counted for something, but couldn't pay the upkeep.

'Good evening, Louis,' said Aggett, boarding a handy table. 'Can we join you?'

'Course you bloody can.'

'This is Nicholas Ranse, whose purpose in Viseu is unclear and none of your business.' Aggett turned to Ranse. 'Good to establish credentials first. Mister Culpeper is the town gossip. An unrefined role for a former Army man.'

'Major,' he prompted. 'They had a go at me in Darwin.' He lifted a spoon to his right eye, covered with a patch. The chin shiny wet with soup.

'Cataracts,' Aggett explained. 'It's due off in a couple of weeks. Also the town liar.'

'Plenty of them,' said Culpeper sloppily. A jacket was crumpled around the skeletal frame, with epaulets hanging out: the only military link Ranse could see.

'What are you doing up here?' he asked.

Culpeper lifted his face and turned his operative eye to the newcomer.

'Waiting for my pension cheque.'

It was a drab affair, hungry or not: an oily soup, duck buried under loose pineapple sauce and strange greens. The ingredients had lost their punch, or Ranse had lost his appetite. As the odd pair bickered at his side, he gazed about the room being filled with an assortment of uniforms and racial types. So this was Inhumas, he thought. He'd come to sort out Goddard's death and they were trying to resolve the aftermath of civil war, which it pleased them to call a revolution. He didn't care about that. His eyes shifted further into the haze of cigarettes and noise, and stopped at a more refined couple: a man of Portuguese blood, and the vaguely Oriental girl he was sitting with. Ranse watched. The two of them – husband and younger wife, or father and child – ate silently; but he couldn't decide if it was a barrier between them, or something they shared. The spoons they lifted so carefully could have held mercury.

'The secret's out, Louis,' he heard Aggett whisper loudly. 'You've been drawing cheques from the Australian taxman on outrageous *noms de plume*.'

Culpeper was messing up his duck. 'So?'

'Including your deceased wife's name,' Aggett charged. 'She would have appreciated the irony.'

The old soldier turned to Ranse: 'I'm a confined bachelor.'

'Spinster, more like it,' said Aggett.

'Watch it.'

'Louis used to run the – wait for it – Novo Viseu School of Physical Culture. Hence the muscles.' He leaned closer to Ranse, confidentially. 'I think you'll find she has nothing in common . . .'

'Who?'

'Over there.'

'The Chinese one?'

Aggett sat back, disbelieving. 'Come on. She's not Chinese, anymore than I am. Look at her.'

'I already have.'

'It wasn't obvious.'

He smiled. 'I've seen her somewhere.'

'Wishful thinking.'

But in Ranse's mind a woman of olive skin and round eyes could still be Chinese, after you'd spent a few years drifting the continent.

'What about her, anyway?'

'Oh nothing really. Her name's Ancora Dias, the father's in charge of finance. *Ancora imparo,* I am still learning. Michelangelo's favourite saying.'

Culpeper scoffed. 'Hmmph.'

'A lot you'd know about culture, Louis. Other than the physical kind, of course.'

'I mean about him.' He nodded to Dias, who was leaving with the girl. At the door they stepped aside as a dozen soldiers spilled noisily into the room, tugging at shoulders and grabbing seats. Ranse saw his driver from earlier in the day – da Cunha from the Central Committee – and gave an uncertain wave. He hardly knew the man. And then the girl and her father were gone.

'Fragas,' said Culpeper. 'Eating up.'

'Who?'

'Fragas,' he growled. 'Freedom something or other. The army in other words. Not bloody much of one.'

Aggett corrected: 'The party, actually. The army backs them, otherwise there'd be no party.'

'Not bloody much of one,' Culpeper repeated.

'Look,' said Aggett quickly. 'Eduardo's here. That's rare. He's coming over.'

The youth grew older as he approached, the face slowly revealed until a few metres from the table he was a man in his twenties. It was the same Eduardo, the fuel boy from the airport.

'Como está?' asked Aggett.

He didn't reply, but looked at Ranse. 'If you want to go up to

18

Senhor Goddard's house tomorrow, I'll get you at eight
o'clock.'

He nodded. 'Here?'

'Yes, outside. At eight.'

'Thanks.'

They watched him circle da Cunha's boisterous crowd and
the Englishman turned. 'Doesn't mix. A genuine local,
Eduardo. Haven't seen him for a while.'

'He looks ill,' said Ranse. 'Or tired.'

'Well, that's it. His sister was knocked off by the Livres.
Arrow in the back.'

Ranse sat up. 'You're joking.'

'No, two or three weeks ago. Up in the hills, I think.
Right?'

'Somewhere in the sticks,' said Culpeper.

The sand was uncertain and their bodies bumped as they
pushed on, drifting into wider arcs of the night and returning
with fresh thoughts. A steel frame loomed, with a tin roof.

RANSE   What is it?

AGGETT Used to be the ... Hippy Hilton. (Veering
        closer) Dropouts in the Sixties, grass and
        stuff. Kept them out of the Tropicala and guest
        house. Five 'scudos a night. On the floor, all
        shacked up. Portuguese flushed the place out,
        in the morning.

RANSE   (Wandering off) Who cares?

He felt the breeze coming. Not from the sea, but gently off the
land. It confused, disoriented him. *The moon is new,* he
thought.

AGGETT Heard it from Eduardo. Very scornful.

RANSE   Got hair like Jimi Hendrix.

AGGETT And a seat on the Central Committee.

RANSE   (Stopping) Him?

AGGETT Course. Got to start somewhere. Half the gov-
        ernment at dinner. He's in charge of security.
        Doesn't volunteer it, of course.

RANSE   But he works at the airport.

AGGETT People's democracy. They take turns.

19

RANSE	You're mad. He's the security chief, of the whole country?
AGGETT	(Nodding excessively) The whole shebang. Something like that. Father was a native prince or king. Quite a story, the way Gecko tells it. (Smiles broadly) You'd need a spare four hours, though. Eduardo's brother hit a tree in the mountains. No more tree, no more brother. And sister's gone. One after another, like flies. Eduardo gets the inheritance. Seat on the Central Committee these days. (Pausing, turns to Ranse) Oh, the heart's in it too.
RANSE	His father was royalty?
AGGETT	Dead now.

Yours, his and mine. *Everyone's sooner or later, unless you collect a tree on the way.* Ranse chewed his lip, walked silently up to the ancient cannon where the beach ended in a rocky outcrop. He felt his eyes playing up. Too much spirit, though actually port. They turned back, Aggett leading on the sand.

RANSE	How long you been here?
AGGETT	Few weeks. Since things died down.
RANSE	Weren't here for the fighting?

Aggett halted abruptly, and looked at him: as though struck by the very word, the way *booze* could hit an alcoholic. He hadn't come back to Asia or even this southern tip of it, Ranse realised, to take up old taboos.

AGGETT	Fighting? You mean the *liberation* . . .
RANSE	Yes, that.
AGGETT	As liberated as peas in a bloody pod. With as much room to move in. Ranse, the fighting hasn't begun. (Throwing his head back, chin and throat forming a funnel to soak up the stars) Malta's so different. The nights were never like this.
RANSE	Yes. (Relieved) Strange place to go, isn't . . . wasn't it?
AGGETT	No. Ever been there?
RANSE	Once, to Valetta. Only a day.
AGGETT	Better on Gozo, not as noisy. Been to Italy?

RANSE	Two days. Goddard warned me not to. Bunch of idiots, he said.
AGGETT	Greece?
RANSE	Yes, once. Remember it clearly. It was Thursday. Very hot and dusty. The Acropolis was closed.
AGGETT	Great memory you've got.
RANSE	Could have been a Friday. I had the shits.
AGGETT	What's it matter? Your whole life flushes past when you die. You'll see it then.
RANSE	Just when you're not expecting it.
AGGETT	Right. (Throwing his arms out) Only in this sort of place it might take a few weeks or months to *really* die. And the longer it takes, the more you forget. (Slows, stops) Have to keep revising your life in a war, I've found. Because then all the really interesting things – *important* things – are going on. That make sense?

He knew Aggett didn't expect a reply. It was the alcohol wearing off, and he felt his own senses sharpening; but couldn't make head or tail of the concept, of memory and death. A ghostly membrane was slipping over the channel, fell away and reappeared in the darker troughs of the outer waves. It was smoking underwater, and surfaced again at his feet. Ranse bent to the damp sand and held up the glow.

RANSE	It's phosphorescence. The blue tiger, evil in the sea. Get it in Queensland.
AGGETT	I know.
RANSE	(Vexed) What about you? Ever been to Australia?
AGGETT	Once, a lifetime ago. Cultural exchange. God knows who they swapped me for. (Chuckles grimly at the memory) Better get back, we're close to curfew.

It was hard to imagine Aggett's opposite. Perhaps it was Goddard, huddled in the hills above them: the hills thickening now under a mist. Peering down the long night of a microscope, still for hours at a time, his careful eye detailing the *rauwolfa sumatrana* or a fossil lump. *Calling up their mutual past on a rusty telephone line over half a dozen years; but no answer.* Those hills were dark now, almost evil; and the hotel drew him easily.

THREE

The streets. A grid of unhappy circumstance, crossing the indolent centuries with more recent neglect; until they'd finally achieved a visual odour of permanent rot. Appearances and progress were forgotten. Only newcomers suffered this unpleasant time warp, Teppy Zervos would tell him later: the rest of us in Viseu are constantly busy in our minds. '*Viva os soldados patriotas Inhumas*' called the sign, as if to prove it. But the revolution had swept through their lives as swiftly and violently as a cyclone, leaving a change of flags and graffiti. The people bent past it, and walked on.

'What do they buy?' he asked.

'Some vegetables, fish,' said Eduardo. 'Cloths. Fuel for burners, lamps. There isn't much to buy.'

'Or money?'

'Yes, there's no money,' he said bluntly, 'and not much to sell anyway. We really want a middle class, da Cunha says. We could work in the morning for them, sell to them in the afternoon. And attack them at night.' A smile appeared and expanded – the Prince in him, or devil – but diffused and reworked itself into suspicion as he searched the faces passing slowly along the footpath. They drove by the Banco Ultramarino, locked up for the duration – faced with the Wider Sea, and meaningless exchange rates.

'You looking for someone?'

'Yes,' Eduardo said, turning the car down a side street to the water.

From the broad fronds of poinciana, the sign Happy Bay Guest House was crudely suspended; though on a Portuguese map they'd confess there was no such place. The flag on the roof was bright blue, and below an American convertible floated on the drive of crushed earth. It was old and battered, but lovingly preserved in wax. And suddenly a pert seagull landed, pecking tastelessly at the dirt. The bird kept moving away and returning, hoping whatever it was – stone, stick, shell – would turn into something more to its liking. Ranse watched for a second, or ages until it finally gave up and took off into a gleaming sky, spreading its wings and ballooning up from Earth's false seductions. Unlike us, he thought, with no bloody choice. *Those whom the hurricane had just thrown on this coast were neither aeronauts by profession nor amateurs. They were prisoners of war whose boldness had induced them to escape in this extraordinary manner.* Edging from his memory in alcoholic fragments: the alpha, beta, gamma rays that carried Verne's inflated heroes to their island. The inside of the car was getting hot.

Eduardo stood at a distance, a gnome with frizzy hair. To fight through the heat, the mounting confusion, the ballast of another culture to work him out: it would take that at least. If he stayed here long enough, he'd probably learn more about all of them. But there wasn't time. Even on a sunny day, a stockpile of dark secrets waited in those hills to fill the gaps in his own rattled existence, his own meagre revolution of sorts. If nothing else, it had taken the boy Nicholas and turned him into Ranse the adult: a reasonable being at last. We're all pretty reasonable when it suits, he thought.

A woman appeared, clutching the top of a white blouse and smoothing it, or else wiping the moisture from her palm before taking Eduardo's dark hand and moving into conversation. They took cover under the tree, though there was nothing hidden about the encounter. When their hands separated, she alternately stared at the weedy lawn and listened to Eduardo or gave what might have been suggestions, instructions, questions or even commands. But from the car Ranse heard only the shorelife; and the fine, concentrating hum of his ears. If he was thirty, he guessed she must have been closer to forty. She

seemed slightly irregular, at odds with the moment. The play of
shade on what looked like a high forehead and strong chin
made it difficult to be sure, because other features swam in the
light as she moved and refused to lock into place. Eduardo
remained silent, fuelling the contrast in their energies. She kept
moving her feet, legs, whole body to make points. She shifted
like an actress, out of place and not easily brought to silence. A
performer, a dancer even: until Ranse realised she *was* dancing, skipping back into sunlight across the grass, coming
towards the driveway. His feet tightened. *Was it too late to
wind up the window, to keep her out?* Eduardo followed like a
tired old friend. *Even in this heat, to seal off a dancing guest-
house keeper?* And then she slowed, turning to collect Eduardo
but waiting no longer.

'Hello,' she said. 'I'm Teppy Zervos. You're Ranse, aren't
you?'

'Yes.'

'You flew in yesterday, about your uncle.'

He nodded. 'I'm going up to the house now. Did you know
him?'

'Yes, of course.'

'It's too late now,' he said, hoping to stop her. He wanted to
get away from the heat.

'Of course,' she repeated. Her fingers tapped the door. 'If you
need any help, ask Eduardo. He'll let me know.'

'I'll see what's up there. But thanks.'

He turned to Eduardo, who was grappling with wires under
the dashboard. She wanted to say more – had something prepared, he guessed – but her hands slipped off as the wires
sparked and Eduardo pulled the motor to life. They backed
away from Mrs Zervos and the convertible. The vision of Paradise was reduced to a waving hand, the diminishing sway of a
lone anemone in a blister of dust.

'Whose car is this?' he asked.

'Someone's.'

'She seemed very excited.'

Eduardo looked at him: 'And beautiful. Don't you think so?'

'I suppose. It was hard to tell.'

'She changes often. But very excited and friendly.' His own eyes were shining, inwardly for Teppy Zervos or encouraged by the sudden opening of dimensions as the last of Novo Viseu slipped by. All around the signs of jungle were rapidly gaining on them, but dotted still with leftovers from the flat: a stick of palm, bananas, a lonely cluster of papaws. *Going back to the friendly Thai who laughed: you have nuclear war in the West, guerrilla war in the East, but here – farang – we have papaw warfare. Whole plantations, to eat you up.* Could it be like that here, he wondered; but after a few minutes that changed too and they left the mosquito hideaways, until by tracks switching left and right they were almost on top of Viseu, looking down to its sheet iron and clay roofs, onto the blood-pungent bracts of poinsettias and privacies of old courtyards. And not too high to see even the tangs of butterflies and birds darting to tropical branches. *L'oiseau exotique* by Kandinsky. The island was coming alive, and he saw the hospital cross and simple maze of streets; and the guest house of the mysterious Teppy Zervos with its flag flying against the rising sea breeze and then the absolutely emerald sea itself rising out and up to the horizon, a full but empty hundred miles away. Wasn't the mythical Cipango out there, somewhere? It was sweeter now in the heights, he thought.

'She a lover of yours?'

Eduardo smiled faintly. 'Too old for me. But my brother and her,' he said.

Everything was black and white, of course; or accidentally coloured in red. 'I heard last night, about him. And your sister too. Your family has . . .'

But he wouldn't go on, couldn't reject condolences one minute and offer them the next. He suspected anyway the privacy needed for some appraisal of death, beyond simple bereavement, would not be offered in Viseu: to either Eduardo or himself. Only as a public function, posted for all to tap their feelings on. And to prove it, Eduardo was nodding. Yes, had suffered.

'Why was she laughing then?' Ranse asked.

'Oh. She is nervous, so much. She was really not laughing.'

The straining motor filled the air, alerting every strand of flora and beating heart of fauna. 'Goddard knew where to come,' he whispered to his hand. The drop at the side was camouflaged but still there; the occasional orchid and wildflower shook to the petals. And it came back to him: the game he used to fill not only moments with, but hours and days. His loving uncle had said – was he three, four? – collect all the flowers you can and take the petals off, and count them carefully, then add one to the number and put them under a rock; when you come back to count them, there'll always be one less, because *one gets lost every time in the counting.* The words were tapped on his chest, trapped there even now – what Goddard said was always right. And sitting and bumping now – scraping the car's underbelly – the memory of petals was not with Eduardo at the wheel in these tribal hills, but always in a classroom – his first grade, his mother's old school – because he often saw in his head an abstract setting that had nothing to do with the problem, event, or recollection being shaped. And so Goddard's place, which he'd never seen, was always imagined as the tin shed of the Pegasus Reel factory, leading not onto the broad Brisbane River where it was – or used to be, before last year's flood – but into a flapping, vacant field of grass. That would be wronged soon enough: the last minutes had pulled them away from any chance of flat earth. But then, Goddard wouldn't have taken any chances. The setting would be scientifically determined: the best climate, the most prolific plant life, the least contact with human nature. The ground they tackled now would be above the worst malaria, and lower than hill diarrhoea would come; and only the birds had prying eyes up here. *And then he took all the chances, being neither high nor low enough himself to escape confusion and loss of hope.* The setting for suicide could not be transferred; was abstract enough, he thought.

The track edges softened, and Ranse worked at imaginary pedals; but at every turn Eduardo anticipated his moves a fraction sooner. He was firmly in control, slipping from the contradictions of culture and town into his natural world of silence. And then he lifted his chin to where they were heading.

'Why did Senhor Goddard do it?'

'I don't know. I'm here to find out. What do you think?'

He shook his head. 'People killing themselves, it never happened before. Not here.'

'No,' he replied. 'But they kill each other.'

'Only for good reasons.'

'I'm sure Senhor had one. He never did anything without a reason.'

And he looked about as the wilderness pressed the car's flanks, halting their progress. The climb up, the tossing stopped.

'Is here,' said Eduardo.

The secrecy was supported by vines and no entrance was obvious. Eduardo led through the tangle, twisting and snapping back the creepers that spread at eye level, and bougainvillea laced with thorns. The branches lashed at Ranse's arms, flicked back by Eduardo's surge into a familiar world. And he felt his own teenage years being recycled, coming at him like cane stalks down at the river: so he knew that somewhere behind a few trees, the house would be silently there and waiting. The exotic birds were laughing overhead.

Eduardo turned, and pointed down.

'Where they found him. The gun over there, he fell back before going down. Across these bushes. We checked it before.'

'Thanks,' he said.

'I'll leave you here. In two hours? I have to see someone in the town.'

And standing quietly, Ranse could only think of the sister's funeral; of the beautiful girl cut down by a single arrow somewhere in these hills. So far from undertakers and death, it was.

He saw Eduardo moving down the track they'd just created, watched him being sucked into the tunnel of vines. Until the car started and the exhaust challenged the bird-calls, and even smaller sounds of the island.

Then he was alone. The vibrance of that mechanical echo faded and silence came down like a sheet of glass that cut the life from the moment. And without warning, into that enormous chasm rushed all his fears, doubts, inabilities; the recurrent solitudes and emptiness of too many places; the misplaced hopes that sprang from some inside well and ran amok in a jungle clearing. He came almost to tears, standing at the confused border of the Other's life. *I've stood in this moment before. I've somehow been through all this, but in no other place or even here.* Again he could hear noises – the wild screeching of untamed animals and birds and the hammering vines and trunks – and the day's blistery heat itself came smashing through the glass wall; the years of doubt collapsed, and Nicholas Ranse was running hard – crossing the death spot in the rushes, stepping on puffy lizards and frogs, squashing their hearts in – to find out the secrets of those weary timber walls.

FOUR

'Of course,' he panted.

And drew harder for something else: trying to comprehend on his shaking feet the apparition before him. Ranse went forward. He could feel the weeds and then wood through his soles, the raw front steps cut by the weather, and the verandah. He stood at two beaten chairs set to fight off the empty days. One on its side, the other facing it. He could hear soft footsteps, his own though lighter than a moment before. And then his childhood, and youth was everywhere: a small corner of Queensland far removed from his adult world. Around him the creeping vegetation touched the house and crossed the rails, escaping the dry season and disappearing like a platoon of snakes up the rafters into the warm, dark oven of the roof. In there a mixed can of vines was feeding on the silence. Ranse stamped his foot, watched the dust rise from the boards. *So that was it.* The house of his adolescence – a replica, near enough – with its ironbark stumps and decaying lattice verandah and rotting teeth for steps and a galvanised roof that flexed in every summer's Blow down from the tropics, until the place shook not only by the rafters but by the knees in the Brisbane floods and the April In Portugal sign broke away with the rest of it. So that was the reason for hanging on, for six tortured years: on that bend in Goddard's memory where the River held its colonial charm, he'd built a counterfeit, a copy insured on higher ground against ill-tempered nature but also against dementia and fears of going back. The house of growing up, and being held down; of bitterness and love. There was the hallway, the lounge, the front bedroom: as they'd been two thousand miles away. The shift was continuous, there was no way Goddard could have explained this in a letter. *And our exchanges dried up, took the form of those weird clumps of mud that had to be chiselled off my boyhood shoes and could never be eliminated for good. Mrs Perkins always complained about the carpet.* He moved past the windows and doors with their wire screens so rusty they'd taken odd brown shapes like animals, down past the rooms so embedded in his growth that he could see things that already weren't there and smell things not possibly in the air: the glue of balsa aeroplanes, the sweet ink of English comics, and how to describe the odour of Condy's crystals unless it was the taste of fear as Goddard tipped the steaming purple solution over the inflamed boils he'd brought home from school. He stopped, held his arms to the light: even now the emblematic scars sat against the fresh scratches.

Off the back landing, Ranse descended into the garden and beyond. The wooden dunny with its honeysuckle creeping in all directions was here nothing more than a latrine, a trench with uncertain offerings: tomato and sardine cans, rusting in the fertile pit. His smile retracted a little. Of course you wouldn't need privacy up here; there was enough of it to drive you mad, and passionately so. All he could see were dark, poisonous stalks and blooms of oleanders rising from the surrounds and swaying about the latrine, the dead ground alive at the edges. In that labyrinth by the River it wasn't possible to get lost, only pleasantly confused. By contrast, the simplicity here was over-whelming. He went inside, feeling the heat above; but whether to escape the sun or to explore the deeper recesses of his heart, he couldn't tell.

The benches were clean. Sunlight drenched the kitchen on one side, darkness the other. A tea caddy recognised by its English pattern, a new and insincere clan of saucepans hanging from the wall. A few medicine bottles on a shelf, shaken to reveal seeds and brittle specimens. Ranse left the bottles intact, ran a finger along the shelf and although three weeks had passed since Goddard's death, there was hardly any dust. *He began life without trace, and left before me.* It was too clean for that house by the River, or for an isolated death. Ranse crossed to the cupboard, the door ajar. A bucket pressed from inside, the mop was still damp and the lino clean to the edges. He looked up, to a face moving in the window.

It was his own image, hinged and swaying in the morning breeze. But for a moment he couldn't recognise that face or where it had come from; because he'd never been here as a man, only as a teenage boy shifting from one uncertain leg to the other. Ranse leaned back to the wooden bench. It wasn't death but loneliness that touched every surface in this house.

'Anyone here?'

But the silence continued. He picked up a Portuguese cookbook, splattered with the blood of a thousand tomatoes. It smelled of crude fish, and refused to lie flat; buckling and warped under coffee and onion tissue and watermarks. On one page the author – lost in Lisbon, a stranger – preferred the cold grilled eels, the *enguias à Aveirense* with their curious flavour and bones everywhere. Clean the eels. Fix the tails inside the mouths to form a circle, and season. He put the book down, annoyed for wasting time; and hoping Eduardo wouldn't hurry back from the funeral or wherever he was. *At the graveside, a growing list: the dead girl and Aggett the brave and Samuel Goddard of course, and Eduardo's silence and even the mercurial Mrs Zervos or Teppy to her friends and lovers, and the schoolboy Ranse standing at the fringes.* He'd been hovering mentally for what seemed like hours around Goddard's study, the second room left off the hallway. It was teasing him like an animal stalking its prey even though he was moving and it was still, and Goddard was already dead and he was still alive. He felt the kitchen sliding past his sides, the familiar giving way to shadows. Then the relative darkness that had nothing to do with light entered his eyes and Ranse knew it was his own slowness standing there, as he had waited for punishment so often before.

The door was stiff. He pushed hard and stepped inside, waiting for his eyes to adjust. *Entering the cinema on a glaring hot day, the screen emerging from the depths of sweated canvas and wood.* He could smell it now, and his eyeballs buzzed and assimilated the swelling points of light: a canvas blind first, against the small window; white sheets of paper coming out of the broody desk; the shine off a cracked glass lamp; an empty aquarium with its sandy bottom rising in miniature dunes; a skull fragment placed incautiously on a shelf; and then books, hundreds of them stacked around the expanding room and coming off the floor. And butterflies too, pinned and labelled white and yellow; except for a lone dark set of wings – up close, *cethosia leschenaultii* – caught in an upturned cage once reserved for small golden fish. All forming Goddard's world. He had, for sure, a collector's mania for collecting; letting the pieces pile up in the way that all his passions – personal, academic, sexual too he supposed – were lumped together and fed off one another as much for convenience as strength; until they went down together in a mental depth charge and these loose bits floated to the surface of Oceania as evidence of the destruction done, as planned, to himself. These were the bits that detectives would collect elsewhere, but they said nothing really of the collector, only of the viewer, and Ranse touched them cautiously as his own mementos.

But the books: they were the Old Man's alone and would prove harder, he knew, to extract from the wooden shelves they'd grown into. *The spines might even be booby-trapped, give way at the slightest interference, be glued together for defence.* Every one would be on natural science, there'd be no fiction ('the grovelling of loose minds') and several would carry Goddard's own name – a catalogue of academic authority, some called it brilliance until he went barmy on them and then everyone knew why he'd done it, cleared out to the islands. They'd have their opinions on more recent events too. And would voice them in the hushed but scraping tones of the department before shifting to more comfortable topics. He could see Uncle Sam explaining – in an early Sixties, buoyant way – that he'd reached his own conclusions about the titles of academic works. The universities were emerging from their cocoons, the lecturers were finally coming out of their shells: the hermit crabs of a beach society! Things were going to be different, the country was opening up ('pioneers') and you had to expose those clumsy crabs to fresh ideas; or find new ways of disguising the old. They were all stupid, but he was game and 'Tropical Fruit Culture: The Papuan Experience' was despatched and 'Going Bananas Up The Fly' replaced it with an almighty fart and smile at the same time. *An artless being full of air and farmerish gusto and for all his brains, not even clever enough to tell the helpful lies that other people expected of him and understood in themselves to be the genuine lubricant of a viable society, the allowances that made all things possible. He had no idea about that, or where to go to achieve the completeness he desperately sought: until the protests of that stormy decade shook his confidence and shot him into the Milder Tropics, to the tranquillity of Portuguese Asia and ultimately to this house, to the false reserve of this replicate past; and for that, the perfect place to take up a gun, go outside and die.* Some of the critics had laid siege to his style, but the advice within was sound enough – with a kind of bright Victorian wisdom, a radiant good sense that even Ranse wasn't immune to. Somehow it had kicked him towards a career – hardly his own, or chosen – among the volatile orange clusters of the papaya. He shuddered, and smiled: not for that, but recalling how Goddard's fellow academics were alienated by it.

'They give me the shits, Nicky! All they're worried about is posterity, and pensions. Absolutely gutless they are.'

Always looking like he should have been tramping through the jungle, even coming home from the campus in coat and tie. An energy about him, a humanist creed that had long lost its currency, but was Goddard and had something to do with suicide too he guessed. It was his stump, his baseline until it was beaten out of him – out of lungs, head, heart, soul – not by the Laceys and Goodlucks or even struggling tutors but by hundreds of chanting warriors mistaking him for either a Vietnamese general or a Pentagon well-wisher. Barricaded in his office, furniture and books everywhere: news cameras whirring and notebooks out, the right to reply. *Why should I be held prisoner by well-fed students? Shuttling to protests in their parents' cars? A victim of right-wing slander, and left-wing gossip! What the hell's going on? I've worked in the Third World, among the poor.* A general pandemonium was sweeping over their lives, the baby crabs were running from their

34

shells with banners calling for change, and professors of natural history were not immune; next week it would be zoology, or civil engineering. Goddard couldn't understand it. And smiling at the secret enjoyment of seeing his uncle besieged by frenetic youth, Ranse had seen then how it could be done. His own liberation from Goddard's tenacious nets was closer. He had seen it done and had stood back and watched, not with his own eyes but had heard it happening and hadn't run to join them, or save Goddard, but had seen it all on television that night; and hadn't joined in Goddard's verbal rampage against them but had gone quietly and deliberately to his room down the hall-way; and was smiling the same smile now that he wore on that longest walk away from his uncle, who was fuming. Goddard was mentally snapping twigs for the fire in his head, and the smoke was coming not from the warmth of his pipe but from the flared nostrils with their deep insensitive pores. He'd thought it was political then, but now he understood why. The university's Staff Rebel was cut out of his own territory by a bunch of kids, was being denied his right place as Head of all questioning and change. The pandemonium was theirs, and would be while Vietnam went on. Ranse looked down at the twig between his fingers – still intact, as much as any twig is complete – and replaced it on the cluttered desk, to the earlier point where Goddard's energy was unbroken. He'd been to a meeting on the coming exams, his green tie askew.

'When the jacarandas bloom, kids get constipation! Their brains are so damned busy they forget about their bums. And years later the bowels give them hell, just thinking about those purple flowers. How's school, Nick?'

Well, the college was all right. A vague memory now – form masters, serge pants, Latin, eternal ringing of bells, the cane – all tied up with being fourteen and without parents, and enjoying and fearing that sudden shift in his life. They'd taken their separate, characteristic exits: his father into a shallow, alco-holic grave and mother silently crushed, reduced by a single collision to numerous pieces of memory and touch. The suicidal havoc their deaths had already played in his life would always be there. To make sure of it: Goddard had stretched the membrane of his remaining chances ever tighter and now he wished he'd never held that cruel and secret desire of all children, to have different parents. But in 1960, it was different: a new start, and free to grow in that gigantic empire of gumbark and cane by the river. *At last I'm going to live there: like shifting to another country.* He'd come not from a broken home, so much as a shattered one in which broken glass was always in danger of slicing his well-constructed hopes to pieces. At the end of the salvage line, Goddard was waiting. *Come inside, follow me.* And bluntness had taken care of things: after a week, he began to realise how little he might have cared for his own parents; strangely he could lie awake in bed and miss his loving mother even less than the drunk he'd had earlier for a father. He could never explain that feeling, or others.

Ranse slumped into the chair and swivelled and gazed through the half light not only at books but catalogues, charts, drawings, note pads and maps of the barren peaks beyond the room. *Is he really dead? Or am I asking only to prove I'm alive and – if not quite the person I was yesterday, or the day before that in Bangkok – still able to produce a human child, the one adequate reason for going on. It could happen yet.* As such there were no generations in 1962 and they were both – Ranse the teenage orphan, Goddard pacing the worn carpet divorced and childless – a bit lost. They were more tribesmen then, looking for a tribe to belong to.

'It's not just their bowels. There's fear in their eyes, locked behind their desks. I thump my fist in some kind of *mock* anger – they should all be hooting. But they stiffen with fear.'

Goddard was smiling, though even then for different reasons. They were sadly misplaced, both with their trickle of common blood down his mother's side that suggested more than it delivered; and even that had dried up and now he was dead, and that was truly all. *It had worked then because Sam was older but still young enough to smile it away. The failures came when I grew too much like him for his own liking; and then pushing him, testing him to see how much love there really was and how much he could really stand of being pushed and being loved too.* His mind leapt suddenly to that one blow: to seeing Goddard's large hand blurring his vision and striking the very core of his head, as if to extricate something he regarded as alien from his nephew's newly intoxicated being. He had never wanted to harm, let alone kill and yet he had struck hard – the year that followed was almost blocked from Ranse's memory – and three weeks ago had struck at himself with terrible force and a gutter of discontent seemed to run between those two unnatural points. The imprint of Goddard's hand was still there; not as a memory but as a presence. He could feel the exact placing of it now in the tropical room, no longer against his face but away from his body and then the mixture of chill and heat forced him out of the chair and he raised the blind. The sun hit everything.

He reached to a loose stack of books, a couple from university days: the Wallace opus, and Forbes. For the final years, Goddard had thrown in *The Malay Archipelago: The Land of the Orang-utan and the Bird of Paradise* as much for the title as its contents; with Alfred Russel Wallace defending all that was spiritually pure and scientifically correct, and finding in these islands too the germs of evolution. Though beaten by Darwin, a little too late. Goddard approved even when 'the fat Christian' lapsed into enormous stupidity and ran about urging men everywhere to hang up their weapons and onto their hats for the coming century. Ranse smiled at those lectures. It was left to Forbes – with inoffences like *A Naturalist's Wanderings in the Eastern Archipelago* – to restore some credibility.

He looked back, to the room. The cushion in the chair was sunlit and empty, with the impression of his own buttocks and nothing more. *Those were the better times and in all the years – from best to worst – we never talked about death. And yet we talked around suicide always, so that its encirclement alone was a guarantee neither of us would do it. But then, that pride of yours: the other possibility. If you were still breathing but hardly living, you would have turned Death into an experiment of your own undertaking, on your own terms. Is that precisely why you did it? Surely you weren't that stupid, that far gone.* The options left him floundering in the heat, and it crossed his mind that ordinary men were pretty dumb detectives. A sagging shelf of twenty or thirty diaries would be a reasonable place to start, at least.

They formed a dark row, the same ones Sam had kept for as long as he could recall, in those five-by-eight weatherproof covers that not only enhanced their durability but gave a sort of imperviousness to outsiders. He reached for the first; then moved his finger and whole body to the last, where Goddard's final pronouncement might be. He took it down and sat at the desk, and cleared a wide space as though the volume itself might explode.

The pages were fresh, even those written on. Inside the cover he recognised the writing: Goddard's name and 'Viseu, July 1975' and a blank first page. Followed by notes on *leucopogon obovatus,* where the professorial hand had taken extra care: the inky hooks and jagged strokes were smoothed for the record, growing not sloppier as usual but finer and more perfect until the last couple of lines '. . . calycis laciniis latis obtusis mucronatis ciliolatis 2½mm. longis; corolla calycibus longiore lobis actuis . . .' were close to copperplate. Ranse stared at the transformation. From a contemporary scrawl to Victorian script, it became more scientific and less human; at the same time cleaner and more pristine and less like the Goddard he knew. And then the perfect handwriting stopped, blank pages followed and there was nothing else. He fanned them back and forth, feeling the dangerous breeze against his face, his sweating upper lip which he wiped, even the slightest noise of the pages collapsing from one side to the other; it was taking Ranse into his senses and away from them until the flow suddenly reversed and he opened his eyes and looked down. The sun was crossing his legs and detaching them from his shadowy form.

Before him, around him the books, the diaries in heat: a million words on those walls and not one could audition a man for death. He suffered his own stupidity for thinking otherwise. Of course there wouldn't be a trace of anguish in his journals, or regret. And if the writing was impersonal, the littered room itself felt increasingly empty. The privacy of Goddard's world meant to enter it was to destroy that intimacy, to turn it into nothing more than a confusing shell. Goddard the man had vacated the room long before his body had; what remained was not his, and no amount of investigation would prove otherwise but would, in fact, make the whole episode of his death even more inaccessible and blurred.

The heat was tiring, Eduardo would be back soon. He could smell the timbers of the house, like sandalwood or teak underfoot and heard the planks stretching in the day, shifting about, biting into their allotted nails and crossbeams; and he had no desire to open up the mystery of Goddard's death. The only obligation was to close it for his own sanity and get back to Thailand, to dinners in Suriwong and satisfying trips to the hills. And then Goddard would be placed in context; in *his* context for once. Ranse heard the car coming up the track to get him. He lifted the inoffensive diary to replace it, to pretend he'd never been here. But from his browsing, sweaty fingers it slipped and surrendered its hidden contents to the floor. He knelt into the shadows.

A dried flower and a yellow note, folded once and again. The writing wasn't Goddard's, but a finer hand collapsing and recovering with every few words: an inscription from the tomb of Majmuna, daughter of Hassan, son of Ali al-Hudali. He looked up, bewildered. She died, on Thursday the 16th of the month of Sa'ban in the year 569 (21 March 1174 AD). Ranse scanned the passage, the twisted script and read on: *'See for thyself – is there anything on this earth which can stay or thrust aside death, or charm him away. Death wrested me from a palace, and alas neither doors nor bars could save me from him, I take with me only the records of the works I have performed, to be assessed at my judgement; the works themselves I leave behind me. Oh, thou who regardest this tomb, I am already wasted away within it and dust clogs the lids and sockets of my eyes. On my deathbed and in my present unhappy state, and at my resurrection, when I shall come before my Creator, my faults reprove me . . . Oh brother, live wisely and acknowledge thy sins.'*

The force of the day hammered into the study. Slowly he watched his hand turn into a question mark, with the flower inside. He looked again at the note. A woman's hand for sure. Planted by somebody, at some point to be connected with these unfolding events. With someone or something. Instead of fading away, Goddard's death was falling on him and wringing sweat from his body. What was it supposed to mean?

He picked up the journal, put the note and flower back inside the cover; and pulled down the blind. The room sank into a steamy darkness, but alive now with the confusing snakes of memory and suspicion. Ranse shut the door behind him and walked slowly towards the verandah, clutching the single black volume. As though his whole life had been an incredibly slow procession down this hallway, either that or being propelled through it too quickly to absorb life or comprehend it. *I'm shaking, and standing alone at the front door and it's not Goddard who appears trudging home but Eduardo crossing the front garden. With a gait that's neither happy nor sad, but never changes.* He went down to meet him.

'You ready?'

'Yes,' said Ranse, wiping off sweat.

'All right?'

He nodded. 'What about you? And your sister?'

Eduardo looked blankly, and lifted his arm to the house. 'You find senhor professor's things? A lot of books in there.'

'Taking this one back, now. The rest later.'

'You'll come again?'

'Maybe. I'm not sure.' He hadn't decided anything. 'I need more time, really.'

Eduardo nodded. 'The house won't be touched. We said so.' He turned and headed through the tangled vines to the car, and Ranse was again scratching his limbs to a mess.

'Were your family there?' he called.

'What?'

'Your family. At the funeral?'

'Yes,' replied Eduardo, puzzled. 'That was last month. She was buried next to my brother. He was killed in a crash.'

'Oh. Yes, I know.'

As they edged the car down the hill, Ranse turned: 'Is that where they put Goddard too?'

Eduardo shook his head. 'He wasn't Catholic, you know. Senhor Goddard wanted to be buried on Corguinho, the highest mountain. That's where he is.'

He steered the car down the rutted track to the flourishing coast.

'Good,' said Ranse.

FIVE

A few streetlights were already popping to life, although the sun behind the Tagua Mountains was still giving light and people were shifting with purpose along the dusty footpaths. Soldiers were appearing too; at corners, around the fruit juice stalls, in uniforms borrowed or stolen. *So the streetlights were hopelessly early, and they were just boys with thirsty mouths.* Ranse was reeling and soaking up the town.

'Culpeper's place,' said Eduardo as they passed a clapboard hall. 'With weights. For the tourists.'

It hadn't been a joke after all, the Novo Viseu School of Physical Culture. He could imagine the dumbells rusting with age, growing lighter by years until eventually they'd disappear into the salty air.

'A gym. You ever go there?'

Eduardo gave his usual nod. 'Only for films.'

'He showed, movies?'

'No, not Culpeper. But da Cunha had some, Spanish mostly. They made him close it.'

And through the peeling paint and Fragas banners emerged what could only be a film poster: *El Angel Exterminador* de Buñuel. The angel was wearing jackboots, clutching a thonged whip and rising to heaven.

Eduardo turned: 'You smoke?'

'What?'

'Smoke?'

'No.'

'For you,' he said, producing a cigar. 'We found them at da

Cunha's house. Where the governador lived, sometimes. Bahia, from Brazil.'

'Thanks. Where's the Governor?'

'Gone back, of course. To Lisboa. Somewhere over there.' He smiled for no apparent reason.

And the footpath boys with rifles were laughing and rough, and controlling food queues with inefficiency. People gathered at the back of a truck, for green bananas and corn. The car slowed almost to a halt. One of the soldiers dipped at the knees and combed his hair, using the back window as a mirror. He smiled too and went away.

'What are they doing?'

'From the garrison outside. They parade tomorrow for the President, the first national day. You'll see.'

Eduardo scanned the crowd and stuck his head out, but quickly pulled it in. And was driving towards the Tropicala where the neon tubes were already alive and flickering through the trees.

'Someone,' he said. 'A celebration tonight.'

Like a shape forming at the oncoming dark, compressing the revolution into the distance between Goddard's house and the moody hotel before them.

'For the country?'

But whatever he thought, Eduardo was silent; and saying that it wasn't that, or anything else like that but something else. Ranse held the journal tightly in his lap, and looked out over the Unnamed Sea and saw the huge reflected sunset bouncing right to the edge, and couldn't remember if Australia or Asia waited out there. It didn't matter, for now. He was playing with chance, not just geographical or even physical chances like things happening or bumping into people, but the essence of chance: being unconscious of it. *I am not thinking Goddard's misled me, or he's been murdered or blown apart, I am not thinking maybe I'll still be here in a couple of days or a fortnight, I am simply not thinking. All the while I'm buzzing around Viseu like a pregnant father more than a bereaved nephew, hopping in and out of cars and distracted by faces and the Changing Sea, but I'm not concentrating. I'm not thinking, and chance is moving up quietly and laying its marvellous accidents around me with deliberate error.* So this was Inhumas, he thought: the pearl of distant suffering, the geographical prisoner. He would have to investigate, without knowing where to start. Why the learned Goddard had come, and why he had gone: Ranse tried to keep these mysteries afloat in a rising sea of uncertainties.

The diary was on the bed. He crossed to the basin, and picked up the razor. *The fortune in those eyes. But the darker they are, the darker you see and become. And if all romantics have blue eyes, that only gives them a few more years to dwell on it. That's why Goddard died, because he had brown eyes too.* It was a mystery only because he was too close. Anywhere else – in Sydney, even Bangkok – the police, coroners, the authorities would all agree on the quirks that lead a grown man to pick up a revolver and remove his entire being from the world. Or in the end, perhaps nobody knew. *It's getting through my pores, this place. Close them off – like the Old Man, with a decent growth – and hope like hell you don't suffocate or catch whatever's going around.* Aggett would probably joke 'Out of razors?' because the cues were already in place after twenty-four hours, the whole place and its unfathomable people were getting through his pores. In the middle distance he could hear cathedral bells, announcing 7 o'clock Mass. And noise too coming from somewhere inside the hotel; he realised it had been there all along but was rising now, growing louder and happier in the night full of bells. For a few hours he could forget Goddard and death, and join the celebrations. *Well, why not?* He looked over to the dresser; the note and crushed flower were still posing questions. And the awakened memories of adolescence were cruising through his mind looking for somewhere to rest. Going back to the house where Mrs Perkins would neglect the vases, or leave them till last and sometimes forget, and he – Nicholas Ranse – had wandered into the spare bedroom where a bunch of jonquils had surrendered their sweetness and their erectness and form, and then life itself, and the water had turned into something quite dark and not quite liquid either. In that decaying and vaguely rancid mess he'd seen something of his own evolution – at fourteen, clearer then – and knew his own personality would change, or split, or cave in sooner or later to the pressures of his earlier life. And at this crucial moment, Mrs Perkins had suddenly appeared at the door and said casually, 'Oh Nicky, I'll just take out these dead flowers' and had slipped into the sunlit hallway with his murky future held like some kind of offering to the day, and tossed the lot into the gangly ferns and mulch over the verandah. He shook his head at the memory, and threw it back into Mrs Perkins' grave where it truly belonged. The bells were still chiming. And the flowers tonight were fresh and wild sprays of bougainvillea, floating into the Number One room out of hibiscus clusters and palm fronds. The shutters were closed, and the privacy was both spacious and close. Before the mirror Ranse dropped the gritty clothes from his body; until sweated and warm, he stood naked. His penis had lengthened in the heat, and he chanced a smile. Even longer, it looked ridiculous for a moment.

'Come and join us!'

He waved, for help almost. Strangers waved back but returned to drinks. The lounge was packed with wondrous faces and filled with the disturbing comfort of small talk and glasses knocking about with ice. Someone was crooning a long way off, and it was spilling into the beer garden under the bloodless glow of coloured lights – strings of rotten pearls, alchemy – and floating across the warmest night air. The path to Aggett's powerful voice was blocked. Ranse shifted uneasily through military greens and khakis and was confronted by the unlikely circle of da Cunha, the ageing Louis Culpeper and an overweight lady in flowery chiffon. The owner of the Tropicala, of course.

'Mr Ransey,' said da Cunha. 'Good evening.'

'Ranse, actually. Hello.'

The Minister for Information was poured into a Napoleonic ensemble, like a defeated actor. He was swaying slightly at the edges.

'Senhora, here is – Ranse?' He smiled. 'And this is Maria Mendonça.'

She held her distance, and Ranse moved to shake hands. Closer up he was reminded of a famous opera star, and to prove

44

it she turned her feet to Culpeper, removed a Cuba Libre from his unsteady hand, deftly placed it on the tray of the passing waiter and returned Ranse's smile, all in the space of a second. Behind her, a clump of palm trunks framed the disappearing waiter with the warm and sticky glass; and Culpeper's unpatched eye floated after it. While heart and lungs and tongue stayed behind, swaying to the croon.

'Ranze,' he slurred, 'you dish see mya tchezk camun, djooh?'

Maria Mendonça turned and snapped: 'Louis, belt up or drop dead!'

His bottom lip moved to resume its thwarted inquiry, but Culpeper lapsed into a sudden, voluntary silence. The long night stretched ahead, all questions and no real answers, and drinks going to the head.

'So many people,' said Ranse.

'It's tomorrow, our first big parade since the revolution,' da Cunha stated officially, but tailed off. 'To thank old Presidente for his leadership.'

'Some ability,' scoffed Mrs Mendonça.

'Why don't you come?' he said to Ranse. 'It's a national holiday, everyone will be there.'

'Not all,' Mrs Mendonça chipped in haughtily. 'Those at the Museum won't be attending.'

He thought for a moment da Cunha would belt her, but the Minister's gasp was followed only by the casual delivery of his attack. 'There's no division now, you know that. You're simply trying to make the revolution fail, and my job more difficult. What's going on at the Museum? These are just rumours circulated by enemies, who want to create artificial divisions within our country. We're united under one leader and a common denominator. We are proud and free.' He stopped, and looked about for a waiter.

'I won't be there,' she said.

'Good,' he said, like a defeated child.

Maria Mendonça: with her enormous body and strong will and inventive humour, making up for physical defects. Beside her, da Cunha: a small man, sinewy and confused. Ranse shifted his eyes from one to the other; but what he was thinking was surely not possible. She was resourceful, he was probably not. On her nose was a mole so large that she'd turned it to cruel advantage by resting the bridge of her spectacles on it. Da Cunha would have had it removed, or tried to conceal it with charm. She dropped her large chin and looked over her glasses.

'That's not why Mr Ranse is here, anyway. Is it?'

'No,' he said. 'What?'

'No,' said da Cunha happily, as though Ranse had come to his defence. 'Of course. But you'll be staying a few days?'

'Depends. I might go back tomorrow.'

'Bud daz tchezk sha . . .' spluttered Culpeper, coming to life.

'Shut up, you pathetic idiot!'

A group madness was setting in but the small talk swelled to compensate. Ranse buried his lips into the neat whisky, aiming for relief. Or escape.

'When you're waiting for someone to die,' Mrs Mendonça announced, 'they sometimes become a memory even before they're dead. Have you noticed, Mr Ranse? I'm afraid Louis here has been so long on the end of a life that we think of him as just a fond memory. And that's why we're surprised to see him materialise in the flesh every day.'

The laughter that followed was led by Culpeper himself, who was also the last to stop.

The Minister for Information held a glass to the corner where a pair of tanned strangers were drinking with gusto. 'The pilots for tomorrow,' he said to Ranse. 'But you should be patient, anyway. My own father used to say: sometimes you have to wait, and sometimes you have to wait on top of that. It's true,' he said, shrugging to Mrs Mendonça. 'Perhaps it doesn't translate very well.'

Ranse said, 'That's a lot of waiting for a man in a hurry.'

'But that's life, exactly,' replied da Cunha, now with a true ally against the rages of Maria Mendonça. 'The man in a hurry always waits for the rest! Unless he's the governador, of course. Can I get you both a drink?' And he set off, the brass on his shoulders catching the artificial light.

'Is it true you're here about your uncle?' Mrs Mendonça asked bluntly.

'Yes. Just to collect his things.'

'Books, microscopes, dry leaves I suppose.' She was openly
cynical. 'I'm afraid I was never invited, though he stayed here
at the beginning. Your uncle and I never got on. Absolutely no
reason why we should have, I suppose.'

'Perhaps he didn't have time for friends . . .'

'A few,' she cut in. 'One or two.'

She looked about casually. But he could feel the information
still tight in her mind, held there by some negative passion or
twist: what had Goddard done to her, he wondered? This oasis
of stability, who drank only the purest of waters and gave
nothing away.

'Ah,' she said, 'da Cunha with my drink. And yours, there.'
She tossed her head back to the kitchen or some inner room.
'But you took too long, Thermo my dear. The earth is surrounded by a gilded cage, isn't it? Stay away from the things
that fascinate you.'

Before the Minister – perplexed, utterly alone in this – could
retaliate, Ranse saw his only chance and excused himself with
a smile. Which in its dying moments, fell on Louis Culpeper's
eyepatch and dropped away.

The mango branches chattered with the nightlife of insects and
birds. He could see the monkey's beady eyes too; shifting sideways, diagonally, up and down with intense curiosity. Ranse
muttered a few words. If it was the ghost of da Cunha's father –
the proposition he'd just put to it – then da Cunha should do
something about the wretched thing. Teach it some manners
for a start.

'Come and join us!'

The party bulbs shook in the breeze and sent ripples across
the metal tables and over the heads of steady drinkers. Ranse
was mesmerized by the immediate, and the call. And was
being drawn again to the Englishman's table, which had surely
moved with that internal momentum that crowd and furniture
seemed to have developed and couldn't be stopped. He went
over.

'Nicholas,' said Aggett, 'at last. Meet my friend, Sergeant
Oscar e Sousa. He's down for tomorrow's parade. You know
about it?'

'Yes. How do you do?'

The soldier's hair was crumpled and he was plainly tired, but extended a hand. 'Please sit. A journalist, also?'

'Sorry,' Aggett interrupted. 'This is Nicholas Ranse, from Australia. Here on . . . business.'

The sergeant cocked his head. 'Good. We need trade. To buy or sell?'

Ranse wobbled a hand. 'Not like that.'

'Oh?' e Sousa looked away. 'Guns?'

A jolly English laugh: 'Caught!'

'My uncle. He died here last month.'

Sergeant e Sousa nodded. 'Of course. I know who you mean.'

Aggett jumped in. 'Wait till you see the Sergeant's boys, Nicholas. This . . . *army* of boys, they train at the Aguema garrison. Kids without familes, parents. And runaways too?'

'Just orphans,' said e Sousa, on comfortable ground again. 'Village boys, of family killed by fighting. The discipline is good. And hard work, they need it. Good for them.'

'Like needles,' said Aggett 'and taking medicine.'

'Yes, yes. Good medicine,' smiled the sergeant, loosely shaking his fist. 'Are you coming tomorrow?'

'How could he miss it?' said Aggett. 'He's the original orphan, after all.'

Ranse shrugged. 'Can't get a plane anyway.'

'As my guest.' The sergeant leaned over, and smiled. 'For your uncle. I wanted him to see the boys.'

'Did you know . . .'

But already e Sousa was up and leaving. With his raffish hair and strong frame moving quietly through the beer garden; not in the way sergeants are supposed to, not with efficiency and purpose in his veins: but almost gracefully, like a fluid swallowed finally by the dark.

AGGETT Discipline's good, eh?

RANSE Terrific. What's he, a killer?

AGGETT A veteran. Back to the Japs. A killer *par excellence*, according to da Cunha. *Feels lonely when not being shot at.* Lot of good it's done him. Kept him out of jail, that's all.

RANSE   And in orphans. Why jail?

AGGETT They've locked up half the regulars, in the
        Museum. Put a kid in charge of the army and
        sent e Sousa to exile in the mountains. To
        train orphans, ten and twelve year olds. If
        they were smart they'd pull him into the com-
        mand of course. He'll be back, don't worry.
        (Smiles) Defending the revolução, and show-
        ing kids how to tie knots.

RANSE   He seems happy enough.

AGGETT They all are, here.

RANSE   I know. It's getting to me.

AGGETT Just a device, Ranse. Something he pulls out
        to cover his wounded pride. (Pauses) Every-
        one's got one.

RANSE   Perhaps. What's yours?

AGGETT (Smiling) You'll have to find out, won't you?

RANSE   I think I know already. Underneath the bluff
        you're really a nasty piece of work, aren't
        you? (Grins, looks about) Goddard must have
        felt balanced among this lot. How do they
        cope?

AGGETT You're being too dramatic, Nicholas.
        (Worldly) It's the same every time. Agree
        with their politics, denounce the West, pray to
        Jesus or Allah – make sure you get it right –
        and don't fuck their women. Or at least don't
        get caught. This is no different.

RANSE   It's no holiday. What if you're an atheist?

AGGETT (Considers) Better tell them you worship
        Marx.

RANSE   Supposed to be nationalists, aren't they?
        Maybe they don't.

AGGETT What?

RANSE   Worship Marx.

AGGETT In that case, tell them you're only joking.

RANSE   Maybe I'm not.

AGGETT Oh, then. Better see a psychiatrist. Or a

	bloody undertaker, if the Livres get back. You don't worship Marx, surely?
RANSE	(Smiling broadly) You'll have to find out, won't you?
AGGETT	Couldn't be bothered. (Lights a cigarette) How was it today anyway, up the road? You're a little rattled, if I'm any judge. Didn't find what you were looking for?
RANSE	Perhaps. (Reflects) It's easy on the surface. (Shrugs) Goddard killed himself. After that I'm not sure *what* the hell I'm looking for.
AGGETT	I dare not suggest.
RANSE	(Smiles) I found more than I bargained for. The house is incredible.
AGGETT	So I'm told. Never been there. The whole bloody island's amazing after a few weeks. Gets you in. Interesting people.
RANSE	Come on. (Surveys the crowd) Some of them, perhaps. Who told you about the house?
AGGETT	A lady told me.
RANSE	Not Mrs Mendonç . . .
AGGETT	No, not Courgette. As da Cunha calls her, affectionately. (Mocking) *No, no, Courgette.* He's a poet, after all. I have my suspicions though.
RANSE	About everything, it seems.
AGGETT	With good reason. And a fair bit of leg-work. Nothing is what it seems. Take her – Mrs Mendonça – for example. The general thing is she's stayed on because she's got so much invested here, in this place. She owns the hotel all right but (blows smoke) there's more to it. She had the chance to go to Brazil . . . but she met a man in Lisbon, at least thirty years older. This is just after the war. He was rich and heading for here. So forget Brazil. She married the old codger and headed east. She thought the isolation and a few years in the Tropics would finish him off. But he

thrived, and she withered. Classic, eh? He
finally packed it a few years ago. He was
ninety or more. So her investment here is
more than money. (Looks up) It's a wasted
life.

He topped the whiskies for the third or fourth time. *No, the
fifth.* So that explained Maria Mendonça's passage through the
time warp, through the colonial and revolutionary island and
the steel rods clustered like nerve endings on the roof, waiting
for the slightest expansion of prosperity: a legacy of the husband who refused to lie down and die. *She can't go back now,
it's already too late. Like the others, locked in for their own
survival. Perhaps in Goddard she saw that too. And having
suffered, would have no time for a man who took the easy way
out.* He could see her arguing now with da Cunha; and could see
them not as physical lovers, but as one more set of spiritual
partners wasted in the heat.

RANSE   So who told you about . . .
AGGETT   Over there, in the skirt. Teppy Zervos. Books,
         books and more books. Right?
RANSE   (Nodding) Mostly science.
AGGETT   So she said. Natural science. (Leans back)
         Fairly exciting stuff. But not for you I guess?
RANSE   No. (Watching her move) Sometimes.
AGGETT   Like everything. I used to like chasing house
         fires, now even total war gets lumpy and dull.
         The effort gets you down.
RANSE   Who's she with? Is that Zervos?
AGGETT   Hardly. She gets around. Over there (finger
         shifting) is your man, apparently knows but
         doesn't care. The ultimate apathy. He's a bit
         like Courgette, a good pair even though
         they're rivals. All the others pulled out except
         those two – only he stayed for the business of
         course, not the memories. All the little
         responsibilities were left at his door – the
         resident outsider, he's Greek of course – and
         one day Zervos wakes up and he's all things:
         pilot, merchant, farmer, banker and guest

	house proprietor, though that means nothing anymore.
RANSE	A bright fella.
AGGETT	Just clever. He's got his eyes set on some airline deal – tourists from Australia, that sort of thing. The pilots over there are part of it. When things ease back to normal. And all the other expats return, and when new ones turn up, Zervos will be chief among them. A father figure who knows all the ropes and angles. That's his strategy, anyway. (Smiling) He told me all this secretly.
RANSE	A man of integrity.
AGGETT	Me, or him?
RANSE	Both of you, by the sound of it. So she's out of his grasp?

An actress, a dancer: at that moment Teppy Zervos had one foot on the ground and one on a chair filled by a European gentleman, her tanned toes pointing out of white strappy shoes. The skirt formed a purple tent which the night breeze rippled and loosened. *Into suggestions of. Yes, she would be. The problematic woman, offering no comfort. If he stayed, sooner or later he would have to decide. If she really was as beautiful as her aspirations wanted her to be. She was awkward enough to be enticing. To be that dancer, the sculptor's model, to be framed only briefly. The intelligent face promised no peace.* She turned, aware of being watched and waved to them. Aggett was jovial and waved back; but Ranse felt his tongue dry with questions, and took another gulp of whisky. Control was hard to maintain in foreign territory, and he emptied the glass.

AGGETT	The night, the night air. I'm quite enjoying it.
RANSE	I think Eduardo might have something with her. We stopped by the guest house this morning.
AGGETT	Quite possible. (Resting his drink) Who knows when love will strike, not to mention lust. (He shrugs carelessly) Mine's a bit long in the tooth

for that. But you might like to investigate. Perhaps you should do something about the shadow.

RANSE   What?

AGGETT   On your face. What happened, run out of razors? (Getting up) I'm curious to have a talk with Zervos the apathetic. Wouldn't recommend it, unless you like bores.

RANSE   (Happier) Not particularly.

AGGETT   What's so funny?

RANSE   Nothing.

AGGETT   They fascinate me. Bores. If you have to stay, might as well enjoy yourself.

RANSE   (The whisky working) Not why I came. Seems to know a bit about Goddard's place, that's all. She does.

AGGETT   Wonder why you did?

RANSE   What?

AGGETT   Come.

RANSE   (Uncertain) My uncle died. That's why. What about you?

AGGETT   My dog died.

The performers had moved back. With their bodies all pressed now towards the lounge, he could see Viseu's human knot like a rope trick gone wrong. *Stay there, all of you.* He wanted to identify the importance of it. To keep them all in sight while he – Nicholas Ranse, of Nang Linchi Road and elsewhere – gazed not through the instrument of night but time itself, down past Darwin and the Christian naturalists, the idealistic men of honour and into the colonial world of physical culture, of the British and Portuguese spirit, of cafes and bars where ladies dressed up in chiffon and skirts, and every trace of breeze would blow away unhappiness and fighting fear if only for a couple of hours and hold the promise of an exciting future. Yet for that, the performers were all living in some glorious past; even the new rulers who wanted to be revolutionaries, or reactionaries like Zervos who only wanted to be kings. He and Aggett were the only people who might know what the real world of the

Seventies was like, with its tough angles poking into you and its displacements shattering the soul, its spirals taking you into the void. *You had to be careful, out there.* But in this chancy wilderness, the possibilities were accumulating and endless: the potential for happiness, for disaster, was all about. In the air, the trees; in the eyes of the arrogant monkey in the tree. It was everywhere open and alive, they were living at the edge and flaunting the odds. The tables they were playing at were hermetically sealed, with no touching point to the world beyond, to lands where nobody cared about the misfortunes of a small Oceanic island, because they were preoccupied themselves with staying afloat in the latter half of the twentieth century. This they knew, the performers. And happily took account of it. The chances here didn't involve winning or losing possessions or money but the stakes were made up of sanity and madness, of prim courtliness against belching vulgarity, of reason against dogma, and in the end the strange dice that emerged couldn't be thrown but had only two sides – life and death – and had to be flipped like an old coin. But when it came down it was so rusty you couldn't tell, and the game went on.

Stepping and counting, pacing himself against the alcohol, avoiding the beer garden – all those gregarious lies – shifting into a darkened doorway: to catch up and overtake this whirling confusion. The back bar and Gecko stood there, wiping the same glasses. Ranse looked about. Nobody else in the small pool of light.

'What are you doing?'

'Working,' said Gecko. 'Drink?'

He shrugged. 'Why aren't you outside with the rest?'

'Washing glasses. Some things the same,' he smiled softly.

'No, I guess not.'

A glass went under the lamp, and despite Gecko's age – sixty, seventy – he had graceful hands even where the thickened veins were spotted and wrapped in worn flesh. *They could easily define a man, and Gecko had wonderful hands. He'd heard once about a Casanova who'd seduced hundreds of women with his quiet charms. And taken their money. Most of them wouldn't testify, say a word against him. It was like da*

Cunha's father and the monkeys: he took their hides and they loved him for it. What a world, what opportunities for bluff. All we need are hands that promise the shivers. They were holding a damp towel and he leaned across the bar.

'Senhor Ranse, some water.'

But he stopped. Ranse looked up and recognised the woman filling the doorway. She pushed her frame and its high floral dignity one step into their cavern. Maria Mendonça stood with head flicked up, like a monarch about to order their execution. The common enemy, it seemed.

'We're running out of glasses. And you're delaying Mr Ranse,' she said. 'Do your job properly,' and left.

A hand touched the bubbling glass and Ranse pushed it back, and stood to button his jacket. Now there was nothing to share: already Gecko had withdrawn into silence and duty, and was working his faithful towel through a tray of wet glasses. Ranse dug into his pocket, found some money and left it on the bar.

The front terrace was flagged in stone, and he shifted twice before the chair stopped wobbling. Ranse was still unsettled, unsure. Was it the place or Goddard, the smell of toilets, of greening water on concrete and cool dirt, and urine? He could sense it from somewhere, and beyond that he could hear music babbling into the night. It was all terrible stuff, coming out of a few drinks.

The sky had closed in several times in the past hour. He could have been locked in a dark, windowless cell. Was that where the odour was coming from? He'd never been in jail, but it always made him think of some dungeon with piss. And now he waited, like a condemned man – not at the hands of Mrs Mendonça, but at the silent invitation of Teppy Zervos. *She heard my cry, I didn't call.* Their eyes had met, and he waited no longer for the clipping of her shoes.

'Hullo,' she said.

'The last person I expected to see.'

'Really. Been out here long?'

'Couple of generations.'

Teppy smiled. 'Wise. The usual dramas going on inside.'

'The drama*rama*, as Balzac would say. Always happens

when the drinks are free.'

'Balzac,' she said, sitting down. Slender arms were lifted, and hands flopped into the basket of her skirt. 'What would someone . . .'

'Like me?'

She stopped. 'I'm sorry.'

'Not in French of course.'

'No. What are you reading now?'

'Verne,' he said with slight difficulty. '*The Mysterious Island.*'

She burst into laughter. 'You're kidding. Boning up on us?'

He ignored her. 'Anything to do with science, Balzac was crazy about. Dedicated his best novel to a zoologist. These days science and art . . .'

'A man of serious convictions,' she pushed up her sleeves. 'It's hot.'

'Should all be in the water. No pool here?'

'No pool. Few comforts these days. We've got one but it's empty. Saves cleaning it.'

'What are you doing here anyway?' he asked.

She looked at him, blankly.

'Why stay?' Ranse repeated. 'Everyone asks me, so it's my turn.'

She gave an exasperated sigh. 'Having a wonderful time. My husband came here twenty years ago, looking for oil and . . .'

'Oil?'

'Nothing but sand and mud. So, he built a tourist trap instead. I was his first victim. Came for a holiday, and stayed. Is that what you wanted to know?'

Ranse paused. 'Why did you want to see me?'

'Did I?'

'Others would have thought so.'

She smiled. 'I was curious about Goddard, that's all. About the house. How was it?'

'Still standing. Same as always.'

'You've seen it before?'

'Of course not. Why ask, anyway?'

She tossed her head to the sky. 'I like the place, I suppose. We were good friends.' She looked at Ranse. 'The house was a

56

refuge from nights like this. The boredom and madness of Viseu.'

He almost laughed. 'To get away, you visited my uncle?'

She pursed her lips. 'Goddard shot himself, playing dominoes on the hill. That's all.' Her eyes enlarged and for a second he could see the harder years in there. She was closer to forty, or past it. 'But you're right. He killed himself so what would I know?'

He shrugged. 'Such a lot of interest . . .'

'You remind me of him, that's all.'

'It's possible, something rubbed off. He brought me up.'

'I know. He told me.'

'Say nice things?'

'Yes. He did, actually.'

'Then he was lying, we didn't get on. Did he tell you that?'

Her eyes settled on his, and then Teppy Zervos overtook him: knew more about Goddard and all Ranse himself had been through than he might discover in a few days, or possibly a lifetime. 'Yes,' she said, 'nearly everything.' His thoughts of vague seduction were swamped by anguish, over the form it might take.

'What are you drinking?'

'I'm not,' she smiled. 'I suppose they've besieged you inside?'

'About Goddard?'

'Yes.'

'Not a word, hardly.'

She thought aloud. 'No, I guess not. Suicide's the big taboo. They're all mad Catholics. It's forbidden by some kind of divine authority,' she giggled. 'To kill yourself is forbidden, can you believe it?'

'He must have been popular. With his evolution theories.'

'At least Sam believed in something. It's a great levelling out, Nicholas. Like the natives, they worship animals. A lot healthier than flagellation.'

'He was into that, don't worry. Always the tormented soul. But only in private.' Ranse looked at her. 'You were up there today, weren't you?'

'At the house?'

'Yes.'

'No.'

'The kitchen floor. Someone cleaned it before I arrived. The mop was still wet.'

She paused. 'Yes, me. I went up early.'

'Why?'

Teppy sat up. 'He was pretty scruffy. I thought you wouldn't like to see it like that. Was he always?'

'Yes, and no. A lady came to clean up. Mrs Perkins. The place was okay. Except for dead flowers, she had a thing about leaving them. To die.' His thoughts shifted suddenly to the dry flower, and the strange note folded now in his pocket. But a warm and slight laugh – Teppy's – stopped him.

'Wouldn't have servants here.'

Ranse heard his own voice: 'It seemed he wanted to get away from civilisation as we know it.' But that wasn't entirely true.

'Most people down here thought he was crazy. I mean right from the start. They didn't know him.'

'And you did?'

'He wasn't crazy, I know that. Though in the end he didn't exactly love the place, the life here. That's what pushed him over the edge.'

'You've seen his work?'

'No, only what he told me.'

Ranse pressed. 'You haven't been into the study?'

She shook her head. 'Once, I stopped at the door. It was usually closed. I stood there watching, he was immersed. But he looked up, rushed over and slammed it in my face. He apologised later, said he'd been frightened by me. But I've never been inside the study. Not even now.'

A quietness came over and between them, not powerful enough to cancel either his suspicions or the noise drifting from the beer garden. Ranse slipped his hand into the deep trouser pocket and pulled out the yellow page.

'I found this.'

She took the note and began reading.

'Did you write it?' he asked.

She kept reading, and finally looked up. 'No,' she smiled. Then the quiet itself was broken with a heavy rap, and another.

It was Zervos leaning up to the smooth pane like a frog, nose pressed on it, his belly flattened too and round like a pie. He was looking at them both with a stupid grin.

'He wants to go,' she said. 'I have to drive him everywhere, just about.' Ranse saw the American convertible lumbering through his mind. The rapping was part of the car, an extension of it.

'You know what he told me tonight?'

'No,' he said.

'Drink only to get drunk. You shouldn't leave a party when not yet fully drunk.'

'Oh.'

Teppy Zervos handed back the note, and gathered her purple skirts about her. 'Right then,' she announced with determination. 'Until tomorrow.'

'What?'

'The parade,' she reminded. 'Nuremberg.'

The rapping grew louder, but less urgent: the Greek was beating a slow and irregular drum on their interlude. Ranse nodded to the beat, eyeing the crazy figure preserved under glass. 'You didn't fully answer my question.'

She began moving, not all that pleased with either of them. 'Happy reading,' she said. 'Don't stay up too late, will you?'

His head was swelling with something other than drink as he watched her disappear. And no loving, he wondered? Under the weight of suspicion, of stars? Out there perhaps it wasn't possible; but Ranse closed his eyes, and could see the coming together of love and lies. A figure in his mind: a person but shaped more like a country, with so many faces. And yet to each person, a different place again. *Where was he tonight?* On steady ground with the complete form of Nicholas Ranse: the old, unmistakable person he'd been all his life. But coming out of that was someone else, like a new country inside his own life. It was disturbing: even the face he gave himself was alien. It was a country he'd never been to: had never wanted to visit, until now.

He crushed the note in his fist, and staggered off.

Could have taken a simpler path, or shared whatever spirit was guiding Aggett at that hour to ask what could be done with a drunken failure, early in the morning; but walked on, tired of drunks and celebrations but not tired of course. He tried to read in bed, but couldn't.

The clumsy black thing with a twisted cord. Where did it lead to? Out to the world, to real life or further back to this? A call to her perhaps, so late. Could see her pressed against the bed edge by Zervos, held there hard and soft too. The phone as plastic, a function of war. *Invisible to the enemy, from above. Also presupposes a zone the enemy can't penetrate.* No, he didn't want to talk to her; or anyone else. Only he would call up Goddard if he could, and abuse him. Or thank him for dying. But gone to the mountain, no available lines; it wasn't death anyway, but a question of whether sleep or confusion would overtake him. And the bells started, those of the church with their mysterious pattern of tolls to test if he was sober, awake, capable of performing complex mathematical things before bed, or just the other. And she's lying naked now and maybe they tried to, and maybe not. Or lying there thinking of Nicholas Ranse and what a dream it would be after a drunk. If and when they eventually did what his whole body pretended they surely would. If he stayed here, if he stayed up and entered certain parts of her fluid body; if he stopped confusing the sound of automatic gunfire, the clinking of whisky and ice, and the drumming of his damp fingers on the hardened covers of antique volumes to the point where. Several houses in a bright line. Shutters with lace fronts. A man outside, happily chipping ceramic tiles off the façade. A purple jacaranda, a skirt blowing off the branches. (A little shooting outside tonight, senhor, nothing much.) Ranse, are you there? No answer, but the whole room flexes like a black sheet and comes at you like night. A rose-coloured lamp sways in that tension before storms, an earthly tremor. (Beware the calm eye, it eats you up.) A definite pulse in the air tonight, yes. But the sun is everywhere too: how confusing to be in Bogota or Lima on a Thursday afternoon! The bed shakes in the darkest corner, a cyclone coming down. 'Who is it?' she gasps, wants to know. Clothes falling about her limbs. Yellow abounds, splattered with blood. And wallpaper, on which dense inscriptions form a pattern.

(A pair of thick black spectacles, and a mole has developed on his right ear: so large it conveniently holds the plastic frames in place.) All over the walls, it says Arab things. Now we're getting somewhere. After waiting for cyclones out to sea. Or taxis on a rank, or phone calls on hold. 'Who is it?' she asks. And her fleshy nipples – raised up – sit in triangular frames of pale white flesh, on her tanned body. And the whole structure of a lost day in Novo Viseu suddenly tosses and turns. But spinning out of control, the stupid mole is discovered on his left palm – you'll go blind, causes hairy palms, it's a playful marble of boyhood, one of his balls – and the cruel glasses are gone. The white pyramids dissolve into darkness. And a night of sleep either begins or ends.

SIX

The blades were long, soft, grassy; cooling in the rising heat, and free. Ranse wiped the crust from his ducts. The morning was already scattered like shell fragments along the beach: and bits of daylight and then sunshine bounced back at him. The boy in shorts was clipping the lawn with shears. Clip-it, clip-it; and the sea out there was incredibly blue. Already the air was moving in several directions, but none could stretch past the previous night; the roomful of strangers, the dark reality of drinking, and some of the dreaming too. Houses, wallpaper, and Teppy Zervos: the roomful of strangers. Transients who come and go. Goddard came, and Zervos came, and Aggett came; and then Goddard had died, and he'd arrived; and so on. And clip-it, clip-it: the locals went nowhere, come rain or revolution. *They either clear the way, or set the traps for the rest of us.* His arms clashed around bare shoulders, with a shiver. There was nothing that Viseu or its crazed inhabitants could offer a total stranger. But out there: where did he belong anyway? And whether in dreams or reality, Mrs Zervos had entered the long night just flown and was waiting. Dreams. He'd never been through anything like it: the way the dreaming had suddenly taken off, filled his recent nights of sleep and even days. As distinct from fantasy, the panoramic images of desire. He'd spent his whole life in controlled fantasy, but these dreams were endless, weaving, great curves with no point at all. No focus he could identify, unless the crisp and shadowy Teppy Zervos had something to do with it. The sea was a beautiful blue, Bimbo; and his eyes passed it on to his brain, but the message was intercepted before it got there.

He realised the clipping had stopped. The boy stood up; and was no longer a boy but a grown man of at least sixty – a mistake so tragic he could only laugh. The fawn bloomers dangled around spindly legs, the bones would have snapped like twigs if the flesh wasn't there. It was Gecko, the barman. And he remembered clearly, almost desperately the events of the night before sleep had swamped him; and now checked his internal functions as he stood at the window, desperate for a leak. He waved, and the ageing Gecko returned it. The inconsequence of standing alone in the morning sun, shears in hand and skin turning to leather; he who couldn't hope for more than a couple of decent meals, a quiet listen to the radio and a scratchy letter from his sister upcountry once a month. And for company, the monkey – in the tree above – playing with itself all day. Ranse shook his head with a smile, and felt a terrible buzz.

The activity foreshadowing the National Day parade – the sergeant with ragged troops, sole artillery piece trundled in, stray pockets of resistance – said nothing of strength, or splendour. It wasn't expected, but the two Americans were hot and pissed off.

'How far did we fly for *this?*' asked Racovic, his chest littered with cameras.

The reporter Eisner shrugged. 'I can't believe it,' he said to Ranse, who waited idly for Aggett. It was nearly ten, and the British weren't represented.

'I guess it's not much in the way of pictures,' he offered.

'Not *much,*' Racovic cut in. 'It's worse than a dog show in Oregon. Sooner we get to the hills the better.' Agreement on that.

From the stand, Ranse looked out to the crowd gathering under a few trees. The rise of hot air was rippling the leaves, and children were crabbing their way into branches.

'Can't do much till the parade's over,' the reporter said. 'Just relax.'

'No pictures?'

Eisner was uncertain. 'Get something here, in case the

mountains are no good.' In case you fall off, he means.

The photographer turned. 'But they're killing each other, Howie.'

'Just shoot the kids, okay?'

Racovic gave a weary toss. 'Always the same,' he said to Ranse who was expected to agree, but couldn't raise a nod in time.

Eisner turned. 'Ravi, go have a juice. We'll get the stuff we want up there.' Try a mother's helper for starters.

'Yeah, we'll do that.' He pushed off to the refreshment tent.

'Boy,' said Eisner. 'Is he edgy. Half a glass of parsley milk. No wonder he's losing his cool. Who you with?'

'No one. I'm a fruit chemist.'

Eisner looked out. 'Oh.' *Yes, fruit.*

'Yes.'

And the two people he most wanted to see – or least wanted to see, he wasn't sure – could be vaguely identified as a butterfly and a brownish bug coming through the dust and darker faces on the far side of the João de Peres sports ground. They were like lovers, a breath apart; and for a moment he put Aggett here with the American and he was there with her. He knew he couldn't leave yet.

'Some of his buddies got wasted in the 'Nam,' Eisner was saying. 'He's keen for the action.'

'You're from Singapore?'

'About seven, I'd say. Thank hell it's over,' Eisner reflected with intense brevity. 'Right. Just a fireman's trip, this one. Got a nice deal with Overpress on the fighting. Whatever we come up with. And you?'

Give him a smile. 'Visiting a few days.'

'From Australia, right?'

'Indirectly. You been there?'

'Yeah. In and out of Sydney couple of times.' He began moving off. 'Great place, not like this dump. Have a nice one.'

Already he looked pensive, tramping down to the petulant Racovic at the drinks tent. What could be done with people like that, Ranse thought. Theirs was no reality.

But as the guests assembled, he could feel his own identity

dripping away like ice in the heat; flowing into that common pool of humanity he might have been with at the Tropicala last night. All except the mysterious Ancora Dias, who had failed to appear. *Was she really absent, or was one always lost in the counting?* Along with her father, the silent pair. Over there was da Cunha, switched from Napoleonic drunk to defender of the revolution; and there was the slouch hat of Sergeant Oscar e Sousa, gathering his motley tribe of warriors before the President's stand. With aquiline noses and frizzy hair and shiny flesh, the orphans were an untraceable blend. He gave up thinking of them as Asians – with none of that sullenness and sparkle in equal doses – or Polynesians or Malays, but more like Papuans of the lower islands. But that spirit of boyhood he remembered all right. To outshine each other and the whole army, they were pushing and shoving into a rectangular block of heads. Barely supervised by e Sousa, where others might have struck with force. *Like our form master having it off with the art mistress, screwing her in lunchhour and bullying us in the afternoons. Striking a balance, of course. One day a kid found a packet of condoms in the teacher's room. What was he doing there if not looting a man's preventative wares? But they had to be obtained at any price; and theft wasn't too high a price. It turned us all into sexual outlaws, into urchins of the body.* Even in physical order, the boys all displayed a kind of raggedness. They were hungry for exposure, and then he saw Racovic taking shots after all. Ranse shook his lonely head. For the boys who'd come down from the hills into the plastic hands of the media, such as it was. The camera hammered at their egos (and probably Sergeant e Sousa's) and Eisner took a few notes: meagre it seemed to Ranse but enough to propel the event – the Day itself – into an occasion.

'Enjoying the show?' asked Aggett. 'All eyes glued on the teen-age army?'

He shook his head. 'My attention's nil, thanks to Johnnie Walker.'

'Don't blame me.'

'Mine's demolished,' said Teppy, her face emerging from under a floppy hat. She hadn't slept well. 'It's not being helped

65

by that, either.'

The old speaker next to them was pumping out a garbled cry. It kept coming, a subterranean hymn which defied the heat and technology and flies to bellow the Song of Inhumas. A clandestine bark that could never again sound as pure as this.

'Bloody awful,' pronounced Aggett. 'You need a stirring anthem, at least. Ranse, don't you think it's awful?'

'No. There's hope.'

'Like hell,' Teppy flared. 'The way they run the country. It's worse.'

'Perhaps you're right,' Aggett said, to Ranse. 'If everyone leaves them alone.'

'Everybody is,' she hissed. 'Portugal got up and left, who else cares? They haven't even *got* a victory to celebrate. Against the Livres, that's all. Look at them, it's pathetic.' She stamped her foot. 'The Fragas hearts aren't beating as one, but all over the place. Or barely at all.'

'Like being in love,' said Aggett.

Just as Teppy Zervos herself had something to do with confused sexuality; and with attractive dangers, he thought.

'But look at their love object, a midget.' She broke into a cruel giggle. 'Felix Galvão. Can you believe it?'

The leader of the nation *was* very short, with a uniform tailored so exactly that he looked boyish against the officials and guards who urged him to the platform. A leader who could wisely ban full-length portraits, Aggett suggested. But the perceptions of scale didn't escape Galvão completely: at his side wasn't the usual persuader, but a pearl-handled pistol that he covered neatly with his palm like a lethal toy. *He might have to squeeze the trigger, have to kill one day to survive.* He sat happily in nothing more than a wooden office chair, showing too how easy it was to shift public attitudes with the right set of robes. What was good for one outing could be disastrous for another: the grotesque sight of Emperor Haile Selassie commanding Ethiopia's golden future from a diamond-studded throne, or that Peacock Shah in Iran dripping with fruity pearls and medals, or having to stand to attention at Saturday matinees in the State Theatre watching his own Queen Elizabeth atop a large brown horse; they burned away and he admired the littlest President for the chair he was sitting on.

Aggett was nodding patiently. 'Oh, it's irrational,' he said. 'But so appropriate. A revolution *is* a form of love. Because it's blind, has to be. The only problem about being in love is how to stay that way. The same with revolutions – the job is keeping them alive, not to question them.'

'Clap, clap,' Teppy said, joining the crowd. 'They're so naive, they're dangerous.'

'Only to themselves.'

'To all of us,' she declared. 'Anyway, this is really dull. I'm going down to see the Americans. You want to come?'

'Maybe later,' said Aggett.

'Me too,' said Ranse. *I want you.*

'Boring pair,' she said.

They watched her clip down the steps into the daylight where the Aguema boys waited nervously for their entrance. He couldn't know Aggett's thoughts but Ranse knew he was attracted himself by something almost unattractive in her; and that's how it might happen with Teppy Zervos, he thought. A generous ageing had toughened her attitudes, but left her peculiar beauty intact. For at this point, the youthful Asiatic charms of Ancora Dias were nowhere to be seen.

AGGETT	How was it last night? Seems you made some impression on her.
RANSE	(Surprised) Teppy?
AGGETT	The story goes she sat up all night thinking about you. All stars and moon.
RANSE	Your story, I suppose?
AGGETT	She tells.

The boys were stripping rifles. 'G3's,' Aggett said. 'NATO issue.' They were deliberate, fumbling, anxious to impress: in the way of growing men. The fastest to reassemble their weapons were giving bursts for joy. Bullets sang in the air. Ranse turned, even Aggett looked apprehensive. The more Galvão and his supporters clapped, the more they turned delinquent and fired. 'Jesus,' said Aggett. And the slower ones caught up, shooting with double eagerness to prove they were almost as fast. 'Yes,' Ranse said. *He knew from school cadets and machine-gun bursts in the bush. At little straw men, a* *hundred miles from home. And how little it had to do with proving or losing your sanity, which came later with the draft: the call to arms, to madness. Going home from classes he knew the ugliest envelope would be waiting for him; and Goddard would only say there's a letter for you, with the full impact of what that meant tailing in his heavy voice. And you weren't sent to Vietnam but deferred, and so not released but only imprisoned by the draft; every day of your life encircled and conditioned by it. You weren't free to leave your country, and now – like Goddard – you really had no desire to return to it. Was that the reason? Or would the disciples of Freud take me by the hand and lead me down through the university days and school cadets and growing up with Goddard and being an orphan too and lead me into a wattle-filled valley where I know my forgotten parents consummated the desire that planted me here, in Nova Viseu, thirty years later with live ammunition in the air? It's the persistence of memory that's disturbing.* The boys had emptied their clips and stood vacantly, either forgetting what to do next or waiting for e Sousa to say.*

The President got up and moved his small pointed shoes to the microphone, itself newly unboxed for the day. It caught the sun. Galvão tapped the microphone anxiously a couple of times and slowly returned his hand to the belt. And smiling once more, began without notes.

RANSE   What's he saying?

AGGETT   The domestic situation has been normalised. We have advanced with firm steps. The country is being rebuilt with the help of the army of the people. Want me to go on?

RANSE   Go on . . .

AGGETT   How should I know? It's dialect, about forty to choose from. Take your pick.

RANSE   You've been at this business too long, haven't you? (Moistens his lips) It's not helping me.

AGGETT   Ranse, listen. What do you want to know? Goddard was murdered? Because really I don't think so.

RANSE   I know. It's a waste of time.

AGGETT   You want to know why he killed himself, is

	that it? Teppy Zervos is a good place to start. I thought . . .
RANSE	I know that too.
AGGETT	Then you're on the right track, aren't you? (Feigning interest, the President's speech more impassioned) She might seem silly and vain, but nothing about Viseu and surrounds she doesn't know. You might have to push a bit harder, that's all.
RANSE	What's that supposed to mean?
AGGETT	Guess.
RANSE	Come on. Anyone else?
AGGETT	In a day or two a doctor gets back from the mountains. A weed called Barthel Peyrot.
RANSE	Eduardo mentioned him. Not in those terms.
AGGETT	Eduardo? (Pauses) All right, listen to me. Wait till Peyrot gets back, and have a talk with him. I'm told (points to drinks tent) that Peyrot did Goddard's death certificate. They do them for Europeans, not the others. He's with a Swiss group, an agency. I had a beer – one beer – with him. As boring as only the Swiss can be. But again I'm told he was one of Goddard's best friends in those last weeks. (Smiles slightly) Maybe your uncle was too polite to send him away?
RANSE	Hardly. (Looks up) So it's worth staying for. How come you know more than anyone else?
AGGETT	(Folding his arms) Because I've been in this business too long. (Pauses) But don't expect miracles overnight. Because the domestic situation *hasn't* been normalised. That's what the President says.

Eisner was struggling up the steps. 'Aggett,' he called, 'we're going to the mountains, after lunch.'

'Oh. Not staying for dinner?'

'Funny man. We got three days to wrap this thing up. The

69

Livres are getting together again. Local murders, ambushes, the works. You heard much?'

'No.'

'Balldust,' Eisner smirked. 'Aggett, what are you doing here?'

'Poking around. This might be paradise for an old hack.'

'There are good stories here, that's why.'

Aggett nodded: 'Of course, but beyond the reach of journalism as you know it.'

'Fuck off,' he said loosely.

'I'm too old. So many things I've been putting off, and now I'll have to do them.' He gave a friendly smile. 'The ultimate deadline creeps up.'

'You're not likely to miss it.'

Aggett leaned back. 'Only when I'm good and ready. Which brings me back to you, Eisner. And that blighted photographer of yours. Don't go in with a shopping list, knock it together in a way that says there's trouble – *maybe* – and every man and dog flies in. We'll have two dozen hands here all looking for a bloody war that doesn't exist. And then,' Aggett snapped his fingers, 'to keep them all happy.'

Eisner grinned. 'You know the procedure, fairly well. But nothing's as dead as last month's revolution. We're going up to trip over a few bodies.' He paused. 'It's hard work.'

'You don't say.'

'Getting a reputation like yours.'

'Keep trying,' said Aggett, without a trace of waggishness. 'When are you going?'

'About three. They're lining up a jeep. What's the road like?'

'There's no road, just the track to Boim. A couple of days it takes. If you get that far.'

Eisner looked at him, trying to figure it out. And even Ranse could feel the whole thing turning around. As though Aggett was despatching the animated reporter on his own behalf, using Eisner's ambitions to keep the legend alive. *A journalist and a clever one: how many nights I've come down from the hills to rob you of your emotions, to present the facts and steal your greedy souls.* It was no discouragement, none at all: the

70

danger was tempting and alive.

'I'm used to the rough.'

Aggett got up to leave. 'It's not the Asian war, old boy. There's no artillery to soften up first, no B-52s, no field hospitals, no Medivac, no choppers. I know it's still in there,' he tapped Eisner's chest, 'but this one's different.'

The American shifted. 'So?'

'I've already been up,' said Aggett, 'had a look. Plenty of risks, and I'm too old for that. But no easy escape. Once you hit the mountains proper, you're on your own.'

'Thanks,' said Eisner, struck with confidence or uncertainty: it was difficult to tell. 'Right for copy?'

'Don't worry. I'll send it back, uncensored if possible. They're pretty good.'

'Thanks again.'

'By the way,' said Aggett, 'did you know Kuroda in Saigon, in the early days?'

Eisner smiled. 'I wasn't even born then.'

'Too late now. He's dead. But he had a running battle with Toshio Fukuda for three, four years. Fukuda's still alive.'

'And covering wars, I'll bet.'

'No,' said Aggett.

Going back on foot, Ranse passed a group of native houses. They weren't huts, they were houses but the walls were easily conquerable. Below the sea, stuck at the level of reclaimed swamps, they waited for the single tidal wave that would remove all the evidence. And the families sitting in yards, cooking on simple stoves; they lived in transparent immunity from what he had just seen and heard. The bands of armed orphans could not be dismissed, nor the machinations of others. If there was to be more fighting, the fabric of their walls would be torn by a single shot. If that was to happen, he hoped the wave from the Nameless Sea would get them first.

A herd of human goats, they straggled out of different backstreets: Ranse and Aggett, and Teppy Zervos and the indispensable da Cunha with his willingness to forgive. They pulled up at the brightest relic of all: the ice cream and juice stall in the heart of town. Laughing like children.

'A glass of Chocolate Quik,' called Aggett. 'I'm in a hurry.'

Released from school, from boredom and arguments and revolutionary obligations.

'Thank god that's over,' said Teppy to the vendor, who stood wiping the fridge with a mildewy cloth. He ignored her, serving others first.

'The geographical centre of Viseu,' da Cunha proclaimed, 'from which we measure all our distances and doubts.'

'Bravo,' said Aggett. 'A little honesty into the cause. But you think that's real?' he asked, pointing to da Cunha's lime cone

'Artificial,' Teppy said.

Ranse agreed: 'Definitely false.'

'I don't care,' da Cunha shrugged, 'at least it's colourful.'

'And probably fatal,' said Teppy, with a touch of hope. 'We still have to pay, don't we?'

'Of course. The tourists used to love it. What's yours like, Mr Ranse?'

'Lovely, more or less. Vanilla.' But nobody was listening.

In the distance Ranse could hear the buzzing too. It grew louder and more constant, until he mentally ducked for cover as a light plane swooped overhead and tilted its feeble wings in a dubious gesture. And was gone.

'My husband,' said Teppy, almost to herself. 'Biggles.'

'Going where?'

'Away,' she said. 'We've probably run out of milk.'

'What do you think?' said da Cunha. 'He's gone to help the others, of course.'

'Don't be bloody stupid,' she snapped. 'If you must know he's going to get supplies. So much for your piddling revolution.'

'Well,' he spluttered, 'you haven't supported us.'

'Us?' she mocked. 'The Portuguese? Fragas? The people who . . .'

'The *country*, that's who! You and your fat husband have not supported . . .'

'We haven't given it to anyone. Is that a crime? We run a guest house, not a political machine. And we're not about to surrender it to a bunch of amateurs.'

Da Cunha's ice cream was shaking. Some had dribbled over the back of his smooth hand and sat there, awaiting further instructions. He licked it off. 'What you run is a lot more than a guest house.'

She waited for his eyes to come up, seeking her reaction; then she gave a terrible giggle. 'You should have married, Thermudo. You need more than ice cream to cool you down.'

He recovered his pose. 'All the good ones went to Brazil,' he said. 'Only those like yourself made it here.'

'And Mrs Mendonça. I'm not Portuguese even.'

'Come on, you two,' said Aggett. 'Settle down, you're causing panic and disruption.'

'It's all right,' she said. 'He's blind.'

'Forget it, da Cunha. Let's get back. I won't touch the stuff till midday, and it's already ten past.'

'You go,' said Teppy. 'We'll be along. I want to buy Nicholas another ice.'

'I want to buy Nicholas another ice,' mocked Aggett. 'I hope that's what Nicholas wants. He's been dumbstruck for an hour.'

'Why not?' said Ranse. 'I'd love one.'

The two older men pulled away, looking like uncomfortable brothers. And da Cunha had forgiven, could be heard lecturing: 'In 1911 – no, 1913 – Salazar,' but the Englishman was shaking his head; the sun was breaking through his hair and he wanted a drink, not history.

'Anyway,' she called after them, but spun back to Ranse with exasperated hands. 'Oh. The heat, of course. Every year's the same. The fluid builds up in their hot little brains. It's like a pressure headache all day, then the monsoons come and they're free. Happy and home again.'

'What about you?'

'No home,' she smiled. 'Well, no business of course. No tourists means no work.'

'No husband either.'

She ignored it. 'I'm not sure why *you're* here. Is it really about . . .'

'Yes. Of course.'

'The others are talking about it. You're not an agent, a spy or something?'

Ranse smiled to himself, not her. Why on earth would he be standing under the blazing sun in a crumbled Portuguese paradise clutching an ice cream – artificially flavoured, no doubt – if in fact he wasn't a spy or something? Because he was coming into the maelstrom and she was coming out of it and they'd clashed by accident; he was investigating and didn't trust her one inch and she was fleeing and thinking like crazy, he knew, and he wasn't thinking much at all but hoping chance would take good care of him.

'Yes,' he said. 'Something like that.'

Teppy grinned. 'Good. Two of a kind. Now we can be lovers.'

But at the moment he was expected either to laugh or drop his cone in shock, Ranse turned his eyes away; past those of Teppy Zervos who probably wasn't kidding and wanted to make love and on through the dusty foliage to the lone figure coming towards them. He knew the walk, the loneliness of the walk. It was Eduardo, cutting a late path from the sports field to the town. They could both see his supple form slipping past the papaw trunks and banana fronds; and weeds and cleared grasses, and buildings and lawns. Ranse was moving with him through all this, and wondering what she might be thinking too. The lover's invitation had evaporated, a thin golden message that had missed its target and sailed into the unknown. She watched Eduardo like a hawk, ready either to attack or embrace. But the face softened and smiled as he came near.

'Watch out for landmines,' she called lightly. But he paid no attention even when she offered the remainder of her cone.

'The President wants to see you,' he said to Ranse. 'At his house, for afternoon coffee. I'll drive you.'

'Oh gosh,' Teppy exclaimed, 'it must be important. You be careful, Nicholas. Won't you?'

SEVEN

This time, roles are changed. Ranse goes first up the leafy laneway, pushing by prickly branches of lantana to reach Galvão's shelter: a cluster of three or four rooms in white stucco. The garden is surveyed by the little President himself, a small picture of happiness standing among the imported shrubs he loves – hydrangea, azalea, cassia, other statements of pleasure.

'Ah, you've come,' he says, spreading his arms. Out of uniform they're not so small, but like fleshy paddles touching the air for balance. The shake is warm, infantile.

'Thank you.'

He moves inside, at a pace that surely frustrates change. Ranse accepts the offered seat, but Eduardo stands awkwardly at the window. The light catching the walls, untreated and bare. The poverty of Galvão's past, some lack of love perhaps, hangs on them like dust.

'You wanted to see me?'

'Look at this,' he says, passing a shoddy object in brass and wood from the shelf. He names an Eastern Bloc leader. 'He sent this, wishing me well. Can you understand why a man would do that? Send this around the world?'

'I don't know. An insult, I suppose.'

Galvão puts it back gently. 'Perhaps. We'll pick our friends very carefully, anyway. To bring a country out of the past is full of tensions. The colonial links are broken, but we're still as dependent as ever on Portugal – not politically, but economically which is worse. And even *she's* in turmoil – Left, Right,

Army, all sorts of parties. I ring from the Marconi office to Lisbon. I'm the President of this country, I tell them. Who's in charge of the former territories, I ask. Nobody knows. They say I'll have to call back in a few days, a week, a month.' Galvão rises from his seat, angrily. 'So I tell them here – don't shout about Marxism, because the others won't come with money. But we're the abandoned children of the West, they argue – and if the West doesn't help us then the others will. What can I say? We must have trade.'

'Yes.'

'Don't you agree?' He pauses. 'Otherwise there'll only be more fighting. I can see you're bewildered.'

Ranse immediately tries to appear so. His forehead creases and he realises he has a slight headache. 'No,' he says. 'I was thinking about tourism, perhaps.'

'Ah, no tourists,' replies the President, 'and that's good. A lot before were loud and didn't understand things here, didn't want to learn either. And always make us see things through foreign eyes. We would distance ourselves from everything first, then wait to see if the tourists approve. Oh, they'll be back,' he says, 'and we need them too. But it's good for now. You agree?'

But as he prepares to, a young woman enters. With a cheap tin tray, carrying three coffees and cake. Galvão watches her politely. 'My helper,' he says before Ranse can reply. She looks at him in a tangle and quickly leaves, carried away by shyness. And still he hasn't breathed out, not even thought to. The girl is Ancora Dias. For two days her Asiatic features have been playing on his mind. He stares at the doorway.

'Let me show you something.'

Galvão walks past Eduardo with a smile – not returned – and opens a glass cabinet, a European relic crying for care. He takes out a photograph. The tropics have got to it, curling the edges and coating it with years of trouble. So that strangely the image has gathered the potency of true nostalgia. The dinky President displays it happily, as though taken that instant. 'A photograph,' he says.

The stained print shows a younger Galvão – a teacher perhaps, some sort of clerk in a charming family group. A towering palm juts from the coiffure of someone's grand-mother and Novo Viseu is unmistakably the setting. Galvão holds a baby, with all the love of a father; but against his lighter skin the child is quite dark.

'I was already a priest,' he smiles.

'Of course.'

'But do you recognise her?' And his betely teeth appear for the first time, a jigsaw around that pink tongue which speaks English in such a perfectly modulated way. Ranse can't concentrate, and hopes a smile will do: no, I don't.

'Of course not,' says the President. 'The child of a friend's servant. And now my helper, the one you've seen.'

A bolt of electricity circles the earth, searching for likely targets and at that instant Nicholas Ranse is the perfect target and feels it hit: the photographic baby has become Ancora Dias, who in turn becomes the President's euphemistic helper, which is converted easily to something else.

The silence forces a stumbling reply. 'Yes, yes,' he says. 'You're very fortunate.'

The President considers and accepts. 'She's very helpful to me. A teacher before all this, an early Fragas member. She helped to organise many students, with my support. Soon after the photograph, her mother died. Of disease. She was adopted by my friend,' he says, 'the Minister for Financial Reconstruction in our government. Julião Dias, this is him on the right.'

'Of course,' says Ranse, bewildered at last. 'I saw them, at the hotel. And you've stayed together too?'

'He went to Lisbon to study, I joined the Church. After that I was teaching at Maracacume, in the mountains – yes, Eduardo remembers, I taught him too – and then all this happened. Julião was working with the government, an economist here. We were fighting for our rights first, and then proper independence. It didn't happen as easily as that, so I took off my vestments and took up the gun.' And the President smiles at this well-rehearsed point. 'Ancora.'

She lapses back into the room, bringing glasses of juice. With a little more confidence she stays and slides into a cane chair, but is still uncomfortable in his presence.

'The terrorist is another man's liberator,' continues Galvão, 'and what you call it doesn't matter. The results are important. Your uncle taught me that.'

Ranse is dazed. 'My uncle?' He sees but can't imagine the ponderous Sam Goddard dispensing advice to the tiny leader, one on the other's knee. He even begins to smile, but Galvão presses on:

'To be truly alive, he said, is to be active. And then came the popular movements – some of us joined the Fragas, and when they saw the Church was no longer united, the people followed their natural feelings. That's why we won. Because suddenly there were priests saying the struggle against oppression was a Christian cause, it was all right to shoot in the name of God. But it wasn't easy.'

Galvão paces and ignores his guest, letting the words find their own way through the room. Eduardo shuffles out to the garden where – Ranse suspects – he has sought respite from Presidental history on several visits at least. They watch him go.

'And I am no more a Marxist,' whispers Galvão to the ceiling, 'than the Bishop is. And he is many stupid things, but never that.' He gives a peculiar, lonely chuckle. Ancora looks at Ranse, and stops only when the President comes back to earth. 'But these are my problems,' he says casually, 'not yours. I wanted to speak with you.'

'Yes. About my uncle.'

The President looks down. 'Again, I must be honest with you. We weren't close. He came here only once, in six years. I've never been to his house. We saw each other at the stores. Perhaps he had no wish to be seen alone with me. I think so. I was a priest but a political suspect too. When we talked, it was only about life in the West and why he came.'

'He told you?'

Ancora watches both. Ranse observes the leader cultivating his memory, turning over their brief alliance. 'Because,' he starts. But too much has happened since those days. 'No, really. It's always been a mystery to me. Why a professor, a university man should come to a poor island colony and build a house on a hill, and live by himself.' He turns puzzled to Ancora. Who comprehends neither, at all.

Eduardo appears at the door, hoping the visit is over. But his unsettling presence only reinforces the unsteady air that Goddard's life and death has blown into their circle, like an unwanted guest.

'As I say, it's a mystery to me. The things which make a man kill himself are deep. And he can't know why he's doing it, they are so well hidden. Do you agree?'

Ranse shakes his head. 'Yes.'

'There is no family?'

'No, just me.'

'And you live in Thailand, they say.'

'I might go back one day, to Australia. Or maybe not.'

'There's no hurry.'

He looks up, to Galvão's stilled eyes and Ancora now at his side. An edge of concern slips through his mind and goes. Eduardo is staring out the window, to the eternal garden.

'Yes?' he pauses. 'I don't understand.'

'I wanted to see you,' the President repeats. 'We need an agriculture man. An expert. Senhor Goddard was a great naturalist, he taught you. And you have much experience in Asia.'

Ranse halts. 'But not . . .' And pauses to accommodate the full naivety of Galvão's proposal, or lack of serious consideration. Or loopy ultimatum, of sorts. 'You want me to *work* here?'

'We don't expect you to join the Fragas, of course. Just to improve the crops, for us. To get trade going.'

'I don't even know the country.'

'Of course not. But when you visit your uncle's grave,' he suggests, 'you'll see much of Inhumas on the way. You wanted to go there?'

He stutters. 'Yes, of course.'

'Surely,' says Galvão and grants approval with encouraging nods. 'On the next convoy, to the mountains.' But almost immediately he reconsiders. 'It's better, Eduardo will take you. They are his home.'

'Yes.' Quietly.

'Oh, of mountains,' says the President. 'I've just heard on Radio Australia that Mount Everest has again been conquered.' He looks at both, waiting for a reaction. 'On the radio,' he repeats.

Eduardo goes out, and Ranse moves to follow but Galvão stops him gently. 'He'll look after you up there. Are you worried?'

But there's no reply. Ranse is past the danger of higher altitudes because he hasn't even left, is opposite Ancora Dias and doesn't know what's going on. He turns and again she's gone.

'About this,' says Galvão, 'there is really no hurry. We've been waiting for four centuries,' he smiles. 'But when you return, we can talk about it. Between us of course.'

'I will, yes. Of course.'

And the President smiles again. He is truly slight, for all his apparent influence; and Eduardo with smooth and untroubled skin is young and impatient, and something in them both helps to define the strength and weakness of whatever Ranse is plunging into.

'Galvão knows nothing.'

The bar was wiped with a damp cloth, and Gecko pretended not to listen.

'You're crazy, Ranse. Like the Americans. Just because you can't hear it, or see it.'

'You weren't too concerned for Eisner.'

'Professional foul,' said Aggett. 'A few tacks on the road to success. Anyway that's his job, not yours.' He drank his beer. 'Look at this,' he said finally, pulling another note from his pocket.

'What is it?'

'Under my door. Bloody keen staff,' he said, tossing a grin at Gecko. 'Some of them.'

'But what's it say?'

'Just a Livre victory before the Wet, the government's a bunch of Commies.'

'We could both do better than that.'

Aggett smiled. 'Our old mate, propaganda. Or Fragas themselves – always handy to have a few enemies of the people, you know. Helps to keep the revolutionary fires burning. Pass the ice, will you?'

A photograph was floating by, and Ranse caught it. There were four figures, all natives judging by their clothes and lost expressions. A simpleton with a wild, unaccountable face and eyes totally out of focus under the swirling madness of his headband. An elder beauty with eyepools of holy water and a bangle through her nostril, the bold circle supported by a decorated chain to her ear. And dividing them, the correct specimen: a figure with moustache sweeping to his ears, and broad face and chest framed in pure white with a tribal cloth spun off either shoulder. But on inspection the authority seemed fragile, no deeper than the bromide of the print itself; a power base to fit the image. *To fool the truth that all men tell lies, off their lips, in their hearts; giving away what they no longer contain in their hearts.* The words aren't his or theirs, but belong to the fourth figure – a woman kneeling before them, as she too faces the camera obscura, circa 1910 of the other world. In his mind her face screams, the enlarged lips are tightened and bronze flesh is bunched into eyes which show no sparks but only the effect of incendiary flashes on them. The others won't know until later what she's telling the tripod, the man in black, the devil: about their lives, their existence, the hopelessness of all things under the tropical sun. These guardians of the young, they always walk their babies into the shade. *At this moment the figures of Julião Dias and his adopted daughter are gliding past the doorway.* If suffering is personal, it burns and holds power like a candle. But when it's shared, the pain surely eases and some of the fire goes out. *She again pauses, looks at him and is gone.* It was a suffering that couldn't be fixed, and wouldn't be halted or lost in the night like others. He would eventually speak in some mutual tongue and ask her why it was, and what was the point of leaving while that mystery was unchallenged at least?

'The ice.'
'Sorry.'
'Ranse, pack it in. You're a bloody scientist, not a soldier of fortune. It's not . . .'
'Goddard was a scientist too.'
'He was, but he gave it away.'
'I'm staying for a while, that's all.'

Aggett sat up. 'Look. Goddard got sucked in. It happens. The world ceases to exist. Your own troubles float to the surface, they seem as big as wars or revolutions. But they're not. Goddard kills himself – and now you want to go to the mountains, to put flowers on his grave? And get shot to pieces.'

'It's their revolution, not mine.'

'And your bloody life,' fired Aggett, 'not theirs. They won't care if you're in the way, Ranse. Won't ask you politely to move.'

But the argument was drowned by a louder commotion in the hallway. He could already see the shadows shifting and growing larger, and da Cunha and Mrs Mendonça soon appeared and spilled into the bar.

'. . . of Tuscany, I can only think of chianti,' said the hotel owner, 'and then the straw wrapping hides the awful truth. These are pale imitations.'

'But you're never tried the Montalcino, I know.'

'How do you know what I've tried?'

The Minister for Information opened his mouth, holding the coral beads at his neck. 'A wonderful red. Dry, balanced, well . . .'

'Balanced? The *last* thing I look for!' bellowed Mrs Mendonça. 'You need edge! Edge!! No, no,' she waved them down. 'I'm not staying. Work to do. Gecko, clean up the beer garden. Your wretched monkey got excited.' Without stopping she moved in a broad sweep to the adjoining lounge, and was gone.

Da Cunha drew up a stool and sighed. 'Good evening gentlemen, how are you both?' He fondled the necklace as though continuing the argument. 'She's quite mad.'

Aggett downed his Scotch. 'We're just sitting here and making plans for Mr Ranse's early departure.'

'You're leaving? For Australia?'

'No.'

'Oh, for Thailand of course.'

'No,' Aggett cut in, 'nothing as sensible as that. Quite the opposite. He's heading up to the mountains.'

'The mountains?'

'Yes,' said Ranse. 'I asked the President, he agreed to let me go. To see my uncle's grave. And the country where he worked up there. Eduardo's coming with me.'

'All that way for two metres of dirt,' said da Cunha. 'But you were close.'

'They'll be bloody closer if he doesn't keep his head down.'

'We were,' Ranse replied. 'And besides, Galvão thinks it's a good idea. I've decided to look at the fruit industry too.'

'Oh, lord,' Aggett moaned.

'Fruit, up there?'

Ranse shrugged. 'Something could be done, it's cooler there.'

'And drier,' said da Cunha.

'I forgot,' said Aggett, 'Senhor da Cunha was a weather forecaster. Tell us about your days as a meteorologist.'

Da Cunha looked puzzled. 'But why would you want to know that?'

A stopwatch appeared in his lap, from the folds of his reddish sarong: the one he'd carried around his neck on the first day. He stopped and started the mechanism, as though controlling the movement of secret actions, of his own thoughts. He held it up. 'I've been timing Benny,' he said.

'Who?' asked Ranse.

'Ben-n-y,' Gecko piped up. 'Monkey.'

'On average he touches himself every 2.9 seconds. Disgraceful. My father said they were all like that.'

'I thought your father loved them,' Ranse smiled. 'Didn't he?'

'My father even loved me,' said da Cunha, 'up to a point.'

Out of laughter, he grabbed the whisky bottle and poured a round. Da Cunha seemed to pick up remarkably as the day wore on. The mornings were reserved for recovery; the mid-afternoons for steady drinking; and evenings like this for invention, and mischief. Later in the mountains, Ranse would recall da Cunha in a single mental image: a lean clever man of silvery hair, an edge of voice always, a glass in hand, a stopwatch. The eyes were complex, and shone with plots. The artist was always alive in him, at work; even after death it would be there.

And the drink was never wasted; for there were no incumbrances that a couple of whiskies couldn't wipe away, like Gecko's counter rag. Da Cunha lived for the moment, but only because he feared what the next moment would bring; tried to appear fatalistic and perhaps was, but – as Aggett pointed out – to be fatalistic in wars was often silly, or appeared to be. His moral lessons in the end might be dangerous only to himself, thought Ranse, because nobody else took him seriously: and like the Fool, he veered closer always to self-destruction. The anodyne was alcohol, and the bad feelings it drained from his body reappeared in verse, in his understanding of misery and defeat: the lines that lifted the inside man above his frivolous manner, caught the limb of a private life, and carried him through another day – the Portuguese ascendant – to the bitter end.

'Zervos,' he called suddenly. 'Hello.'

They looked up. Through the clutter of chairs and faded umbrellas, the Greek was moving directly for the bar. Gecko remembered his chores, and shuffled out.

'What's this?'

Zervos threw down a fresh copy of *Imagem*, the local paper – the work of da Cunha as editor, chief correspondent, censor and critic. *Because the Minister for Information administers the information, naturalmente. And then publication becomes no problem, senhor; you can always get around the incumbrances in life.* And he probably could.

'What's this about my mangoes?'

Da Cunha lifted his shoulders. 'Again you're causing panic. And could I introduce my guest, if you'd allow me. This is Mr Ranse.'

Zervos tilted his head back. 'So you're Ranse,' he said slowly. 'Hello friend.'

'Hello,' said Ranse.

There was a doomy silence, until Aggett leaned across and pulled Zervos over by the jacket. 'Forget the mangoes. What's this?' he inquired, drawing the lapel almost to his glasses.

'Do you know what it is?' the Greek asked.

'A bottle top?'

'Look closer.'

'A tin badge,' said Aggett. 'Good god, it's Gerald Ford.'

'The president?' asked Ranse.

Zervos screwed up his mouth in disappointment: 'I had thousands made in Hong Kong, but he's not coming now. Thanks to this lot and their war-games.'

'It's spelt wrongly anyway,' said Aggett. '*Gelald Ford*, it says.'

'Small problem.' Zervos flattened his coat and felt backwards for a stool, placing the weight of his body on it, it not much of the body itself. He was glaring again at da Cunha, who forced a smile.

'All I want to know, from the Poet here – what's this rubbish about? Overcharging for mangoes! You can have the bloody things, they're falling off the trees. Anyway no one's got a brass razoo.'

'That's true,' said the Minister. 'So fold your umbrellas and leave.' The smile faded. 'Oh yes. Leave, get out. Because you'll die here otherwise. We'll all be fighting soon, the whole country. And you and your wife will be killed with the rest.' He turned to Ranse. 'And you also, do you want to die? It's not time to go anywhere, only a flight to Darwin. Perhaps with Zervos here.'

'Exactly my thoughts,' said Aggett.

Da Cunha got off the stool. 'This is my feeling, anyway. I know, for example, the Central Committee as a whole would shoot me for saying so.'

'Such honesty!' Aggett cried 'What people.'

'More *bullshit,*' said Zervos. 'He's just setting me up. Another peaceful takeover by force. That's how they do it, like their mates in Africa.' He turned sharply to da Cunha. 'Want me to fly out, leave everything and twenty years' work – and piss off, just like that? You think I'm crazy? With your pink beads.'

But there was no answer. Already da Cunha – Poet of the Revolution and Minister for Information and Propaganda – was walking away from the arena of bruised pride, slight frame carrying him through the maze of chairs. Into the early evening of Viseu's relative peace. His shuffle left a cloud of dust, all that remained: a smudge that took only a few seconds to go.

'Little prick,' said Zervos, holding out the paper. 'Look at this shit. *Who is this man, Zervos?* Character assassination in a small place, eh?'

'Well,' Aggett drawled, 'maybe da Cunha's right. About getting out, I mean.'

'What's this about mangoes?' asked Ranse.

'I'm holding on,' said Zervos. 'The trees, the whole business – till things settle down. Got a deal with the pilots to freight them – to Darwin, the southern capitals. And bring back tourists.' He looked closely at Ranse. 'You're a fruit expert.'

'Only research,' he smiled awkwardly. 'I don't go round selling advice.'

'Like me,' Zervos said. 'I like to touch things. Be real. Across the North I was buying, selling, just hanging on. Cars, food, anything,' he smiled. 'These idiots don't understand – they think everyone gets a neat slice. But it's not like that, never will be.' Zervos leaned forward, and caught his balance. 'Money's got a life of its own. Whole economies too. You can't fool them. All you do is watch like a bloody hawk. See which way they're going, and then – snap! That's how to make profits. I learned about deals in the Territory, what it takes – force and intrigue. Lost a lot too.'

A course in melodrama, and survival. Ranse was looking at an optimist of such open vulgarity that it sent shivers back to his own uncertainty. 'Perhaps you should go,' he said. 'If things get rough here.'

'Both of you,' Aggett chipped in.

Zervos slumped a little, and looked up. 'No,' he muttered, 'back there it's bricks through the windows, if I'm lucky. Maybe a bullet in the brain. I mean, you can exhaust yourself. Looking out for people like that, can't you?'

He lifted his eyes sluggishly but with a smile, not to Aggett or Ranse but past them: up further to where the ceiling fan was rattling, and running slow. Zervos seemed to be chasing the newness of some idea and was unable to catch it.

That sea, at night: where could it take you? South to an Australian past, or north again to Asia and half of humanity? On these November nights, Ranse remembered, he'd slipped from his humid bed a decade or two before to the open air;

down the grassy bank to the River, bold and flat under the early summer sky. The river rats, he could hear them scampering their rubbery forms by. Through the slimy tunnels they'd been hiding in all day; now they were getting relief with the tide and more mud for a cooler night. And then a boy of five, or was it fifteen, joined them in reverie of the brutal stars: every sparkling dot a question without answer, and beyond that a deeper mystery which even Goddard couldn't solve. At the top of the bank, the light in his uncle's room glowed. The eternal riddle of his youth, that a man larger than all the human life around him should huddle through long, hot nights screaming silently into a microscope for the relentless joy of it. *Secretly hoping never to find the answers to the questions that puzzled and pushed him on; but always having the satisfaction of the answer, to show himself off to the world.* On those astral nights, hearing the muffled protests of frustration behind the glowing blind at the top of the bank, Nicholas knew his Uncle Sam was slightly mad. The river rats went about their business all night, like the man at the microscope.

And that was it. The centre of their being had slowly shifted, from Brisbane and its subtropical incandescence to steamy Asia for one and this baffling colonial dump for the other. For ages, Goddard had tried to get him here: besieged with letters, invitations to talk and relax; and he'd read them in Bangkok's bars, as finely but absently as one might read the chemical analysis on the label of a bottle of aqua minerale, of how certain elements had come into force to make this healthy water and why it would be good for him to fly down for a couple of weeks. But nothing could induce Ranse to restore that tangled alliance to the present. And now he was here, because nobody else would gather up the wreckage of Goddard's peculiar existence among the boiling palms.

But there was more to it. Suicide or whatever. A last diary, with empty pages. A crumpled epitaph, from Arabia to nowhere. And the lonely grave with Goddard's earthy remains held nothing for him. And yet these were the hands pulling him upcountry and pushing him on. *I'm not here as a tourist or snoop, but as a man looking for his own life; and the solution's in that house on the hill, or the mountains as much as anywhere else. I suspect you've already guessed, Senhor da Cunha – for me, getting out has to wait. As a poet of deeds more than words, I know you'll understand. It's like coming through the back door of that house, where Death is announced as a visitor might be. And perhaps only then can I know what's behind death, not just Goddard's but my own life and death to come. As it surely will, sooner or later.* But thinking about it outside his thoughts made him cold with fear; and he wanted nothing more than security, to hide in his Number One room and dream of release. It was hard to see the damp sand at his feet: the moon moving towards its first quarter was lost for a moment and pure blackness like oil covered the sea.

He stopped at the edge: the sea and night drew closer and became one, though he could make out the stars and at the slowest speed of light could barely see the phosphors as they slipped to another channel and came up for air, to make more light and disappear. All night they kept moving through the channels. Ranse looked up and down the beach; and the broken lights from the foreshore, he realised, were not beckoning from the direction of the hotel but came from the Happy Bay Guest House. At this late hour Teppy Zervos was up. The light plane had departed; and her unpleasant husband who was huddled not over another woman, but probably over plans for another deal or coup. Ranse could feel another danger or force growing, menacing his head and whole body out of a few patchy lights through the trees. He tried to ignore it but couldn't, and was at the point of entering the possiblity when it was crippled by the image of another man – perhaps Zervos, or not – spilling himself on her. In confusion and excitement and fear; and in frustration he pushed away from the beach and into the treeline, but not towards her place.

The curfew was still on. He'd forgotten about it, but the soldiers ignored him. They were chatting somewhere in the dark with cigarettes. Ranse was climbing a little, he could have been a climber. It was the warmth off the mountains; but he could feel the swampiness too, the muddy feet and dirty hands, scratched by native trees and the scrub he reached out to grasp, exotic birds opening the night, diving into the shadowy swamp and they were gone, probably watching from some distant height, seeing his clumsy and mysterious silhouette; he could make out forms in the trees, and Goddard's high temple of a house where he used to live. But he could see no danger.

EIGHT

It could have been Brisbane. There was no mirror, no reflected image to suggest all the subsequent years that had, with waste included, turned him into a person much older: no way of telling where his Australian past had ended and life on this other island had begun; in that Sea of Middle Age, even at thirty. The stars above in November gave no clues, or relief: a million or more light years away, they burned on his eyes like firebrands. Ranse looked up – all time was like this, unstoppable – and stumbled inside.

In the kitchen he lit an oil lamp. The room swelled in a trance. The timber cupboards held it, and underfoot the same cheap lino gave off a sheen riddled with stripes and dots. Ranse swayed in the confused perspective, and groped down the hallway. He stroked the frame of the study door. Where had the builders come from, for god's sake? The lamp swelled again and he held it back, and moved the latch; and pushed forward into darkness. The study which had always been Goddard's, now his. Around three walls the books were whispering for attention; and he looked up and saw the diaries like black bricks. Suspended by the thinnest of planks.

The first was dated 17 August 1967: the day Goddard had arrived. Squarely lettered on the opening page was: *Samuel Goddard. Notos One.* And further down, scrawled as an afterthought: 'I've been waiting so long for this I don't know if it's going to work.'

Over the page, the diary began.

No sirens here, no banshees of progress. It's taken me two hours and forty minutes to realise I've done the right thing – all my life I've wanted nothing more than to sit on the terrace of a comfortable pub and watch the sea. The endless greenery, sky's cloudless. A botanist's utopia – even a monkey up the mango. All over the archipelago of course, macacus cynomolgus, only this one's a pet. Its name (says the barman) is Benny – no doubt a human equivalent lurks somewhere. One thing, it can't stop leaping about – even though the rest of the place seems to be drifting somewhere in the past. I've come for both – to rest of course, and also to be a fairly decent scientist again. I wonder – after the mess – can I be happy here? (Don't even want to, but I'll have to face it sooner or later.) Just for once, look after yourself a while. Look at the beach, the plants. And the future, you're not that bloody old – not even sixty. All those wasted years, and in their place an island like this with the totality of natural experience to draw on. It's what they all wanted – Darwin, Wallace, the rest – an outdoor lab. They weren't stifled by history or straddled by it, and I won't be either. Let's shift in ways the department wouldn't know of – perhaps I can take off, or end up the last of my species? (Long pause here, thinking about Nicholas. It's asking a lot, but I want to get him up here. He'll end up at a bloody desk, I know. What the hell happened there?) Anyway (why am I noting all this – for myself, posterity, inspiration?) here's something in Wallace that would challenge him, if he hasn't given up science altogether: 'The fact that potatoes and wheat of excellent quality are grown in abundance at from 3,000 to 3,500 feet elevation, shows what the climate and soil are capable of if properly cultivated. From one to two thousand feet high, coffee would thrive; and there are hundreds of square miles of country, over which all the varied products which require climates between those of coffee and wheat would flourish; but no attempt had yet been made to form a single mile of road, or a single acre of plantation!' And I guess there are still openings, a century on – though I'm told (again by the barman, full of it) that the Greek who runs the guest house does a few hundred acres of coffee in the hills somewhere, and fruit here on the coast. For the first time in twenty years I'm challenged myself – perhaps Nick could make a real start here too? Better than zipping off to

*Asia, to Green Revolutions and Five Year Plans and agencies –
they've got him by the balls. He hasn't got the guts, I know, to
go it alone. With me it was different, but that's better not spoken
about. Only depresses me.*

Ranse closed the oldest diary, leaned back into Goddard's
chair and shut his eyes. He had no idea of time: two, three in the
morning? Was there some hour that was longer than an hour,
more like a day or half a lifetime? The softly burning flame
wouldn't rest but troubled him. 'Oh god,' he whispered, and
lifted his fatigued body off the chair. He found his way through
darkness to the verandah and the cooler night.

The limits of Viseu were dotted like a child's game. And
joined up, the individual lights showed a town hardly bigger
than the average suburb. Ranse was bothered by a single
extract. What could diaries tell you about a man, other than a
capacity for self-delusion and lying? The years apart had been a
long and slow-burning fuse. And now at the end of it, he was
waiting only for the day to explode. To throw him back to the
undulating and open coast, where the full extent of his
emotions would be drawn; or could the mountains have a say in
that too? He stepped along the creaking boards.

It was like looking at your entire life through that rusting
flyscreen over there. You could never – even on the clearest,
sunniest days – get close enough to it. Life was going on but the
distinct features wouldn't come out and identify themselves.
*You must find out; with directness and clarity in the middle of
the day.* But the resolution seemed as fragile as the rusting
flyscreen; he wondered if the events unfolding on that coastal
plain and in the peaks high above would force him to resort, like
all of them, to the same evasiveness and lies. Just to save whatever gains he'd made. The lights of a single vehicle were shifting through the town, and one building glowed with more
intensity than the rest: the neon at the Tropicala was still burning, and Aggett and da Cunha were probably getting plastered
on rich and dangerous port. It was down there, six or seven
years ago, that Goddard had etched these impressions of his
destination; the first inklings of self-destruction too. Should
have gone with the flow, gone further into collaboration and
distilled his immense knowledge into finer and finer detail; and

92

all the while miniaturising his soul to the size of a forgotten transistor. But how to overcome that other desire, to spread out and see the nature of things. How obvious and human, and haplessly Goddard to do that. And he could feel the Uncle's presence out here in the open; where anything was possible because the lights were disappearing and the game was up, but a new one was about to begin. The diaries first, then the mountains. He would throw another dice at their fragmented past.

This one, from 1973: *Here at the house I'm working in relative peace. The locals leave me alone from week to week, possibly they don't think much of what I'm doing. A girl comes in sometimes to cook and wash – not that I'm incapable, but it gives me the contact I'd otherwise lose. (But she troubles me, is always shifting about and watching – may have to drop her.) The colonial days are numbered, even here I suspect – a couple of years and we'll be looking after ourselves. I've been alone long enough not to be troubled by that. For the past week or two, been working through old texts on natural theology. (Helps an old atheist pass the time.) Both ridiculous and amusing, I suppose – intelligence always comes a poor second in the godly race. A bible basher first, that's our Paley; then a naturalist, so the writing's full of turgid rubbish too. Like this – 1802, mind you – little example: 'Death implies separation: and the loss of those whom we love must necessarily, so far as we can conceive, be accompanied with pain. To the brute creation, nature seems to have stepped in with some secret provision for their relief under the rupture of their attachments. In their instincts towards their offspring, and of their offspring towards them, I have often been surprised to observe how ardently they love, and how soon they forget.' And what of it? The duty of all love is to perpetrate itself beyond reason, of course it's a bloody mystery. Only a man with nothing better to do would try to work it out. And besides, a little loss of memory can be a wonderful thing – when I think of all I've forgotten about Australia (the most forgettable, selfish of isles) I can only cherish the continuing decline of my human senses. A lot of fat, warm-stool complacency, that's what I remember – mowing lawns after the War, retiring to the back steps for another beer, more cars, television tubes, junk piling up in the confused* corners of six states and two territories of good fortune. And when the Sixties pulled them into the world like a beacon, it still wasn't their world. Certainly not mine. And now it's Vietnam and afterwards they'll get back to their lawns. Don't go dabbling in foreign affairs! The beach is still popular.

Well, he thought, Goddard didn't know much about mowers but he knew about broken marriages and a War he didn't actually fight in; and most of all he knew about universities, and the bullshit there. As a student, tutor, research assistant, writer, lecturer, research fellow, professor, administrator, all those bloody labels and hardly ever a scientist – not the way he'd wanted to be. And that was the frustration behind every jibe. Same as it ever was, thought Ranse. Only a few would ever become great scientists; beyond the material reasons or rewards, out of love.

Eighteen months later, early 1975: *Up and down the ladder a couple of times, and this rung's the most suitable to escape from the burning fortress of my existence. Outside the rains are pelting relentlessly, I can't work – there's plenty to do, it's the noise on the roof this year that's irritating me. Reminds me of Brisbane summers and why after all those years I should find that annoying I don't know. Perhaps it's the business with Nick of course. But sometimes I think he wanted to be forgotten, by me anyway. What he did was probably right. Even back in those Brisbane years, I was more or less deadened to his sensitivities. Of which I displayed none and so perhaps can't be blamed? It wasn't society he was rebelling against, but me – and together we ended up doing a fine job on each other. It was Australia, that place of extreme psychologies I see now – was possible to disguise tortures on each other there, and not feel them in return. Or is it still true – chasing birds, butterflies and the most vulnerable insects, you can fall into traps? Take the mountain villagers – they find spiritualism everywhere because they don't understand the scientific nature of things – plants grow because of spirits, not elements and heat. But the likes of me, knowing the physical realities, are even more confused by whatever's pushing science along. Remember the time at Boim, I had the fever and pumped myself with quinine every day for a week and knocked it out, and I was back in the*

94

scrub again in ten days. But after that I always felt, by dint of a single mosquito bite, a totally different person. That was almost the spiritual thing getting into my bloodstream, my whole system I think. And will Paley be looking down from his perch in Heaven and see all this as a small victory? I'd better be careful, these diaries will turn me to God or the grave.

The lamp was failing. Spluttering and fading in an instant, and gone. But the glow sat there. Ranse was tired enough to see his uncle in that persisent lustre, the long energetic face and beard coming from somewhere inside his memory. And then not as he remembered his Uncle Sam at the cluttered Brisbane desk, the light dangling carelessly over his brain, and the inverse relationship of all this to the perfect order of his scientific mind, but as he might have appeared in those final years, at death: an ageing remnant, past his prime, a tropical failure like so many others. And taking great delight in his atheism, while tinkering with notions of God as the rain came down. Hadn't the nephew been snatched from the jaws of Calvinism and his mother's puritanical desires, and proudly stapled by Goddard to the doorway of secular inquiry? Hadn't they teamed up against the stupidity of the world? But at the very end it was Goddard who needed religion most of all.

He gazed into the dark and saw nothing at last, felt not a trace of Goddard's presence but could hear the shifting of feet.

The doorway to the study framed a light, into which a woman moved and stood.

He stepped back but was going forward, drawn by the torch-light that played across her face. And getting closer, became aware of his own body: hot, smelly and scratched as he approached the litheness of hers; though he'd never seen her so still before. He was the native and she was the intruder, facing each other now in the heart of this timber oddity; as though he had once lived in this house and she, Teppy Zervos, had come to visit.

'It's the middle of the night,' he said. 'How did you get here?'

She lowered the torch and he could barely see her. 'In the car.'

'I didn't hear it.'

'No.' she said. 'It's too big for the track.'

'The convertible?'

'Yes.' Her voice was strong. 'The tank.'

'Must be wonderful when it pours.'

'You can't go anywhere in the Wet, so it's fine. You really didn't hear it?'

'I was reading. What about you?'

'Delirious with boredom.' A bottle of brandy appeared, but was unopened and she was plainly sober. 'For you.'

'Thanks,' he said. 'I'm like Aggett, never drink between the hours of three and midday.'

'Please yourself.'

The torch at her side moved in a wandering circle and he could see the calf of her leg where it was scratched – probably bougainvillea, purple for her. He watched it come in and out of the circle of soft and artificial light; and though it was only a scratch, the random curves of torchlight seemed to magnify it and moved it back and forth until the insected mark swung right off her leg, which itself began to shift. He heard her move away, down the hall and gone. Ranse lifted the bottle but it was too dark to see. He could feel his hand not shaking but almost relaxed and for a second, thought of the independence and purpose of the study around him and Goddard's floundering diaries, and of what he was about to give up. The faintest glow emanated from the large front room.

She sat on a simple chair by the window; gazing through the rusted screen into the bush and from there out to the fallen night, the town and its limits. The torch was aimlessly hard and not glowing at all; and he wondered what Goddard had done for light. Oil lamps, of course. *Or what his lying uncle did for chairs or women or repairs to his body; and had never been asked much in return about his own life. They weren't close, at all.* At the window Teppy started to hum, a tune so soft and pitchless that it was only invented to cover herself with, as she removed her clothes. And the humming stopped without an end, the light on the wall disappeared and he turned. 'Saves batteries,' she said quietly. 'What have you found?'

He could barely see. 'Here?'

'Among his things.'

'Nothing much.' Ranse stumbled. 'I'm not a detective. Not looking for clues.'

'There aren't any,' she said quickly, at the window. 'No police. And no psychiatrists, either.'

'You've been?'

'You must know by now, we're all a little crazy up here. It helps.'

'But not suicidal?'

A long pause, a gap. 'He was pretty down when Fragas took over. But we all were. He started to pick up and got busy with his work, and then . . .' So softly he missed it. 'Wham,' she trembled. And her eyes were still dark, her dark eyes were surely on his. Ranse could hear the night banging into things that weren't there, things bearing down in the Viseu night, the mirror of affection being dropped: the insects demanding his attention and getting it, and his own body shifting now to hers, and she was moving too.

He felt his wrist taken by sweat. She was naked and her hand was naked most of all. It drew his own hand to her neck, and he coaxed her head to his own and found her lips. He couldn't think clearly of the act to follow – gasping out their unholy alliance, or the motives surrounding it – but already the opposite; even as she abandoned all modesty and found, through the remains of his grubby clothes, the coming together of what she wanted and what he wanted her to find, yes, he was stroking her fine breasts and nipples in a lost, childish dream while his adult thoughts swamped about their moving bodies in confusion and waves of doubt.

'Go on, say it.'

'—' He stopped. 'What about . . .'

'Don't worry.'

He was pressing against her fully but his mind kept swimming away; wanting to explain to himself what was happening, not just here on Goddard's humid bed with Teppy but from one end of this island to the other. It had to stop, not go on. And she touched his body and came down the bed to meet him in rustled silence; and on the outside still her flesh was like the inside flesh of fruit to be discovered, even where she was not young. What was this for, his mind asked having swum as far from her as humanly possible and now he was happily drowning offshore, as the slender but forceful reality of her body rolled onto his mind and killed every doubt of continuity, and there was nothing to do but share with her the remaining moments in the bodily life of it. And then her silence too, acting like a brake on his own tongue, caved in through bare teeth on his shoulder; and she threw her head back to catch the obscenities that could not have been hers or his and screamed so violently, loudly that it jerked him to a moment of conscious panic before gripping her waist and then he felt himself slipping into the Oceanic dream, shuddering like the ruined hulk of a ship going down forever and again. And still again, when he couldn't fathom his own thoughts, when he couldn't even think to underpin his weight on hers, when he couldn't stop his whole body from shaking; and then his mind was immersed deeper into the drowning dream, until the streaks of phosphorus in the night had found their channels of love and the blue tiger was everywhere, all over the bed.

Teppy was stroking his damp fingers, in her own. 'Your love for your hands,' she said. 'That's very male, isn't it?'

In that pitch of night, Ranse was awake. He hadn't woken suddenly, but out of a dream about his uncle though he'd thought of her coming out of it and all he could recall now was a dribble of broken lines: over the years I listened, the answers were never in response to simple questions, but vast equations, volcanic oceans and jungles, that couldn't conceal my loneliness. Who could put a face to a dream like that: it might have been Goddard, or her, or me. At one stage he was slapping his own face, fighting off mosquitoes, boxing the pillow to sleep. There might be blood on the pillow: but Goddard's, or hers, or mine? A cotton mesh hung about them – Teppy Zervos had pulled the net down, and slept now without worry and wisely. A person, an island guest could die of many things, he thought: malaria and suicide being two of the local possibilities. And sex with total strangers; near enough to drowning.

A possum perhaps, *cuscus orientalis:* noises were scratching through the old timber roof, or somewhere in the room beyond the net. But there was only silence when he listened close, and her breathing. It came back to him then: the language he had used with her, the ample crudity of it. In her shock was also a revelation that had put him on firmer if more dangerous territory, and her on softer if not weaker ground. She was human too, with a fascination for bad language; had urged him to stop, and not to, and in the end it didn't matter. *In earlier days the words filled the nights with a sexual vigour and the hidden orators were men and women in the making. But her, and here, and now with a war coming on, and bodies, and death – what good are words, even dirty ones? You reach a particular moment, and reach for the right obscenities – when the sun comes up you'll still be facing evasions and lies.* He turned away from her. But almost as quickly she curled her limbs and torso into his back, and he could feel her mouth aimed at his neck. And could sense the arm and arch of the hip and the outer, neglected part of her thigh. He could feel the breath coming from her body – where was she now? – and activating the smallest hairs on his neck. Before he could trace the path of it, another stream of breath came from deeper than the lungs. She was sleeping heavily, and his own fluid was deep within her. Ranse saw these forces at work, at play as they rode up from the Oceanic dream and closer to another day. And back to reality. There was nothing he had that she could want. But she was hanging onto him, her hand was falling across his hip and he rolled his body over to hers until he could go no further. He rolled onto her and she grumbled against it, the barely audible desire to resist and desiring it too.

'Sam,' she murmured. 'Too heavy.'

And pushing down until he had entered her and in the protest of passions she was abandoned, and he released too quickly and slipped to the rough sheet waiting on the other side. He listened, catching breath. She said nothing more, but they knew she was awake. Though both were soon asleep.

The tropical dawn came slower than the sun, creeping into that peculiar abode and illuminating the furniture, the walls, the curtains, the floorboards, their scattered clothes and her extended body. There was a painting in all of it, in his eyes, or in a dream still going on. Only it was real enough with her lying there in the half-lit space they'd enlivened and done eternal damage to in the short night. It could never be Goddard's again, nor perhaps his; but would be Teppy's from the moment she opened her eyes with the insolence of someone who'd slept often in the same bed. He couldn't help thinking about the two of them. So his Uncle Sam was her lover, or had been; and now he was, had been willingly seduced by her and right here, in Goddard's purposeful room and in this place. At this latitude, perhaps he meant. If anything was tropical, it was sex; or rather infidelity, the most tropical invention of all. The heat could slow down a metabolic interest in most things, but not the companion flesh under you or over you and a common layer of sweat under the flimsiest cotton sheet. And the response was always to smile without embarrassment; even as she awoke Teppy was stroking her small breasts in the light. She smiled and rolled away. Searching for the appropriate lie, while Ranse waited. He felt the tension building up in his own chest – could have suddenly released a tidal wave – but when he expelled there was only a ripple.

'You thought I was Goddard,' he said slowly.

'It happens in Viseu too,' she said.

'An affair with Goddard?'

She turned hesitantly. 'Hardly an affair. I would have gone anywhere with him. Only one problem.'

'What?'

'You're not a very good spy, are you?'

'No, I'm not.'

'A girl and boy,' she said, 'eleven and nine. They're at school in Darwin. This place really isn't safe.'

He began to get up, but felt Teppy's hand on his back. She was describing a circle.

'How did it start?'

'Like this, coming up one day.'

He turned. 'You know what I mean.'

'Does anyone know?'

'I've got a fair idea.'

Teppy pulled her hand back. 'It wasn't that. Sam was important to me, he changed my life.'

'Pity he didn't look after his own. Next you'll be telling me he was a great reformer.' He paused. 'Galvão seems to think so. Aren't you worried about the Fragas, coming here after curfew?'

'They're the ones who are terrified. Haven't you heard? I'm the Dragon Lady of Viseu, supposed to be.'

'And mother of two.' He looked away. 'You had an affair with Eduardo's brother.'

Teppy sat up. 'Inside an affair, yes. My god Nicholas, you've really put us under the microscope, haven't you?'

'Yes,' he said quietly.

'Well?'

Her foot was hanging from the edge of the bed, and he watched it. Over the years he guessed it had taken on the splayed and slightly calloused tone of the tropics, and on the underside you could see quite clearly where Darwin had been right. This would have been Goddard's assessment, anyway.

'What are you smiling at?'

'What's that supposed to mean, the Dragon Lady?'

'I go wherever I want,' she said. 'You saw what happened with da Cunha yesterday. Anyone else, straight to the Museum. They leave me alone.'

'Because of the plane, or Zervos?'

'Because I don't go round asking stupid questions. You haven't let up.'

And a deafening, chattering boulder of sound crashed about the house, onto the iron roof and down into the garden and around the verandahs. Gawking through the rusty wire he could make out humanoid faces and flaying tails. The hammering went on until it passed like a storm and stopped as quickly as it started, and daylight was again in place. He looked out, staggered.

'Monkeys,' she said in disgust.

'Just a few.'

'Sam encouraged them, then he was sorry. Benny's relatives. They never stop.'

'Masturbating?'

'*What?*' She smiled. 'Do they?'

She leaned across his body, the dancer's leg draping itself on his thigh and pulling him back and down.

'Come on,' she said. 'Let's make love. Or are you still interrogating? I don't get the chance that often.'

The beginnings are vague. It's difficult to know where one of life's wars ends and another begins. Possibly the Papaw Wars started in Bangkok, waiting for anything to start, hearing the distant thud of mortars: but only papaws, mangoes and fruit. From jaded affairs to delicate partings, and abrupt breaches of love; gone off to fight in other wars. And other beds, all far removed from this: watching her movements from one dying man to another going up and down, the curtains drawn together not for privacy but effect; for intimacy; and it worked. But let me ask again – must life be a collection of papaw phraseology? What can we see in the papaw's amazing transformation, from the haze-green milkiness of birth, giving life to tropical life and the golden boil of tropical love, giving out to age and the rottenness of time? What does it mean? That wars with no beginning have no end, the friendly Thai replied once; and papaw warfare lasts a long time. It's fun, but it can be dangerous. And later there's always death to consider. Ah, beware the cruel papaw. It eats you up.

'Do me a favour, will you?'

She was gathering her clothes. 'Yes . . .'

'Look after Goddard's diaries for me. I want to send them back, to Australia.'

'Aren't you going with them?'

'No,' he said softly.

'But you're leaving?'

Ranse walked naked to the window. 'Not for a while. I'm going to the mountains this afternoon, with Eduardo. We're paying a visit to the Great Man's grave. With the President's blessing.'

He turned and saw the bra suspended, a hand at either end; she wrapped it quickly to her body. 'Eduardo knows where it is?'

'Why wouldn't he?'

'Peyrot took care of the body, not Eduardo.' She looked at Ranse. 'The Swiss doctor.'

'Did you see Goddard, afterwards?'

Teppy nodded. 'I went to the hospital. Peyrot wouldn't let me at first.' She paused. 'He put the gun to his temple.'

'And they found him here?'

'In the garden, at the bottom. I told Zervos about it, that I wanted to go and see the body. He thought I was crazy.'

'Didn't he know?'

She looked to the busted flyscreen, useless and turning red in the sun. 'After a while you can't have secrets here. You learn that. Anyway my husband thought I was the crazy one, not Sam. It pushed me closer to him of course.'

'And you still wanted to see . . .'

Teppy turned to him. 'I was sick afterwards. But I insisted and Peyrot gave in. I'm not sorry now.'

'I'm seeing him – Peyrot – before I go.'

She shook her head. 'Not if you're leaving today. He's still in the mountains.'

'How do you know?'

'By the radio. Zervos picks up the gossip and passes it on. Tells me everything – the sign of a failed marriage, I think. Peyrot's still up there.'

'Then I'll see him up there,' Ranse repeated. 'Only one road, Eduardo says.'

'Yes,' she replied, 'and a hundred tracks. *And* a thousand eyes, all waiting for you.'

'Me?'

'Yes,' she snapped. 'Oh yes.'

Ranse blustered: 'Why?'

She flicked her head and started to button her shirt. 'Because up there you'll see things you shouldn't. A few people killed and kidnappings. And meetings. But it's coming, don't worry. They all see things differently. Sooner or later that means war.'

'I can't wait.'

'Do you know how many sides there are?'

'Two?'

'Nobody knows.' She slumped into the wooden chair and faced the mirror. 'Every two days they change sides, the war of nerves shifts about. How else do you survive?'

'By getting out?'

'By keeping one step ahead. But in your case, yes . . .' She put her lipstick down. 'You can't bring Sam back. Go now, before it gets worse.'

'I think you're trying to get rid of me.'

Teppy gazed into the mirror. 'Don't worry. If it comes out badly, we'll be gone too.'

'Can I have the Pontiac?'

'What?'

'They say the big ones work out cheaper in the long run.'

'The Ponty,' she scoffed. 'His real love. Shipped over from Darwin in the good old days. The boat almost sank.'

Ranse stood there, minus his trousers, listening with confused interest and still thinking in some reckless way that all this could have a future; as Goddard might have. 'Convenient he left yesterday.'

She growled. 'He'll be back, don't worry. But it's not that hard to scare Zervos out of town. I'm his Dragon Lady too.'

And he could feel two of those hidden eyes already staring at him, over her suggestive and tense smile and could sense a final, robust term of privilege about to happen, even though now she was perfectly made up for the day. She couldn't stop him going to the mountains – to the grave, he would let her believe – and in perversity she might choose to despatch him to war instead with a burst carnation in his buttonhole; but there were no carnations in this climate. Absolutely no garden flowers in sight – dried or otherwise – just fearless desire and a screaming need for security. There was no difference really.

She was already parting her thighs to accommodate his desperate thoughts.

NINE

At the hotel, Aggett was waiting.

'But you told me you weren't going,' Ranse said, 'didn't you?'

'I've spent a whole life changing my mind. On reflection, it hasn't paid off.'

'So why go?'

Aggett paused, drew his breath. 'Come on,' he said. 'We're losing light. To get to Aguema garrison by dark, unless you want to camp out. You're not that crazy, are you?'

Eduardo came around the side of the hotel, in a jeep loaded with supplies. He revved the motor a few times. In his room, Ranse thought and packed furiously. He was holding them up and when he tried to think about Teppy Zervos he could still see the Finance Minister's daughter and when he thought of Goddard's room he could only puzzle on why Aggett had changed his mind: what the hell was going on? Things shifted and changed, and in the process, a toothbrush, jacket, passport, were resolved for better or worse, you emerged with a cluttered overnight bag and a head full of doubts. But deeper down, he was starting to enjoy it.

Going out, he bumped into Gecko who was keyed up with stutters and smiles: 'Mister Ranse . . . '

'I'm going to the mountains.' The jeep was waiting.

Gecko nodded. 'Mister Ranse . . . '

'What?'

'You return. I have the room for you.' He stared, not letting go.

'A few days, a week. Don't worry about it. I have to go.'

But even crossing the lawn – and with Gecko's uncertainty – Ranse felt his own belt of confusion getting wider and tighter. He wanted to expel the tension in his lungs and tried, but this time it was trapped and wouldn't come out. The engine could be detected not running hard, but idling.

'See you,' was all he could say.

After the town, Eduardo made a casual detour to the guest house, and searched in vain for Teppy. But Ranse said nothing. The secrets of Viseu were better known than a day ago, and still as obscure. Could it be Eduardo was looking for the other side in her? The mother or missing sister, or still possibly a lover though that could be troubling, he thought, until he considered that Eduardo's brother had slept with her and his own uncle had too, and now he was her lover so there was a peculiar symmetry to the idea of Eduardo's moody and naked presence in her arms. If so, where would it end? *Contain the heart and freeze the soul, she'd sung, only our bodies grow old. And then he'd felt very much older, not young at last.* And what was she doing now? Perhaps sleeping while the afternoon people were moving through the dusty pool of their lives. Ranse could feel the slightest nostalgia for this place of sagging banana trees and troubled causes; for this country which had begun to exert its dubious pleasures and pressures on him in roughly equal doses. He thought of the vocal President, and his unexpected offer. *I'm not young but the Security Chief is only twenty-four after all.* And he thought of Ancora Dias, and found himself slipping from the slightest reality he'd absorbed in the night just passed with Teppy Zervos and into the conceit of love-making with the Finance Minister's daughter and the President's mistress (*'You hear things,' Aggett had said*) and was afloat on the fantasy of it. He thought of everything except the blank pages in Goddard's last diary and why he'd bothered to come here in the first place and he felt the anger rising; because above all he wanted to forget about that and face his own destiny for a change.

They pulled in before the decaying balustrades of the Viseu markets, on drained swamps at the edge of town. The stalls layered with posters – where he might have seen mountain and coastal natives rubbing their bare shoulders, and noisily selling and swapping fruit, clothes, utensils and gossip – were almost empty, and dismal. The only produce was spotted and old, and the few marketeers wore body cloths of reddish-black and yellow, intruded with dust and stamped indelibly as works of poverty. The dyes themselves might have been watered down, he thought: against the recent memory of Thailand's embarrassing reds and bright pinks and yellows, it actually seemed possible. Along with mats, ropes, pottery; though for whose benefit he couldn't see. A few drab ends, was all it amounted to.

'He's not here,' said Eduardo.

'Who?'

'Fevereiro.'

'Who?'

'A man called Fevereiro. He's gone. We've come here too late,' he said, looking at Ranse.

'What for?'

He gave an uncooperative shrug. 'So he can tell us what's happening.'

'Oh.'

But perhaps they weren't late at all; perhaps February hadn't come, or most of the other months of the year either, and those who did brought so little that it was always like this. Ranse gazed about. They had nothing much to sell, they were creatures of some long and almost uneventful famine that was slowly reducing them from the face of the Earth, one by one. Perhaps his friend had gone that way too.

They hit flat ground. No flatter than Viseu itself, but devoid of the random buildings and foliage that had given relief from the monotony they faced now. Around them the truth of Inhumas was geographically bare, the bitumen dropped off and the road was clayey and hard and led only to another fringe settlement, the limit of lost dreams, and then to nowhere. The sky seemed to touch it, the product of a very intense burning: you could have seen it from the coast of Australia or the centre of Mars. A fire that centuries ago might have ripped through a rainforest,

107

ravaging the jungle flat; so that now the sky came right down to the ground, exposing the sparse vegetation and those who travelled through it. Between the smiling but Doleful Sea to the right and the aimless road in front of them stood a line of trees – short eucalypts, struggling here for life – and something that was neither sand nor dirt, which further along became even whiter and hard.

Aggett turned from the front. 'Salt mines,' he said. 'They mine it down the shafts.'

But deserted now, with old rigging, and Ranse could only pretend an interest. He was still distrustful of Aggett's presence, if only because the Americans had been lied to. *Where did that leave him, in some unexplained ditch? What was Aggett up to?* The trust they'd shared was suddenly dry, and he found it hard to revive the earlier responses: the smiles and jovial cracks were replaced by salt mines that hadn't been worked for ages, and the scrubby tumbleweed around them fighting for survival. A hundred yards from the sea, it was strangely arid and bare. And then, the strangest sight of all.

'What's that?'

'Our patrol boat,' said Eduardo. 'To watch for landings. A fishing boat for many years. See the gun on it.'

'The Fragas Navy,' quipped Aggett, 'all three tons of it. They'll squeeze it in Jane's Fighting Ships, between Great Britain and France.'

Eduardo laughed too, even when he couldn't understand and Ranse settled uncomfortably into his cave. It was enough that he wasn't offended, he supposed.

A native kampong ahead, half a dozen large bamboo and grass huts on stilts around a central gathering hall. They had landed long ago and had slowly worn into the setting, and were as natural now as the people who inhabited them: dark-skinned figures in long rough shawls twisted around their fine bodies, tangles of shaggy curls and spirals of uncertain intentions who stared quietly as the jeep bumped past their lives. They stared; at every level of thatched housing, from every tree or standing on the dried earth itself; at every distance too someone with a dark, uneven face was staring at Ranse: but without question, without wanting to know. They stood about, stunned as victims of some great cultural upheaval might have in centuries gone by; and had been muscles, been slaves for their arms, thighs and backs; and now slavery was obsolete and they were free. They could have been happy, might have been sad: had not caught up with revolutionary reality; were creatures trapped in some tropical museum or zoo, and Ranse and Aggett and even the driver were spectators. These were not villagers, Eduardo said, but only a few living in isolation and fear of community. *And lost in their own land, he thought.* Further up, said Eduardo, they'd see the true villagers and real interaction and political gains and support for Fragas and a willingness to fight and defend the revolution; but these people didn't want to know about that, and weren't a party to it. They were left alone.

In each bay, at each curve another kampong of uneven faces and misgivings about the day. It happened once, twice, five times. Their lives were confined by the road. To cross it and head further inland led only to the common malarial swamps; and then the granite hills began and suddenly, almost violently, the huge forms of the Tagua screamed one, two, three thousand metres into the afternoon sky. Up there was another race of people and the coastal natives didn't cross that territory, Eduardo said, didn't go there. So they fought off malaria and lived like Melanesians which they probably were; while the mountain tribes drew their blood not from Oceanic roots or even Asia, but from something darker and more complex going back into time. And more recently, from Portugal. It was higher and cooler up in the Tagua; and on the mountain called Corguinho, where legend said Goddard was buried, the air would be European and comprehensible. Ranse could understand living and dying up there, but not among these difficult faces on the coast.

It was still light although the sun had left the mountains, and the emptiness of the road called them on. The Dry season kept baking the earth beneath the floor of the jeep and would all night and it wouldn't turn cold until higher up. And then Ranse shivered: he wanted to get there, be up there now.

That man in the reeds, the lotus man, what was he doing, was he thinking, slowly dreaming in the lotus sunset, no sunshine sunset, the junk-yards, extensions of man and woman abound, where are the women tonight, lotus lovers all, bound for the hills, heads in heat, lost in sounds of rattling railway tracks, going back to Chiang Mai, cruising up country on Thai tornadoes, those lotus left behind and ever present Thais, silk speeding north, Bangkok behind, south is the sun and sand, north is jungle and all Asia, untapped and unfree, hopelessly tangled in electric vines, freedom is standing by the rusty tracks, mothers and sons, empty hopes and overhead dreams, take me south, south away from it all, but north is my soul, the south is sudden death; as in dreams of night, nightmares and wild horses, all those tired horses pulling us back to the north, a rest.

He saw a fork ahead, though no indication of which way to go, to turn: how would they decide? The afternoon was ending slowly, giving off smells of dry gum leaves (squeezed dry) and a faintly Mediterranean clove. He supposed it was Greek, though Aggett might have called it Tuscan or even Maltese; but the roots of the strangest plants here were always Portuguese, in a distant way. He had never been there either, but imagined he knew. Because the land was more Australian than anything else, he felt it was also a part of himself; of his own geography from the past. People could have spiritual homes too: only the slightest physical connection was needed, the rest you played out yourself, like an actor fitting into a role. On the first visit to Europe, he'd been to Greece and waited to be breasted by herbs and cool Aegean breezes. But what had struck him was the dryness, the pure heat, dust – ruin rather than ruins, life that was at once full of potential and possibilities and hopeless too. And despite the detachment he still wanted to feel, slowly he felt this country acting on him like that; and himself acting too on the fractured landscape it offered. The fork came at them slowly, pushing out of the flat road that one day promised a great sunshine highway and deciduous dreams of escape. It was coming slowly to them and going away, but gradually the fork was on them: and the road dribbled without signs to indicate which direction to take. *It took a war to wipe everything away; then another, and another after that.* But already they'd chosen their path, or at least Eduardo – that strange, dark child of a grown man, a security chief no less, whose head could have been carved from Carrara marble, in its stillness and strength, but with eyes that flicked and darted and changed focus endlessly across the barren land, missing nothing even when nothing was apparent – had chosen for them; or rather – and here Ranse struggled for an exact description of how the decision was made, demanded of himself the precise answer to this eternal problem of choice – had not chosen at all but simply let his right hand fall and raised his left arm and the wheel of fortune that took them everywhere had already turned right and the absence of calculations ensured they were heading in the correction, the correct direction he meant to say but nobody was listening, towards Pojuca, lovely jewel by the sea.

The very name spelt more in his mind than the place or objects it described; like some floral or botanic words he played with, as a mathematician might play with numbers or a mechanic with valves. *Frangipani.* It had ceased to be simply a tropical, overpowering bloom for Ranse the botanist years before, and for some reason beyond verbal requirements, the simple recitation of that endorsement could adequately frame a thought, a response, a late afternoon chill or even a defeat in all its pristine sadness. And now the form of Pojuca was entering his mind, leaping not from blanket impressions but from those humps he could already see, the elongated blisters that just managed to bury but didn't hide the bodies of a dozen or more men of war: the unlucky ones. They stopped the jeep, subdued the engine and got out.

Beneath the first, a grown man's or just a boy's body was already collapsing under the weight of earth and being drawn – though early days yet – to that common core where all of history's deaths were compressed and recorded in inches. *If you need a reason to live, Sam, you need an even stronger one to die.* The oleanders shot up against the walls in poison pink clusters. Ranse walked towards them, his eyes absorbing but hardly feeling the bullet sprays where the underbelly of plaster was revealed in dots. He stood urinating into the branches, and looked down. Buried among them, like a childish secret, was a tombstone: carved in soft marble and falling on its side. It was a child's grave, or even a baby's. He shook his penis, at that premature curve into the unknown; and then saw the words inscribed and half removed by the alternate Wet and Dry seasons. For a few seconds or a minute, a slight and awkward smile came over his face. They all had their stories, yes. But in the name of Mendonça, he would never have thought it possible. He turned and saw the others; and behind them the resort – a clump of leisure, a grove of haphazard trees, the sea – was utterly lifeless.

'Where is everybody?' called Aggett. 'Off to war again?'

'Nobody's here, since the last fighting,' Eduardo replied. 'You know why.'

'Tell me again.'

'Because it's a cage,' he heard Eduardo say. 'The sea, and no cover behind. Don't get caught here.' He pointed to the fresh graves, the ambushed lives.

There was no cover indeed, or pleasure. But he could see how, by rough juxtaposition, the myth of Pojuca could be maintained. It sat in a twist: a faded apparition of some romantic joy against the bluntness of toady surroundings to the rear, where the scrub picked up again. Even now a trickle of spring water got through to the overhanging palms. They'd made it work all right. The rulers of colonial Viseu had created a shore at which they could relax, dream and fornicate in peace. Reminded of home too, but able to do things that home would never allow: here the levers of church, commerce and rule were diverted to other places and days. Ranse still couldn't imagine it. Perhaps life in the old times of Pojuca was just as empty as it appeared now, deserted. But you could only feel that if you stood around these clumps of death.

'Come on,' said Aggett troubled, 'let's get out of this Hollywood dump. It smells like dead flowers. Ranse.'

He could already hear that phrase in his dreams. To signal always the change, a point from which he was unable and unwilling to go back to where and what he'd been before all this had begun. Like dead flowers, at which the push and pull began. *Like something awful in your past; you're glad you can't recall it but frustrated too. If only you could remember, without*

112

experiencing the awful memory of it. And so you reinvent it,
reshape it; find a point of entry where it doesn't threaten you,
doesn't hurt too much and you take it from there and move on.
Always there'd be dead oleanders and frangipanis and that
child's grave popping up in his thoughts at the unlikeliest
moments – but there'd be no unlikely moments from now on.
Life would be blessed instead with a mixture of stale perfume
and guns.

The river spread before them. Its endless width seemed to go
nowhere: the other side was as wide and flat as the desolation
they'd driven through, covered not with foliage as much as
vegetation of extreme hunger and thirst. Only the bougainvillea with its secrets of rejuvenation came up and scraped the
sides of the jeep, and the insides of ears and the tips of his teeth.
And trapped in the back, Ranse was wincing and thinking of
blackboards, of running home from school, of reaching that
house on the Brisbane River, of swimming that river in flood, of
tangled hyacinths – springing from Hyacinthus, struck dead by
Zephyrus and his flying quoit – and bloated cows swept to their
deaths, of dead Uncle Sam and the living and capable flesh of
Teppy Zervos and lastly of decaying flowers, over and over
until the river. It was the flattest he had ever seen.

'Rio Bras,' said Eduardo. 'We can cross.'

'In this?'

'Yes, not very deep.'

'Dry up here,' Aggett cut in. 'Worse than before. Drought in
the tropics, can you believe it?'

'It's not really Asia,' he said.

'Don't worry, we'll be on the other side in ten minutes. And
then,' Aggett stood up, 'off to pay homage to your illustrious
uncle's final place of rest – high in the bowels of the Tagua
Mountains.' The jeep inched towards the water's edge. With a
single word – *homage* – Aggett had shown how simple it was
for a man to find himself in this situation, in this very place at
5.30 on a late November day in the middle of an extremely
troubled decade on earth. But he was wrong too. There was
more to it than paying respects: that was a mental task and
could easily be achieved in another country, over a bottle or
two. Ranse was dragging himself to mountains infected by war

as much to erase the terminal influence of Samuel Goddard as to honour it; not to die alongside his decrepit, glorious uncle but to escape the ties that eternally bound them, even in death; not to worship Goddard's image but to cut it down to size and if the man himself had already done that with a gun, then conversely to pick up the fragments of his own troubled life and proceed to the thinnest edge: just for a look, at least.

He didn't reply. But surrounded by boxes and the splashing water, Ranse accepted it. Because events were taking over, after two hours of track. On the opposite shore were human figures, dark and fleeting like ants; calling to him, to him alone and not the others. The soldiers were waiting.

BOOK TWO: UPCOUNTRY

The gun has got its trigger,
and everyone does just what he likes.

TEN

'Where to?'

Aggett turned. 'They think I'm a working hack. Taking us to the model farm, at this hour. Sit back and enjoy it.'

'Do they speak English?'

'Why not ask them?'

But the soldiers were twenty, fifty metres ahead in a battered truck and Eduardo was fighting the dust to stay with them. Strangers from another war or just another side of the same war; or just from the other side of the river. They were Fragas too, but carried the soil across their bodies and their bare feet. Ranse couldn't stop watching them. Inside thick boots, his own feet were pressing silently and hot. He felt like the enemy. But the soldiers were devoid of curiosity, had already parcelled him shabbily as a foreigner. He'd been quickly absorbed into the muddy landscape of swamps and small, shallow lakes. The effect was unsettling, as they pushed for twenty or thirty minutes into the dry wastes again; but slowly too they were rising, and he saw the Tagua looming to the north. Just as the jeep began thumping like a sick cow.

A flat tyre, half an hour.

On a volcanic lump, he sat watching them. The vehicle was jacked up like an insect and they were struggling with the spare wheel. Aggett was supervising.

He scanned the horizon, from the granite burst high on a ridge above Viseu (obscured by trees that grew dust, and silence) and above Pojuca which sat clearly and forlorn at the water's edge; and beyond it the Sea of one single face curving

117

into a giant smile of escape. *There was nothing astonishing out to Sea, except the places it could take you.* From the same ridge always, the Pacific swept the vast Melanesian shimmer with Tahiti at its fringes; and whatever a person could get away with there. But why had Goddard chosen to come here: to repeat and amplify the joyless dust and heat of Australia, the meagre bush and runtish fauna, like a dried mole or a weasel without teeth, rubbing though the same groove until predictably, you also found it dry and pointless and wanted after six, seven, eight years to move on? Or kill yourself, logically rounding off the unhappy dream that was never quite a nightmare but certainly towards the end, no bliss. Looking out he could see no jungle, or real fertility; but thickets of low scrub and pale grasses of an Australian, desperate kind. He tugged a gum leaf from a branch, and crunched it in his hand – over and over – until the heat drew its fumes and stung his warmed nostrils. He sprinkled the leaf fragments on the rock, to the ground. The almost forgotten reason for Australia was that intense vacuum behind the coast; the thinnest air into which all the words and actions and ideas were sucked day and night, to create the droning interiors of our lives. That was Goddard's theory, anyway.

The softness of dialect was coming to him, and Ranse turned. They were tinkering with the motor, Aggett had wandered off. He leaned back to the rock and could see Goddard sitting at the base of a huge river gum, in paint-splattered Army shorts (conscripted, he'd never fought) with an old testicle visible and resting up his leg. Affecting a strong love of the land, though he wasn't farm material either. And debating for hours whether the Australian ethos had been formed by the Bush or the Beach, by the Outback or the Sea. The uncle had come down from the garden to listen, and talk.

'I've got it,' said Ranse.

'The outback, right?'

'No, the sea.'

'Oh god,' he pleaded, 'let's hear the bloody thing. I've got lectures in an hour.'

'Listen. We scratch our memories. And take an early Fifties pride,' he was reading his notes, 'in swimmers – those sparkling fish, taxing Newton's Law of Gravity, Archimedes'

Principle of Displacement and Einstein's Theory of Relativity. At the same time they're busting Olympic records by the hour. We had heroes . . .'

In the sunshine, Goddard was examining his right knuckle like some prehistoric claw. 'Six out of ten.'

Nicky took a breath. 'And the rest. I know it's crazy, after all They Came From The Sea . . .'

'Pompous.'

'. . . but one more point in its favour. It's *my* theory,' he'd smiled.

And later at the headlands of Sydney Harbour, the gaping rock jaws of a thousand suicides and seasick rides to oblivion and nowhere, cursing the wind of a bleak winter's day, the primaeval moss clinging to those horizontal cliffs jutting out below, plateaux of death, the wave curls up and slides under itself, emptying foam-gut over the green moss, and Ranse turning his grown back on the land: on Sydney, the pulse if not the heart of Australia; his back to it all. And staring out to the sheet of Pacific winter, the longest marine vibrations in all history ended there, losing their weight and gaining a Free Ocean ride, coming in to settle a point, tipped onto a tiny shell below to end it all. Would you ever jump, she asked and her own goose-pimples swelled in a wave, would you ever want to he replied: a suicide pact between himself and the holidaying woman he loved because Goddard despised her, the artist who was free and might even break her neck to prove it; but an empty suicide pact, followed by a cup of tea at the kiosk as the Sea kept coming at them.

'I'll brood over it in Botany III,' said Goddard, wiping his temples. And already Ranse was going back – even as Goddard rose to change and head off for campus – to days with his mother at the seaside, tasting watermelons that had miraculously sprung from seeds they'd thrown away the year before. The water's edge was alive, and had its patterns too.

'Good luck,' his uncle had flung off with the manners of an earlier age, whether meaning it or not. 'See you tonight.'

Like that always – just the two of them. He could barely remember other figures, or people, or faces. Were there no visitors, what had happened to his university friends and other relatives? Just the drifting Mrs Perkins who cleaned, and the odd meals they shared with her (everything being 'in the lap of the gods' she claimed) but essentially just the two of them – uncle and nephew, like father and son – locked across the table, or extremes of the room. He had of course been trapped; seen clearly now, a victim of Goddard's selfish desires. Friends were discouraged and later the women he'd perhaps loved, perhaps not, were disowned and Goddard had demanded to know why he was rejected so and why Ranse had failed to make the pilgrimage to Viseu when it all fell apart. And now he was getting back his revenge, if it was at all possible to extract revenge from a dead man; for already the pilgrimage was reduced to a homage, and then a pointless expedition to a dusty grave. He came back, heard the vehicles starting up again.

'You see, Ranse,' shouted Aggett, walking over and waving his arms at the limping jeep, 'keep your goals simple.'

He looked up: 'Trucks aren't lives.'

'You should have been a bloody politician, you know that? A lawyer . . .'

'Or an artist.'

'Come on,' said Aggett, 'they'll go without us. An adventurer, that's what you are.'

Across an almost grassless plain with the lesser heights in and out of touch, the convoy pulled over. The soil might have been rich in parts – what he could still see of it – but there was limestone too and overall the land was sterile and gone. A simple concrete building stood in the going day, only half-built but already falling apart. A dozen rooms in line, each with a plain wooden door; some shut tight, but most hanging on limp hinges. Inside one he saw an iron bed frame, urine-soaked mattress, flies on excreta. A pile of rude hoes sat neglected in the vast and tortured farmyard spread out behind the crumbling block. Stalks of corn poked out of the ground, crumpling half-way up and dried to straw men. In better times a field of sugar might be possible. Rice, sweet potatoes, greens. A slice of Thailand, transferred to this. It could be done.

'The model farm,' said Eduardo, without emotion. 'The presidente told me to bring you. The Livre fighters took our people here. They locked them up, with wild pigs. Without food. They left them with the pigs.'

The afternoon light wouldn't go away. Ranse wanted desperately to respond but his face showed absolutely nothing when called on – he saw at his feet the scattered, chalky bones and teeth bleaching in the same light as before. *Go away, or go dark.* But the teeth especially sat there, free of betel now. Smiling at him, laughing. *And saying man is structurally a happy creature, sucked into relative sadness only by the addition of muscle and nerve.* They sat on the dirt, these particles. It would be a quagmire, the whole plain awash in the dutiful Wet; but for now it was relentlessly hot and dry, and they showed it.

'Very effective,' said Aggett, 'like message sticks.'

'We left the bones here,' Eduardo explained. 'Always to let people know, what they did to us. About ten killed in this way. But only men. They took the women, of course.'

Aggett was nodding: 'The real scores. They'll be settled across Asia, now the Americans are gone. Just like this,' he said to Ranse. 'They could have killed the poor sods, and buried them.'

'But they had to run,' said Eduardo. 'We caught up with them, two days after. And killed them all.' He smiled faintly. 'We left them in the sun.'

The natives cleared the undergrowth by fire, they glowed in the approaching dark like small gods at work against the blunt mystery of a single line of mountains. And they had always hunted with bows and arrows, and spears with iron tips: all against the deer and feral pigs which they chased into traps and killed for food, while keeping their own skills alive. It worked like this, always had along the ridges. Each village was free to grow and die, to make battle and peace and nobody on the coast had really cared because there was nothing to be gained or lost. No trains, no roads, no cars, no power, no water, no lights, no links he thought. And every year, the Wet slushing even tracks like this one further into the valleys and the settlements might just die, be forgotten. From this Eduardo wanted to build a country, for nation was too big a word.

They were heading for the Aguema garrison, further inland and higher up. All around the view was spectacular and the detail was dropping away and taking with it the depth and space needed to confuse things. The hills grew into a darkish line that was both firm and reassuring; like the Great Wall, keeping out the darker unknown forces which history had placed behind all mountains. Along the nearest ridge, and the one behind that and so on up to the lower peaks, the red fires were burning; not out of control, but almost formally and contained. But the warmth fell away quickly, and Ranse chilled. The others – the Livres – would already be stalking them out there, covering the distance through darkness and distracting fires and the Tagua shaped into a single mass of concern. It was becoming impossible to live without it.

'Boa noite!' he called from the gates. 'How are you Mr Ranse, welcome to Aguema. And Aggett, you too.'

They shook hands vigorously in the colder air and Sergeant Oscar e Sousa, slouch hat on head with feathers, escorted them across the compound. The sergeant's pride and strength of purpose worked out of his face like a continent; even in this light the nose bulged, and wrinkles ran down the slopes of his cheeks and emerged on his hands. In the field, e Sousa was a different man. He was against the elements he loved, and a touch of mystery came down on him with the light fog.

'The men will look after you,' he said, moving off with Eduardo. 'They have dinner in the mess hall.'

Across the parade ground, the men – or boys, urchins – hurried in different directions. All had jobs of a revolutionary kind. Discreet lights were coming on, and he could hear a generator humming in the night.

'Getting us out of the way,' said Aggett. 'So talks can begin.'

'On what?'

'The cost of mangoes.'

Ranse stopped. 'I can do without it.'

Aggett gradually halted, but didn't speak.

'Just tired, that's all.'

'Sorry old man.'

They walked silently for a minute. 'The bones,' said Aggett.

He stalled. 'I guess so. And this, the kids. What's it for?'

Aggett shrugged impatiently. 'Someone has to win. I told you not to come.'

Away from their own, they were less answerable; up here the altitude pushed it along. So he thought, with the orphans of Aguema shifting around them like grown men. They were quietly making boots, and probably guns and making flour and bread, and repairing weapons and printing up texts for the locals and engaging themselves in all the industry that Sergeant e Sousa and the coming battles could throw at them. So far from the outside world; or even from Viseu itself where there was no contiguity with the roots, where Life was simply a layer over all the other illogical layers and processes – like mines of lead and gold, with conflicting seams and veins going everywhere. Down there things could never be stopped like this: by taking needs as they came, and responding with honesty and crude simplicity. A shoe, a grenade, a cup of coffee. Or perhaps their lives weren't improved by it, but drawn and hopelessly confused by the inexplicable forces that drove them into nothing more than circles. A meal, a blanket, a crop of rice. What would they give to ride that top layer, just once in a while – as we did nearly every day of our lives?

'Let's hope it's more than boiled eggs,' said Aggett.

After dinner, they walked into a night as spectacular as he would ever know. The stars in the deepest sky, moon, fires glowed at them and growled at any advance in their direction until he seemed to be walking backwards. You couldn't look up, or down; or find a single direction, there were so many.

'Come on,' Aggett called. 'The mosquitoes will eat your balls off.'

'Okay. Just dreaming, all right?'

'Yeeaahh,' he said, turning his head up. 'That stew, laced with cheap brandy. Kills the germs.'

Ranse smiled, that explained it.

'Hello.' Aggett was waving to a couple of guards, who watched him curiously. 'Fala inglês?'

They picked up their rifles and came across, shaking their heads on the way. 'Não,' of course not.

'What about Portuguese, eh?'

They shook hands. 'Chamo me Tini.'

'Ricardo.'

'I'm Aggett, he's Ranse.'

Hands going everywhere.

Ranse turned aside: 'Ask about the mountains, what's going on.'

'This is the mountains.'

A quick exchange with the taller boy, the other wasn't interested. And Ranse felt his own tiredness too.

'They're clearing land,' said Aggett. 'The fires.'

'About the fighting.'

Another exchange.

'They've been practising dry shooting.'

'What's that?'

'Without bullets. They've heard there's fighting going on, further up. They hope so.'

'Great.'

'They think so.'

'Ask them where we're sleeping.'

In e Sousa's personal quarters, and hosted like nobility: eating small cakes the boys had made; and then Dutch beer in cans, and port from the recent colonial past, the drowsy chat of their own escorts outside and slowly he knew everyone was slurring themselves to sleep, but first he heard Thermudo da Cunha on the radio. 'Nove horas, até já,' be right back.

To bed, to sleep anyway at nine.

It came as a catlike purr, growing louder in a propeller hum, then a drone. As dreams and nightmares ended with the same giddying fear.

'Jesus,' whispered Ranse.

'Bloody hell,' Aggett struggled to his feet.

'Quê?'

The walls shook, the night was sucked from their heads and replaced with a dull explosion; and their eyes widened for the shock that took so long it never came, only the amplified silence broken by the methodical retreat of the aircraft as it banked into the valley and was gone. They rushed to the window.

'What is it?'

But he could see for himself now. The water tank had been demolished by a single grenade. Every drop – the garrison's whole supply – had emptied like dishwater into the parched gully. The tank stand was crimpled in the night mist, poking its limbs at the thin air; and the last whisper of the plane was bouncing off the hills.

Eduardo hurried back, leaving e Sousa to reorganise his oasis of efficiency. The boys were running and clattering, and scared. 'We must go,' he said.

'Tonight?'

'Yes, come on. Hurry.'

'Are you mad?' Aggett protested. 'We're driving into that?' He pointed to nothing, the night itself.

'The road to Maracacume's okay, e Sousa says. We'll be safer there. Come on. They'll give us some grenades. But it's okay.'

'How far?'

'Not very far. Five, six kilometres. Only one hour.'

'God. What about you, Ranse?'

Still confused. 'The plane . . .'

'Come on then, out of here. Before we're reduced to bits of flesh.'

They said goodbye to Aguema, and took the jeep. It wasn't 10 o'clock yet.

ELEVEN

They were still moving, or being moved. Lying on rice bags in the back with the overhead canvas blotting out the stars, and sides cancelling the view. What they saw was a film, disappearing as they faced their most recent past: the road they'd just stirred into a mild and moonlit duststorm. It was one of those boyhood films – Tarzan, Jungle Jim – where the man, woman, boy and dog took forever to get where they were going; they took the whole film, in fact. The journey began to devour itself finally and lost its purpose, you dozed off or spat wads of licorice through buckled straws. Beside him, the elder Aggett was breaking a twig into odd matchsticks, and flicking them out. Ranse was sweating, trying not to feel cold or hot. Beyond the next ridge, who knew what? Already they were sharing the burden of not knowing where the fraternal voyage was taking them: other than to the mountains and perhaps the grave.

RANSE   The water business, what is it?
AGGETT   It's called dropping grenades in water tanks. (Pushing his hair back) There's a drought on. It'll put them back for days, carting water up from the valleys.
RANSE   I know that.
AGGETT   Don't you believe me?
RANSE   (Switching) It was Zervos, wasn't it?
AGGETT   Who can tell?
RANSE   Maybe he was after me.
AGGETT   (Sitting up) Come on. Apart from the obvious,

126

	and that's assuming he knows. Just because you've slept with his wife, along with half the town? Don't flatter yourself . . .
RANSE	Thanks. It's not that.
AGGETT	You heard him in the bar, he moves with the tide. Whatever's going. But he's up to something, of course.
RANSE	Yes.

There *was* a reason and it wouldn't go. Could he afford to think he'd been drawn to the mountains simply by Eduardo's vagueness, by Presidential smiles and Teppy's lies – to inspect farms that couldn't be helped and a grave that didn't exist? Because she'd killed his uncle and Zervos was trying to scare him out of the country? She was confused and defensive, about the ugliest creature in Viseu, and unfaithful at the same time. Ranse shook as the axle scraped another boulder.

AGGETT	He aims for the rocks. (Calls out) Take it easy, okay? (Quietly) He's worried about an ambush.
RANSE	We're going to get killed up here, aren't we?
AGGETT	No, don't be silly.
RANSE	Look at you.
AGGETT	It's dark, Ranse. (Pauses) What can you see? I'm just here for the ride.
RANSE	Or the fighting, right?
AGGETT	It's about time we had another war, to remember. I've forgotten a lot of the last one.
RANSE	Here?
AGGETT	Silly boy. I mean the last big one, over Germany.
RANSE	You were in the Air Force? (No reply, he turns) How could you forget that?
AGGETT	Oh, you do. After the war of course, everyone talked about it. Like yesterday. You always found someone who'd fought, got out alive. But now nobody talks about the war. It's slipped their minds.
RANSE	Only to return in old age?

AGGETT	I'm only fifty odd, son.
RANSE	(Smiling, unseen) Is that why you gave Vietnam away?
AGGETT	Is that why I gave it away? (Pauses) You sound like everyone who fell on that miserable place, like Eisner. 'Will we get killed?' As if there might be some other way around it, the business of war. That's why I went to Malta. Not because I was scared, but they were. And they were making me sick.
RANSE	(Weakly) And so Malta was okay?
AGGETT	Lots of wine, crumbling farms. Gozo's older than the rest, they drink Johnnie by the gallon and go to church. My adopted homeland. (Considers) That's where Goddard should have gone – you wouldn't be going through all this now.
RANSE	He wasn't into roses, or grapes.
AGGETT	Neither was I. What do you want to know that for, anyway?
RANSE	Did it work, that's all?
AGGETT	(Reflects) No man is rich enough to buy back his past, Oscar Wilde said. You know that?
RANSE	No. Or his future.
AGGETT	You can only go with what's there, Ranse. My life is reporting, even when I'm in the bath.

He wasn't lying. He was past caring, for that. But he spoke deliberately in riddles, Ranse knew. He got to the point, or rather the point he wanted you to get to, by a circuitous route designed on his own terms to sort out those who had an ability to understand and wanted to, and those lost souls who didn't have a hope in hell. It was Aggett's way of sorting out people, and only the wise fools got there. Ranse wasn't sure if he'd fallen aside or not. The image of journalists he'd collected and carried over his adult years (times of distrust, contempt even) and the types fostered in the media itself (drunks, hacks, muckrakers, womanisers, dead at fifty) hadn't come true in this Englishman whose very appearance suggested more ease than competition, more style than sloggery. And so he – Nicholas

Ranse, to whom the isolation of Australia had admittedly been the barren crucible of these half-baked ideas – couldn't be sure. Aggett was hinting at fear of something, which he wouldn't acknowledge or define: perhaps the very fear of society that had driven Goddard from his academic gold-mine to the wastes of this neo-tropical Siberia, the salt mine of lost hopes. At his own insistence, Aggett wasn't scared of dying; but that was exactly what Goddard had said, and now Goddard was dead either because he couldn't wait for nature to take its terrible course or because Teppy Zervos had got in the way. *I'm a young man, he'd written – not my intention to grow old, or my need. (To get old, to get infirm I mean. I am getting old.) And Nicholas, there's always the future to consider: even at your age. I mean, don't go groping down the dark alley-ways of life, I know you were always one for darkness. I sought the light but you got the darkness in there early, and it won't let go.* He searched for Aggett's face, the barest outlines of it; and could see an element of hopelessness that was both plain and dangerous. But then Goddard had been older and ready for the next world, in those inexplicable letters; from the earliest days his impatience with this one somehow suggested it. And clearly Aggett wasn't that far gone. He was still the participating observer, if that was possible: the sane man who could also be morbidly enthusiastic, given not to slashing his wrists or killing himself or others but to a reasonably perverse enjoyment of watching general inhumanity at work. Yes, reasonably perverse. That summed him up.

Now leave me alone, he'd added; and Ranse had complied.

'What's this?'

Aggett came to life. 'Oh, that's it. The boys' school and seminary,' he said, sitting up. 'Where Galvão hails from, Eduardo too.'

'Rebel nursery.'

'More like a big, fat whore,' grunted Aggett, getting out. 'Don't think they learned anything revolutionary in those walls. Only by default.'

Ranse spun before the vastness of it. 'I was expecting a church.' In the exaggerated night was moored a neo-classical monument to Portuguese fund-raising, a marble ocean liner

129

with no name.

'It's called Maracacume, that's all. After the village, further on. Possibly a saint or a brand of cheese.'

'We made it,' said Eduardo quietly.

'Grateful. Where are the boys?'

'On holidays.'

Aggett put his arm around Eduardo, and smiled. 'I'll send you to England, for lessons in lies. They do a marvellous job over there. Can't tell in the end.'

He pulled back, quietly. 'We can always tell when you're lying, Senhor Aggett. Because you haven't trained properly?'

'I went to the wrong school, yes.'

Catching their uneasy reflections was a pool for swimming in, though not what Ranse called a swimming pool. It was carved from rock, a Babylonian corner full of algae and the cumulations of nature. From this peculiar setting he looked up. At the top of a vast stairway stood not another classroom or church, but a simple plaster house with an iron cross on the roof. The host was bounding down the steps in a frock.

His skull was shining and deeply impressive in the moonlight. Father Telles reached them heavily but not out of breath, and hugged Eduardo for a moment. The others were introduced with brevity: Aggett journalista, Ranse botânico. He gave an impatient smile, and urged them up the grandest stairs; stopping only for the foreigners to get their breath back.

'It's difficult,' he stated.

He waved them up to the residence, set within the Tagua Mountains. It overtook the rugged surrounds by the essence of simplicity. A house on a hill, nothing more or less. And nothing like Goddard's mimicry of life in another place; buried where no eyes could see it. This one fitted the landscape from afar. But as they approached the narrow doorway, Ranse saw none of that elemental purity, only confusion and disorder.

In the main room, the hissing of a gas lamp and the background crackle of a short-wave receiver; against the bare walls, the furniture was pushed and abused. Two men were slumped in chairs, one was lying in silent pain on a puffy old sofa. He was roughly bandaged and blood was darkening whole areas, so that the wounds themselves seemed to be breaking through.

130

His eyes were afloat, and his head shifted slightly but quickly like a bird to catch sight of the visitors; but fell back quickly to the hissing shadows on the wall. Everything took a hard edge from the lamp. On the floor a bottle of spirits, demolished in pain or anger. From another room, Ranse heard a sob, another and then a groan. His eyes caught a fourth man standing at the fireplace, toying aimlessly with a revolver. Clicking it, unclicking it, his thoughts therein contained; or perhaps shattered. Other weapons smelling of oil and recent use were lumped into a corner. Ranse shivered. He was at last witnessing battle, but through the back door. The aftermath had come first.

Telles stood like a stranger, as reluctant to enter his own house as they were. Ranse was curiously moving forward but it was Eduardo who pushed past and into the room, exploding in abuse.

The men dropped their heads, looked away to things that weren't there. They'd taken their own humiliation, and were too tired now to listen. Eduardo gave up and thrust into the back room. The radio filled the awkward silence with static, up and down. And in exasperation, Eduardo reappeared and paced to the door.

Aggett entered. 'Did e Sousa know about this?'

'Perhaps.'

'Of course he did. That's why we came, isn't it? He told you to get up here and see . . .'

'No,' Eduardo stopped him. 'We left for your safety, and his,' he pointed to Ranse. Behind them the soldiers – messengers of things to come – sat listening. Because after this, the war would get worse.

The radio went quiet. In a second, the night air was free to breathe again. But there was no darkness to bring them together, it was a brightly lit silence. And he wished – as they exchanged glances and fear bounced off their eyes – wished that da Cunha's wonderful propaganda about the motherland, the forgotten child and ultimate victory would return to the airwaves. But it was stunningly quiet, as perhaps it should have been.

The air outside was alive with insect noises, minor traces of doom. Every star was awake, new ones joined them by the second, and the fires were flickering a lot closer now.

Eduardo came out and found them half-way down the steps, and on that classical stage explained the fighting which had taken place thirty kilometres or more from Maracacume, from where they were. The major attack had come in the late morning, close to the sea on the opposite side of the island; and the Fragas forces had been all but overrun by Livres in much greater numbers. They'd lost forty men, nearly all experienced fighters. But too confident for their own good. The Livres had played on that confidence, and now they were playing the old Fragas game of hit and run. Eduardo's voice was steady, reciting not so much a play as an official report – though Ranse knew they'd never bother with such formalities here. He was testing its unpleasant contents on them, they had to accept what was there; and they showed no signs of disbelief.

'I have to go on. If you want to come in the morning, then you can. Otherwise stay with Telles and get a truck back to Viseu.' He nodded to the beleaguered shadows inside the house, moving past the windows. 'With the others.'

And if they wanted, they could swim safely here tonight. He could guarantee that.

'You religious, Ranse?'
'No'
'Good. Ever?'
'No. A bit of Sunday school.'
'Good. Why not?'

He had a reason. 'When I was five, a boy – called Felix the cat – was playing in the dump. He was hiding in an old ice chest. The door slammed, and he suffocated. I could see his face, in my imagination at least. I prayed to God for three nights and days to bring him back to life. Nothing happened. I asked my mother about it every hour. In the end, she hit me. I was the youngest person ever to denounce Christianity. And be persecuted for it. Even before I knew what it was.'

'A child knows,' said Aggett.

Lying at no odds with the stars showering down, Ranse splayed his arms and floated into the deepest Notogaean night.

The water lapped at his sides, at once supportive and mildly threatening: he knew the experience couldn't last, it was already past midnight, but he had no idea what might replace it; because there was no question of going back. Eduardo had not mentioned going up to Corguinho, to the real or fantastic grave. Yet they were moving on, and he wasn't unhappy about it. *To stretch my limbs to the mountains, to show I'm as human as the rest.* There was no way of turning back: not in his head, or by shifting his tired body, or by calendar or clock. *It's a One Life Moon, the aim's not just to survive but to enhance that life fully. And suffer it too.* The moon shone down, up and down. He hadn't come to find out if Goddard had been kidnapped, or murdered or killed himself. That wasn't why he'd come; any more than to collect his uncle's few miserable possessions and fragments of mind, of a head quietly falling apart or blowing itself to pieces. What was he still doing here if it wasn't something darker, or deeper in himself? You had to go forward, move on.

And rolling his head and eyes following the sky, all the jewelled moments of his existence in nearby Australia and tramping over distant Europe like Hannibal with a back-pack and Bangkok from the recent past were stilled into this slimy, therapeutic pool of night. It all suddenly made sense. Now they were real – all those routine, exciting, confusing, prosaic, crappy, delinquent, showy, introspective, childish, regretful, cheating, romantic, wise, hopeless, odd and gemlike events of his life. More than real, they were like the thousands of dots that made up a newspaper photo. There was nothing more real than the dots.

When was the last time he'd floated like this? His memory rolled back through the alcoholic nights and days and slamming doors that wouldn't shut completely – down to Breaking Point by the river mouth but not the Open Sea, in the lap of waves tempered by the off-shore islands seen only on clear winter's days and obscured by haze and humidity in summer – and down to even darker nights like this. At the discovered boat-shed where sex, having been entered upon, wouldn't go away. Shifting the sweaters and bras and clothes of the girl whose name couldn't be forgotten, was never really lost, whose outline was – he realised – almost the same and whose name was Ancora Dias in another language. *With her body rising from the velvet grass, the grass not stiff and shaven but welcoming like no mattress or carpet before or since. Even da Vinci's birds of flight: would they ever surpass those first nights in a tin shed? From the sides, through cracks and a broken window looking onto the Moon itself: the unseasoned movements of their bodies smothered with enough innocence to make it highly probable that they were the finest of lovers. There were thus twelve months, which they reckoned by moons, in their years. How many days there were in a moon they didn't seem to know, for the number was variously given as sixteen to thirty-five. Only the hours mattered, how many were left and how far could you go in the remaining time of the month, of night too.* He could hear the strange cry of the young woman who had to go, and the odour of beginner's luck at their fingertips: his and hers.

And now he admitted the vacuum of the more recent past, weighed against the joyous onslaught of desire and a future as uncertain as the great space being punctured by a million stars above. You couldn't stay, tomorrow they'd move on. And it meant hanging onto nothing but a rocket passing the mottled surface of the Moon, where invaders were shifting, swimming across the Sea of Tranquility in rubber suits and coming out of the water as frogmen might. Onto the beach at Breaking Point and up to the tin shed with guns and knives, with her in there; and all they were doing was looking over each other's shoulders, to grass and moon.

'Ranse, you didn't tell me you couldn't swim.'

He blustered, dropping his legs and hiding his firmness with a nervous grin. It was Aggett splashing towards him. Or it wasn't Aggett, but manhood calling from the other end of life; from the approaching storms of middle age at least. 'We'd better get up to the house,' he said, 'get some sleep.'

It wasn't hard to feel the arrow at his neck, slipping past his ear, shooting high over the no longer simple house at the top of the stairs. And past the highest mountain even, where Goddard was catching up on rest. But it was important now to find out where it was going to touch down, the next spot marked out for him. And was it important enough to die for? He looked across the pool to Aggett, climbing out.

He was the last to awake: waking up in Maracacume, high in the lower peaks, going inland but heading too for the coast on the other side. Balancing between the Two Seas, of half aware and half awake. *So it can be cured, you say, by either going back to sleep or by taking a cold shower? Is that your proposal, senhor, because we must push on.* It was freshly cut pineapple, the Queensland nostalgia that shook him finally to life. They sat around the communal table, eating that vaguely alcoholic fruit in the new morning with brewed coffee in the air. Only the wounded soldier was missing.

'How are you?' Aggett half whispered.

He wasn't sure. 'Fine,' he said. 'Tastebuds are still in the right place.'

'Glad to hear. Pity about the heart.'

'What?'

'You spent half the night mumbling in Thai, strange names,' Aggett smiled. 'Sure you don't want to go home?'

'I haven't thought about it.'

'Liar.'

Ranse didn't look up, but plunged into a disc of pineapple.

The priest too had abandoned any bid at joviality, and conducted the table with industry; but their minds were already far off, and Telles was fuelling only their bodies. They were barely grateful for it, thought Ranse. The Church couldn't win, had played all its cards in the last fighting; only Father Telles had the trace of credibility needed to survive their suspicions; and even then they half believed he'd pass on their miseries to the Livres as soon as they left. On both sides were Catholics but their religion didn't matter. Telles was left with a steaming coffee pot and his empty school and mountain pool and played host to friends and enemies, was in some new twist a missionary in reverse: not preaching, but playing hard to get. At least he was giving God's leftist enemies something to eat. Bloated with rich coffee, Ranse rose from the table and went off to find a few bushes to hide in.

'What's the plan?'

'There is no plan,' Aggett replied.

'Down the village, for the others,' said Eduardo. 'We can't get through to Corguinho, of course. Not safe anymore. I'm going up to Boim – it's still held by our men.' He clapped his hands once. 'But you can stay with Telles. Or come, it will be easier if we stay together.'

His authority had grown as they'd slept, or perhaps it had always been there: either way, the change surprised Ranse and troubled Aggett too. The grenades sat improbably on his chest, and his confidence was too close to the surface.

'You'll attack from Boim, right?'

'The Livres hold the coast. But we can circle them.' Eduardo was impatient, looking about the room at the Fragas getting ready.

'I see. And what if they circle Boim? You'll never get off, they'll wipe you out.'

'They're not in the valley. We know that, only on the coast.'

Aggett turned to Ranse. 'Wait till you see Boim, up there like sitting ducks.'

'God knows.'

'I'm inclined to get up there.'

'Really?'

'Don't ask me why.'

'All right,' he hesitated. 'See what happens.' Sooner or later he'd never get to Corguinho, he knew.

'Yes,' said Aggett. And they both thought they knew what he meant by that.

A small explosion of dust mushroomed off the side of the hill, and Father Telles stood flapping and wondering again about boys going off to war. It had to come, if not today then surely tomorrow; but if not tomorrow the crisis would probably pass, and he'd again be welcoming them into his own version of hell.

The top was down, the day rushed through their heads and out into the wider valley – where Maracacume was surrounded by small dry squares of rice and cane. There was coffee on the trees, cash for someone but nothing much to eat; though they seemed happier here than on the coast. Their bodies were shorter and stronger as they moved, which at least they did here. The jeep slowed on the flat and the villagers walked over and infiltrated their ranks; to learn what they could. Being gossipers of necessity.

This was the true market of Inhumas, and would have to be broken for another side to win, temporarily at least. The valley was locked into another, larger bowl that swept down off the mountains to the unseen coast. And looking out, Ranse felt the ease of it. He could see a kind of Thai balance, even where the landslips had shoved a million tons of granite into the valleys. They had long stabilised; and now the people with bright wraps were moving across them, unaware of any geological fault in their lives: just about everything was absorbed into this united view of the world as a valley, and there was little they needed. Least of all, a war.

But a hundred boys had suddenly milled into the centre of their lives: to get food or water, or instructions half-heard as they walked away, the soldiers of the Fragas revolution retained their privacy only because the villagers didn't ask them to expose it. The old men watched – the drowsy ones, even when awake as they must be by now, denying existence – with their downturned mouths and the crippled women with betel lips fanning themselves behind screens in the huts raised a few feet off the ground, eyeing the world and hiding from it. They weren't happier, at all. The policies of Fragas were aimed at these people, but they were moving in quite different and random directions and he wondered how it would all come together politically as Eduardo claimed it would, already had in fact. Ranse and Aggett moved among them like tourists in a foreign land, feeling more than that and less; were entirely superfluous in the way only tourists could be, free to come and go the way these soldiers were not, the way the villagers could not; and even by commitment and other internal slides, the way Eduardo himself might never be. 'You're right,' said Aggett, 'they're not smiling.' But Ranse had said nothing.

AGGETT   You worried?

RANSE   No. (Lying) I was just thinking about Eisner, the reporter. Wonder where he is now?

AGGETT	Up at Boim, I'd say. Getting shot at. (Two chickens scatter by in the warm sun) American, of course.
RANSE	Not only that, he's eager. For what?
AGGETT	He's fatalistic, that's all. Like you. (Stopping) I'm terrified all hell's going to break loose in those trees, that grass over there. So's Eduardo, shitting himself. (Moves on) But you *really will be killed, Ranse.* You've accepted it.
RANSE	Come on. Sounds like a Buddhist or something. Of course I care. We all do.
AGGETT	Some more than others.
RANSE	I've never been in a fight. Let alone killed.
AGGETT	Obviously. Not even a punch-up?
RANSE	Never. (Thinking) Only once in a bar. Tried to slam two heads together, and missed.
AGGETT	Give it time, Ranse.

The soldiers were lying about, listening to a Sony held together with string. As they passed, the unmistakable voice of Thermudo da Cunha crackled through the day.

AGGETT	Can't get away from . . .
RANSE	What's he saying?
AGGETT	(Squints to the sun) Hang on . . . (Smiling, ripples of joy) Oh god, unbelievable. A country of great contrasts, of small things and great, the gazes of laughing children. . . in earthly paradise . . . from the ocean come mermaids and little sea horses sleeping on the sand.
RANSE	Is that all?
AGGETT	Okay, lying. But that's what he'd say if he could. Seen his tourist brochures?
RANSE	No.
AGGETT	A wonder. He's trying them out on everyone. Says he wants to get the right tone. Land of jewels and honey, that sort of rubbish.
RANSE	Probably works.

But it wouldn't, not here. At least not for a few years; with rifles tossed in the grass, scattered in the dust, a box of grenades loose on a slope. Belts of ammunition hung off trees. A heavy machine gun, out of place. Most of the casualties weren't from battle, but mucking around with bullets. ('Just to get out of fighting?' he'd ventured. 'Hell no, they all want to fight. Just being stupid.') Yet they formed, the boys and men, a mound of human happiness on that troubled morning; like Balinese beachboys – some with sandshoes, with motorcycle helmets – they gathered for a song, a tussle, a jibe for the foreigners who felt unease as they laughed. One of the boys had already lost his left hand, and a stump challenged the sky with a wave.

AGGETT   Wearing a watch on it.

RANSE   Where are they from, I wonder?

AGGETT   I don't know. Look at them. Grit, strictly disciplined, high morale, exceptional leadership, faith in final victory – all the things Guevara ever asked for. Except he got them, of course. It's not going to work. (Turning to Ranse, seriously) And it's not too late to go.

RANSE   Go back?

AGGETT   Yes, why not? (Flops his hand across the village) All this is leading to one thing. A month from now Fragas will be back in the hills, where they started. And the Livres are gaining on the coast.

RANSE   But Fragas have got . . .

AGGETT   What have you seen? They've got Viseu, and the road up this far. Out of 5000 square miles? Ask Eduardo to take you across to the south-east, or up the eastern tip to Ponta Lisboa. He'll tell you the roads are difficult, but it's not that. Listen to me. (Softly holds Ranse's shoulder) Between where we stand and Sydney or Bangkok – either way – is a very clear, safe route home. You go down the road again to Viseu, you fly to Darwin and hop a jet to the sun and sand. Get out, Ranse. Look at you – you even look like a cactus stuck in the middle of an English landscape. You really don't . . .

RANSE   (Shaking free, pointing) There's a cactus right there, look. That's why you said it, I'll bet and because you're English. (Annoyed) This is just as much me as anywhere else.

AGGETT   You don't belong here. Two days from now you'll be slopping up oysters and wine. (Whispering, angrily) Get out of here, Ranse.

RANSE   No, not now.

AGGETT   Listen, you're not going to see Goddard's grave. That's what I think, you know?

RANSE   Course not.

AGGETT   (Slapping his sides, breaking into a patter of slaps) Obviously lives alone. Nobody to curl up to at nights. No one cares by day. No parents?

RANSE   I told you, they're dead. And so's Goddard, if that counts. He *is* dead, isn't he?

AGGETT   (Easing off) I really don't know. That's true. But before we go any further, forget this and go back. Why go up to Boim anyway?

RANSE   (Shrugs) Goddard. That's where the arrow touches down. Perhaps.

AGGETT   What arrow? What are you talking about?

RANSE   No, nothing.

AGGETT   Galvão was crazy to let you come. Maybe he wanted you killed, I don't know.

RANSE   Galvão?

AGGETT   Why the hell do you think I'm here?

RANSE   A story.

AGGETT   This little scrap? Somebody wants you where you're likely to walk into a bullet, or away from Viseu for a few days – for whatever reason. (Looks hard at Ranse) It's more or less why I'm here.

RANSE   What?

AGGETT   Alone you wouldn't make it back alive.

RANSE   And why would Galvão want me dead for god's sake? I'm not the enemy. If anyone it's Zervos who's after me. I'm a botanist and I screwed his wife.

AGGETT   (Smiling slightly) Eduardo was a seminary student. Da Cunha a weatherman. Galvão himself was a priest. They see the enemy in the same guises. Maybe you're suspected because you fiddle around with plants, not other men's wives.

RANSE   But I don't anyway. Plants, I mean. Not lately and not here.

AGGETT   Maybe you should.

A brace of pigs was ushered by, like servile entries in an agriculture show; they were remarkably clean and pink, but then he saw the odd smudges of dust against the sides where the boy had guided them forcefully with a large stick.

AGGETT   And besides, I was getting bored in Viseu. (Kicking the dirt) That's why I'm here.

RANSE   Make up your mind. *And besides,* I don't need protecting thanks. It's a story you're after. Eisner was right.

AGGETT   (Shaking his head, slowly) Eisner's not interested in journalism. What he's up to has nothing to do with papers in New York, more like thick files in Washington. Why do you think I'm so against him?

RANSE   Because he's American.

AGGETT   Of a certain kind, yes. If you insist on going to Boim, we'll meet him sooner or later.

RANSE   That's another thing. Peyrot. Either he's further up or we've missed him.

AGGETT   I'd say our Swiss doctor's back in Viseu, trying to patch and sew all the miserables with one limb and one eye. You know about him?

RANSE   He signed the death certificate.

AGGETT   And the rest. You really are slow, Ranse. Has anyone told you that?

Ranse is silent.

AGGETT   He's an addict, old boy. Can't see him struggling up here.

RANSE   Heroin? (Bravely) So?

AGGETT   Well, you didn't know. Did you?

RANSE   (Exasperated) No. I didn't know that.

AGGETT   Nor did I until someone told me. I'm just passing it on.

RANSE   So you're saying he's *never* been up here?

AGGETT   You might say that. But you'd have to go back to Viseu to find out, for sure.

RANSE   I'm going on.

AGGETT   I thought you'd say that. (Smiling) So am I.

RANSE   Know everything, don't you? But you don't give anything away. You must have some secrets.

AGGETT   Oh, thousands. But they'd probably turn me into a very – exceedingly – boring person. I have secrets, Ranse, about the most mundane things.

They tried to join a queue for water, but were shuffled to the head of the line; by soldiers with guns. The water came out of a rubber hose from somewhere and Ranse channelled it into his gullet. He could have been one of those boys Father Telles watched going off to war: taking communion into the fight.

Market day up north, under grey sky colours, kids in pairs wave at Thai trains, miles away, across the river of crystallised paddies, white brumby horses, implied energy and minerals at the tongue. Going back there, briefly.

And into flight, Ranse like a bird in this: moving in and around its perimeter, ready at the slightest pressure to fly off to safety but always coming back for a closer look; and still closer to feel it. By contrast, Aggett stood still: ever the participating observer, waiting for that change of wind, of season, of fortune. The smell of decaying fruit drafted through the gathering and out of the rags of the wounded stood one man, leg wrapped in a white bandage with a plum oozing underneath. A flesh wound, he wouldn't be fighting today.

Eduardo called: 'Come in this jeep. We'll follow the others.'

'Never fancied lead postion in anything,' said Aggett quietly.

The convoy moved out: a couple of jeeps as scouts, four trucks of troops, the lone jeep at the back. The villagers waved them off.

'Glad to see us go,' said Ranse.

Aggett turned: 'In the past – according to da Cunha – when they caught anyone stealing a horse or a cow, they'd chop his head off and put it on a spike – and chop the animal's head off for good measure and put that on a spike too. Just a warning.'

'That's true,' Eduardo said. 'And they're happy we're going to finish up the Livres.'

'Oh,' replied Aggett, 'is that why they're waving? I hope they're right.'

Eduardo smiled: the prospect of battle had brightened his soul. 'You're taking a long time to support us, Senhor Aggett. I think you're probably a right-wing at heart.'

'In mind too,' the Englishman offered.

The three of them sitting in the jeep: an unlikely trio anywhere, Ranse reflected. The mustard dust was being pumped from each set of wheels into the face of the next, and passed on. And the last vehicle – theirs – struggled to breathe and see. And to each side, alang-alang grass was stilled in the sun. The two Fragas men in the back watched the blades and curled their fingers into nervous hooks. But it was still a game.

'What a day for an ambush,' Aggett sang and orchestrated their fears.

They started to climb towards Boim up the steep hill. But stopped, barely a minute later. A pall of dust was coming down, a jeep was moving quickly and there in the front seat, beside the driver, was a face he'd almost forgotten. It was Racovic, the American photographer: drawn and dirty with contempt in his eyes.

There was no sign of Eisner.

TWELVE

By midday, the Fragas forces were half-way down the opposite hillside to the sea: the lunch-time attack had bogged down in the dry heat that sapped them of nerve. The air, in which insects could be heard mating and dying, gave them no cover; they feared their own footsteps, which instinctively stopped. They couldn't pull back, and their isolation was complete.

'Aren't you dead yet?' asked Aggett.

The words hung there, unsupported by humour and gathering sweat.

'Well. The relief shift come to scoop me. You can see . . .'

Eisner was trying to prop himself up in the jeep, but eased back.

'What is it, the leg?'

Without waiting, Aggett pulled back the blanket. 'Oh dear.' It was shrapnel in the thigh, a small but deep wound and there was no way of cleaning up the mess. 'The bone?'

'Nah.'

The spirit was mildly defiant and Aggett helped it along: 'You'll get a Purple Heart, or the Viseu Star perhaps.' He turned to Eduardo. 'Right?'

'He must go back, quickly.'

'Of course.'

'Not that bad,' stammered Eisner. 'Just drop me with Telles, couple of days in the magic pool and sipping juice. Be as good as gold.'

'Good as gone.'

Racovic was gaping behind them into the valley, for a way out. Without cameras he seemed lost. And Eisner was smiling, and playing down what the battle had done to him. Whether a spy or not, he was still flesh and bone. At least he was that.

'Brash to the bitter end,' Aggett said. 'What happened anyway?'

He tried to smile, but the pain spread: 'They know how to fight all right. They don't know how to stop. One minute something goes off.'

'You don't say. Just have to find another war. To shape yourself against, won't you?'

Racovic spun around: 'Leave him alone. He's been hit.'

'Thanks. You'd be as useful as one chopstick . . .'

'Forget it Ravi, just English humour. Aggett,' he said, 'don't write me up.'

'I keep telling you, the work's over. Lost your hearing too?' He smiled, the same patronly smile. 'Not a line out of here. Got it?'

'Sorry,' he said.

Aggett straightened up. 'This infection Eisner, the heat brings it on like crazy. Get back to Viseu quickly. Wish you were still in Vietnam, I'll bet.'

Eisner waved and dug painfully into his pocket, and handed Aggett a crumpled page.

He looked at it. 'Terrific. Pure shit.'

'Hah,' said Eisner.

And wearing out underneath it all was nerve, being able to adjust constantly to events. It was getting harder, he thought. They'd all have to hold their ground firmly, from now on.

Wrenched into a last act of strength, their own tired jeep levelled out at Boim. The road up, through an arc of trees that lowered in the heat, kept its secret to the destination: only twenty yards from the village did it open out, the sea flung into their sights again. With its luxury of greens and ribbons of blue and black spots of ink. It was, Aggett noted, so utterly tropical in the middle of their day; and facing a barrel of clouds – the first he'd seen here, a hundred miles out. A release against the land, and the heat they were stuck to.

They circled a dusty oval that swelled slightly towards the centre, where something might have once been rooted. A tree bearing enormous fruit. Overlooking the water, the coastal lip. But everything now was dead and deserted. Around them stood a dozen relics of colonial times: a faded house of religion, a cracked general store with two doorways and empty shelves, a few shacks of crusting mortar where later Aggett would find a Portuguese newspaper with news of Spain and the Suez crisis. A portable typewriter would turn out to be Eisner's, left in a hurry. Ranse was walking onto a stage and those clouds out there – rebuilding and gathering strength – were heading south; the war would come ahead of them because a month or two from now, the Wet would start and the fighting would have to stop. It was already here, in clashes.

He looked around, saw Eduardo making plans with the soldiers. And could see in him the science of ageing; though only Aggett – at the other point of this triangle, looking at them both – knew what that was about and how the toll of abrasive years, distinct from ordinary ones, could alter a person's self. *But they were all misplaced persons in Boim village, of course.* Standing there and hoping for early rain, so the Fragas and the Livres could call it off for a few months and come to terms with the harder reality, of everyday life. But for now they were fighting like couples with a romantic past and nowhere to go: on one side the terrain of dust and struggle, and on the other the vast loneliness of the sea.

Even at the end, it would seem long ago: Ranse would have trouble fixing his memory to the time scale of Boim, knowing only that they arrived late one day and left early and quickly on the next, and that time for sixteen hours became as elastic and tricky as dough.

'Bit of a shame,' said Aggett.
'Paint's gone. The plaster's next.'
'Our ammunition store now,' said Eduardo, who wasn't enchanted.
The path had led to privilege by rising to the highest point around, to the old governor's house overlooking the scrub

down to the broad, full song of the sea. All of it once so white, a release from the mania of colony. Ranse walked to the front, where a patio flagged in marble sat on the verge of Asia; at the very end of the Old World, he thought. It might have worked when it was brilliantly white, catching the hopes of empire. But now it suggested the standard reply in these parts of mediaeval purpose, and then the lost cause. *And the Portuguese elements hadn't been properly absorbed but were isolated and lonely like this house, or Mrs Mendonça at the hotel, or an abandoned car left on a country road; of no use to anyone now, overtaken by events, too clumsy to be moved back to the metropolis they'd come from. And here they were still working out what to replace it with: nationalism, socialism, Marxism, Christianity, capitalism, or nothing?* The gap was widening between the colony and its replacement; and the population was filling it with war, and waiting.

'The attack hasn't begun?'

'It has,' said Eduardo. 'But it's stopped again.'

'You said it would be over by lunch. And now it's,' he looked down, '5 o'clock.'

'But tonight they'll move down with the darkness. You and Aggett can sleep here.'

He watched Eduardo go. Behind him to the west, the sun had burned out its hard white core and softened into orange. Did anything really bother him, Ranse wondered? Was he ready to see others die provided he could eat first and read his Mao Tse-tung and comics? Would it be so elemental, in the end? Eduardo's fine bones were already disappearing. In the village behind him: human demands, commands, instructions, arguments and laughter were finding their place. Over this, the growing calls of nature, birds, insects, animals talking to others. And filling in the spectrum, the rubbing of tree trunks and leaves shaking and falling; and the final noise of dust settling over everything.

Ranse grabbed an old chair on the patio, and was happy to be left alone.

After a while, he heard Aggett moving about the house. The empty rooms were bouncing his steps out, stopping sometimes: making a pattern of some purpose against the general

147

hubbub of Boim; he was doing or checking something, Ranse thought. There was, in Mister Aggett, a touch of the snoop; but also a very clear line along which his curiosity stretched, not wormish but investigative. It would be no surprise if his father had been a British detective; or if, in some of his early life plans, Aggett himself hadn't toyed with the idea. He wasn't embarrassed by his own curiosity, like most people: on the contrary, he pushed it forward as a pillar of his personality, so that Mister Aggett would happily be known as an asker of questions and a gatherer of information. But he knew when to stop, Ranse thought. He could always stop just in time, and others would never know. And his caution was well buried, so that he could look excessive (in bars, probably in battle) without risking his life or his image in the slightest. Did that come from his years of reporting? Or was he just naturally careful: an inquirer with multiple chin, a builder of jigsaws who always set out to complete the picture and rarely failed, though he hardly seemed to be taxing himself. It was always rainy in Aggett's mind, and jigsaws were the perfect companion on rainy days. It all came together in the end if you took things carefully. But still Ranse wondered: wasn't there also an admission of some failing, of a man using the cover of questions to hide the weakness of his personality? The years of questioning might define a man, without actually exposing him. And then the footsteps again, growing not louder but softer through successive walls and doors and disappearing into the late afternoon itself. He was walking towards the village too, the lamps coming on down there. Ranse tightened his lips: had he come to find Sam Goddard, and discovered George Aggett by error? The one seemed so obvious, the other a complete mystery.

In the shell of the general store, he caught Eduardo reading by the pale flame of the lamp. His eyes strained at the small volume.

'Waiting to eat,' said Eduardo, putting it down. 'Are you hungry?'

'Depends, on what there is.' Outside on the dirt lay an ox, he'd seen it carved at the belly with its warm, sickly intestines dusted across the ground. Flies buzzed into the cavity and made repeated attempts to sit on the lashes of its opened eyes.

Ranse had stood there watching it. There was no stench from the carcass, only the smell coming off two large fuel drums converted to boilers.

'It's bad food up here,' Eduardo said. 'Only some rice. Goats, wild pony, pigs, maybe a dog. What they can find.'

Ranse shifted uneasily, and picked up the book. An image of Mao in sepia smiled at him, mole on chin and face polished like death.

'I heard on the radio last week,' he said smiling, 'President Ford is going to China for talks.'

Eduardo watched the lamp, and shrugged: 'Mao is just a political model, not a hero. We need models of course. Do you understand?'

He waved the book. 'I think you're wrong. Models are failures of the imagination too. They lock you in.' Ranse opened a few pages, scanning for something that would do. '"Unless one makes the effort,"' he read aloud, '"one is likely to slip into idealism and metaphysics." There, you see.'

Eduardo got up to go. 'We still need models,' he said, and went out at no more than his usual pace.

You and me, we lost that bout. That was no victory, Ranse thought.

'Curious. You dreaming or something?'

Ranse swung around, and stopped. 'Oh god, it's you. Why don't you knock next time?'

'Didn't mean to scare you.' Aggett moved from the doorway to the flickering light. 'Look at this.' He held a copper coin, greened with oxide and age. 'Some kind of Dutch thing. 1945,' he said, scratching the surface. He handed it to Ranse.

'Ten reis. *Dei Gratia Maria.*'

'They dropped by after the war, briefly. Could be valuable,' Aggett said. 'You can never tell, of course. A few years ago in Ireland they put a Roman coin in a musuem. Turned out to be a plastic token given away by a soft drink company. A kid told them.'

Ranse was dubious. 'What else did you find up there?'

'Just grenades, mortars, stuff like that. NATO issue, from the Viseu armoury.'

'The Portuguese left it behind?'

'Didn't have much choice. They wanted to get home,' he said, taking the coin from Ranse and tossing it out the front door, 'to all their lovely Marias . . .'

'Hey. I really wanted that.' But then Aggett's face stalled in the light, and his mouth tightened a bit.

'What's up?'

'A rusty coin won't do much good, unless you believe in charms,' Aggett said. 'Come on, let's dine. I'm so hungry I could eat a small child.'

He tried to ignore it, for once.

Couldn't see into the boilers, but a mist was rising that suggested all the plagues of Asia and beyond. Perhaps the Livres would or wouldn't kill them; but Aggett had reason to believe the food would and had wandered off, prepared to starve if necessary. Ranse was still willing to try. And so the loosely vacant chair sat there, the night rattling its feet on the floorboards. He would spend dinner talking to an empty chair.

In his bowl swirled bits of rice, root vegetable, anonymous meats. Ranse determined not to eat the dog if there was any; but when he yielded to hunger or insane curiosity, it tasted just like the rest.

As though dreaming at two levels: at one deeply, he was finally at peace with his past and Goddard and that summer garden by the river; by manufacturing it from scraps of gold foil, of memory. But higher up, closer to consciousness, came the taut visions of anguish and fear; here now in Boim too and writhing uncomfortably close to the uncertain future. It was so close to the surface, this level, it might have been reality itself. He couldn't tell, wouldn't be able to until he awoke. And yet he was awake, he told himself, wide awake and reading a magazine even: to anyone who'd listen he would relate how that front cover was banned by the city authorities in Dallas, Texas for obscenity. Under a new ordinance, magazine covers featuring either genitals or nude bottoms must not be displayed where children under the age of seventeen can see them. And so the city fathers of Dallas, Texas banned on grounds of obscenity – eleven years, four months and seventeen days after John

Kennedy was assassinated in their midst – the cover of a magazine showing a Vietnamese mother hanging onto her bullet-ridden, naked dead baby. It was a girl, you could tell if you were over seventeen because it had no balls and no future. And wondering: were there any children left in Vietnam, any at all? He tossed the offending publication into the back of a military jeep, but Eisner preferred his copy of *Playboy* which wasn't banned in Dallas, Texas or anywhere else. Except in Queensland, of course. And you could forget that, going down again with green mould on the walls like a grotto. They threw into the colder, foggy night a long silk thread that landed in the dark valley: the thump that ended in a bang. Ranse stirred but didn't wake or sit up; he knew Fragas had started their mortar attack, at some pointless target and dark hour: was it the target they didn't want to see, or the pain? Another thump, a few at random that began and ended nowhere but inside the cave of that long, lonely dream. *The dream is the ultimate lonely experience, he thought. Inside the dream chamber they slept all night: he and Goddard, he and Aggett. Guarding the entry, the gnarled limbs and legs of an old fig tree with its dropped tendrils were like a gate, a maze of possibilities on how to enter or escape. The tendrils left stark shadows on the limestone walls of the cave, which seemed to toss and ache in its role as sleep chamber to undesirables; to foreigners with nowhere else to go. It was then perfectly dark, wrote Verne, and their gaze could not extend over a radius of two miles. Did the sea surround this unknown land, or was it connected in the west with some continent of the Pacific? It could not yet be made out.* And out there, out there. He was retreating from sleep, and not sleeping but suffering a lifting insomnia, up and down in that mulchy territory of the mind that all night was creative and destructive of thought. Feeling the fog right at his arms, and cold and twisting heat; or mosquitoes and malaria perhaps. *It's on the rise. The infected female injects the malarial parasite from its salivary glands. Ouch! The parasites then travel to the liver and six to eleven days later escape – free at last – to the bloodstream where they attack the red cells. There they multiply and forty-eight to seventy-two hours later the red cells rupture, and out come a new wave of parasites. This is repeated over and over.*

It's the rupture of the red cells that prompts the first symptom, the chill that lasts up to an hour. But he was fit, tougher than malaria; it was just the sweating pulse of a foul situation that beat his heart a little harder but looser every time. Or was it the mortars shaking him, pocketing the air and taking their share of night? He could hear thudding, too much of it: perhaps hitting man, or sand? And could see a small fire at his feet, not a raging thing but a softly smouldering fire with flames licking away and a little rise of smoke. *The same fire that began on his wardrobe every night somewhere between black night and dawn, he would fall in and out of its mesmeric glow as a boy and in falling would never be hurt or burned by it; altogether his favourite fire. And his favourite number, U-4343, he thought; what? Their old phone number, calling up Goddard on a rusty wire. 'Where are you?' he would ask, digging in hope of recovering those metal objects he'd buried as a child, expecting to find them completely rusted at some future date. His childhood fascination, above all, with rust. Always bringing in muddy objects to his mother, but the rusted objects among them were never those he'd buried himself; though he pretended otherwise. They'd been there for years, longer than he'd been alive. Rusting was something older than yourself, always as a child. And however close, it was always removed: your own body was immune, like a copper coin. But the man of iron, of principle, of self-inflicted death: Goddard could never be a corpse, it would be up to the centuries alone to etch him out of existence. He could actually see Goddard lying there, the rusting process barely begun; and then Aggett was standing there, soft and vulnerable amid the noisy hum of bees. He could smell sandalwood in the air, see fog in the dark, imagine fire. And food was rumbling, why he dreamed so crazily; so close to the surface, so deep in those swollen intestines where he'd emptied an aggressive bottle of port to clean out the stew, and chased it with a few Lomotils to check the runs. 'Which reminds me,'* said Aggett, *'there was another story about Mrs Mendonça, a finer story that fits her magnitude a little better. She is, after all, hardly a failure.'* It was said her husband – a pseudo-scientist, a research quack called Doctor Avriel Lourenco Mendonça – was working on a system of coloured pills that would clearly mark

152

the body residue (i.e. faeces) of each day: blue on Mondays, red on Tuesdays, yellow on Wednesdays etc. Thus the chronic sufferer of constipation would know which day's motions had passed and which were still to come. But the trials were abandoned when a constipee killed himself, having lost his 'Wednesday Yellow' for over a week. 'Clearly a worrier, ' said Aggett. At the thought of this putrid mass floating inside his body for eight days, he'd taken a gun to his head. The elderly Doctor Mendonça – having fled to Viseu, not really a medical practitioner of course – was described always as wearing outdoors his panama with a sprightly feather cocked to one side and a bright purple band around it. 'God knows why Maria ever thought he would die!' He wore a three-piece suit even in the tropical heat and always read the Lisbon papers from cover to cover, advertisements and all. He was a sparrow of a man, and needed little to survive on; she of course was rooted in the need for stimulus and change, and was never satisfied. The doctor died sitting in a white cane chair at the hotel, reading the paper. It was the same paper he'd been reading for two days. He sat up, fumbling with editions he'd shoved between the blankets for extra warmth. Like a tramp. And over there was Aggett, covered only with his shorts and ample flesh: didn't feel the cold ever, he said. Even sleeping on this patio against the deepening sky, which was blue. There were a million brilliant blue moments in it for a second, and then it went blue again. Another flare going down, on what? He'd never seen a truly horizontal Englishman before, lying on his back; unlike Latins and others, they rarely presented themselves as anything but vertical: certainly upright. But now his head was back; so that the large chin stretched in a line from chest to mouth, like a pelican's gullet; his mouth was gaping wide and it looked quite ridiculous when he breathed in and perfectly natural when he breathed out. And he saw that Aggett was a lot heavier than he appeared; not fat, but perhaps the remains of a fighter. He also plucked roses and drank a lot. There was a quick, clever mind in that sinewy body; and if deduction failed, the burly cop in him could always extract a confession. Another thump in the night, another mortar on its way. But what was really going on beneath that pallid and thick skin? His big heart would hammer open and shut a

153

couple of billion times before it stopped, and nobody would ever know what made it tick; or what opened and closed the endless valves in that ticking mind of his. Ranse watched him snore; and still the questions refused to subside. Because at least Sam Goddard was dead: the mystery of his existence had exhausted its urgency and could – if he really wanted – be resumed at convenience. But Aggett was another matter. He resisted analysis and took off at unexpected tangents and at the height of aberrations, after wetting his lips with the bottle and growling 'Where the bloody hell are we?' in a sort of pained ecstasy, would simply turn and question Ranse's curiosity with a polite 'What's up?' to firmly centre himself at the heart of Western normality; and place the questioner at question, at risk. Goddard had never done that, never been that complex; only made life hell in other, more obvious ways. But that was history now. Below them both, the valley lit up and shook and settled down and he felt no fear of it; and tumbled back to sleep. *And even as he tried to abandon the struggle the voice said, 'Here, take this,' and it was Aggett covered in mud and matted hair and his eyes burning with fever. And leaving the black diary – so black, full of the night – he staggered into the monsoonal rain and scrub. It wasn't Vietnam, over now; what would they all do with their lives tonight or ever? In the Mediterranean it was safe and easy: why didn't you stay if it was so comfortable? There were no mortars, and vines needed pruning and cheese needed turning and that was it. What more could you ask for in life, in your need to get away from life, if that was the problem? Now you're gone again, sucked into the Wet with your desire for more knowledge, questions: all the rhetorical tensions that trouble your race. And the calculating Mister Aggett didn't worry about a thing – that was a lie, was worried about me for a start. 'Here, take this.' The volume was caked in black mud, in blood and the pages were soaked in pissy, Wednesday yellow and it was unmistakably Goddard's hand as rough as ever. The pages wouldn't flip where Ranse wanted them to; and he was forced to read, and read on. 'But again, the weather is disastrous – things are blowing out with the heat. And what can you do in the Wet – the same every year – staying indoors is enough to drive anyone mad. The cleaner's sending me crazy too – she threw out my only liparis aurita on the grounds that it was just another flower! I felt like strangling her. I could go on like this, even last so long that we won't recognise what's happening – about Nicholas, I mean. Or it could go away. After six years I hardly care.' He flipped the pages anxiously but the diary wouldn't turn, had turned to redwood and he wanted to shave it open; but feared it wouldn't take him deeper, only closer to the surface and he didn't want to risk waking because the dream and the diary would be lost forever, and there was so much more. Aggett was watching to see if he could overcome the difficulties but wouldn't step in, and that was just like him too; but the diary itself came to the rescue – dipping from anecdote to approval, memory, balance and bluff – or was it Goddard who was posthumously turning from one fractured entry to the next? 'No plan, there's simply no plan. Just to survive. Tell me what survival means – that's the one plan worth looking at! Wasn't it Horace who claimed non omnis moriar, not all of me will die? Only it will because none of us comes back to Earth, with its attendant miseries! And what a place it is: even here they kill and plunder and rape the very souls of each other's bodies, rip open the Earth they're supposed to love and have no love of beauty but live in states that animals wouldn't go near – they want to eat their own shit daily, suffer gloating remorse for every infidelity, inspect with glee the damage they inflict on each other's souls. What a choice – return after death to live among the savages, or conduct an eternal debate with Him on the meaning of life! No plan, I say – give me just the humble stupidity of not knowing what happens when we close our lids for the last time. Death gives scale to everything we do. Before that I'll go down on my hands and knees to stay mobile, to stay alive and fight off predators. Do you know why insects have six legs? A favourite among the First Years, and I asked Teppy – they have six legs because that's the lowest number of legs you need to stay upright while lifting half of them off the ground. And we, the evolved species, have two. Or four, she replied.' And he could only think of Teppy Zervos in that slumber that wasn't quite sleep, and their own uncomfortable twist of the incest taboo. Goddard was gone and Ranse was being called on to give him life again in* some perverse way, in her flashing eyes. She was pushing her sexual drives through some kind of shaky moral filter in the desperate hope of coming out clean, free of guilt for what she'd done; but it was past that now. He wouldn't fall into the same spider's trap she'd set for Goddard, he didn't want to be locked into that subterranean prison of death, like Goddard he wanted to live and more so while he was young. He should leave, Aggett was right. But he couldn't leave without knowing what the cost should be: at whatever cost, because to go back to Thailand – or even to the murky surface of Boim at the top of his consciousness – without that vital shred would not only mark the start of his own human decline, but invalidate the whole elaborate dream and he was fighting, tossing and breathing hard, and pushing away the invisible hand. Hell, it was Goddard's trying even at this hour to keep the truth from him, to keep his image of blunt honesty intact while his nephew sweated out the diary and the night exploding over his head – until again the scratchy needle of their past took off. 'A gap here of two weeks, I know. Teppy went to Darwin to put the kids in school there – things in town are getting jumpy but you wouldn't know it here. In any event, I've been so ill I haven't really cared. Just about everyone here is locked into some bloody cause – except me. What a joke! Coming to Viseu to escape all that – politics and blood money – I'm heartily engaged in a torrid affair with the wife of a sleazy Greek entrepreneur who'd have slaves if he could! But it intrigues me, how Zervos can handle the affair – he must know, and she in turn goes to incredible lengths to defend him. Why, why? Perhaps it's nothing more than the mutual conspiracy of two waifs – they huddle to sleep as dependants, surely not as lovers. If he knocked me off, then Teppy might start making demands he could never meet – or worse, no demands at all! No, in a strange and mutually understood way, Zervos approves of it. Perhaps he thinks anyway I'm about to die. I still don't know what hit me, that sly little Peyrot was no bloody help – where did he learn medicine, had to guide him through the books. I watched the entire world going sideways and further down and then nothing, and woke up three hours later with the moonlight bouncing through the windows, into my eyes. All right, I *thought. But I felt dead, my head wasn't moving as quickly as the rest, feeling the floor under my wet ear and thinking it was water from the sink and only then – when the moonlight blurred, when I blinked – it was sweat in my eyes, and fever. I got the strength to knock up some eggs and rice, and boiled up water with honey. And rolled all night on the bed and thought I'd die, thought of her and alarmingly found myself erect in the midst of dying – the powers she has over my poor mangled body! I joke about it now but at the time . . . And finally a visitor after three days – Lydia, the old housekeeper I'd sacked was passing by and when I saw it was her, my hopes sank absolutely, thinking she'd walk away with sweet revenge all over her face. But almost as bad – she went and got Peyrot instead. And despite that I pulled through – and vowed to get out, to leave Viseu, to piss off. I'm getting too old for that, at least I need a decent hospital for emergencies and a few European minds wouldn't go astray. Something calm and vaguely civilised and beautiful, in summer at least – away from this hole of a place. It's given me nothing. Except her, I suppose. And she returned a few days later – a full week, I see it was – had even been to Sydney for shopping this time and looked full of life, was simply breezy when I mentioned I'd almost died – and even haughty when I baulked at the idea of rooting her. God – I'd just come back from the edge! She smiled and produced a gun, a smallish pistol. Zervos had obtained it for her in Darwin, because things were going badly here and she might need it one day or night. Can't stand the bloody things, but inexplicably I started to laugh. "What's up?" she asked and I said "Nothing." She put the pistol away, embarrassed, but wouldn't tell me why. I'd never seen her like that before. Told her about leaving Viseu and that was painful – at first she was stunned, then began to sulk (briefly) and then launched into me for half a bloody hour. "I certainly won't be going back there," I said.' As abruptly as that, and the pages were blank again.* It had taken hours and sleep hadn't come, he hadn't escaped the thinner air and greasy stew, the port and fog. Ranse put his hands into his trousers, to work out the force of the dream, partly to escape the tiredness of his own body. And eventually he must have slept because the mortars stopped and the moment came when, quite deliberately, the night went too and it was another day.

But nothing: the Fragas troops were stuck in the valley. In the mist there was nothing to see. The night of loose threads and mortars had wound up, and nothing had really happened out there. What could he trust of his own night? Still lost in the convoluted diary that would have killed Goddard and perhaps himself if he'd gone on; if he'd been allowed to, or hadn't woken in time. Was that it? He could hear Teppy's car coming up the track, see Goddard at the desk, and his golden lover making demands – the affair, Australia, divorce – and then a gun. *As simple and sudden as that?* So that all this had evolved from such an utterly melodramatic cry of the heart, had Ranse chasing himself and his own fractured life and future in Goddard's steps – was this the shakiest reason why Zervos now wanted him dead, was out to kill him to protect his dancing wife from further investigation and whatever he might find? It bundled itself into confusion and anger, and Ranse couldn't find a way out – unless it was through the fighting, or through Teppy Zervos once again, or by ignoring the whole business and returning through the same door he'd entered by. Aggett was no use of course. Eduardo would keep telling his lies, in pure silence. And over it all, the friendly tribal war of Inhumas would go on – for months or years until the bullets ran out and the guns rusted in the salty air, and there was nobody left to fight.

'Perhaps you should go back today, with the truck,' Eduardo suggested.

'I think so. See what Aggett says.'

He was coming over. 'Nicholas. Did you hear the bloody things, the mortars?'

'I couldn't sleep.'

'How many, Eduardo?'

'Oh, twenty. Fifty.'

'They didn't send any back. You sure the Livres are down there? Not just making patterns on the sand, are you?'

'This is very slow fighting. It might take two, three days to wear them out.'

'Yes,' Aggett said cheerily. 'Or we might be all dead this afternoon.'

'We must wear them out.'

'Try using bullets. Very good for wearing out the enemy.'

'Plenty of time,' said Eduardo.

'For the Fragas,' Aggett responded, 'there's no refuge in eternity I'm afraid. Time is running out fast.'

Eduardo ignored him. 'Mister Ranse, there's food in the village. Very quiet this morning?'

'Didn't get much sleep, that's all.'

'Some coffee, anyway.' He turned to Aggett. 'And you, our best enemy?'

'Why not?'

Alone with the flavour of Hibrido de Viseu in his mouth – the world's finest mocha, at least they had the best *something* – Ranse stopped at the frangipani in bloom. It was a morning tree, the clusters springing from the old trunk and stalky green leaves. So damp and intoxicating. The cream flowers nestled in his hand, in his palm, his loose fist. Whenever he smelled the frangipani, Ranse was able to stop his own progress; was forced to yield to the moment that could last a minute or more; and now to spread his badly slept body into metaphors all the way back to birth. He reached up and drew together a bunch of flowers and leaves, shook the overnight damp into his dirty palms and washed them. Could find no place on his shirt clean enough to dry them, and so walked up to the governor's old house with wet hands in the first hours of the day. He'd been denied romance for so bloody long. And if the frangipani bloom could fix that, it should be allowed to. Without glancing over his shoulder. In the next twenty-four hours, the petals would help to cover his gravest doubts; for hope to spring eternal, Ranse thought, it had to be detached from all kinds of human reality.

The first shot: and the long whistle grew louder and heavier coming at them from below. It was an odd sensation, like waiting with a noose around your neck. His tongue was burning dry and for the longest moment it stalled and didn't know which way to go in the cavernous mouth of his fears. Ranse turned, and began his run.

Down there he saw Aggett throwing his weight across the dusty square, the rising sun on a still-waking village; saw

Eduardo almost mechanically turn his ear up for the message, and others like ants digging for cover; saw the bankruptcy of death coming in a second, and was still running when he heard the shell explode behind them all.

'Ranse!' yelled Aggett. 'Get down!'

He was running now and wiping his hands and swerving up to the house. From the valley below came another screeching and all his senses peaked into ears, eyes, lips; and Aggett screaming not to.

'. . . the house!'

A second shell went over, as he pushed inside. His hands were falling, and then his whole body to get some air. On all fours, gasping at the wooden boards. 'God, god,' he choked. 'Where is it?'

Could already hear another shell, draining his lungs; and the heart and head of courage. Long before he might, Ranse was dying with every whistle; he curled inside his body, was a child waiting interminably for fireworks to explode. 'Where, where?' he whispered at the floor. Another one, the intervals were closing: a minute, thirty seconds. 'Wh-eerree? Godddd-daaard!' The floor shook from outside; into his ear at the floor, picking up the rumbling shells on impact: the shock was every-where, and thunder too. He looked about the room, filling with dust and smoke; all around were boxes, with stencilled codes staring at him and stacked into castles. 'Again,' he said irration-ally. He knew why Aggett's voice was warning him. 'But where,' he whispered, 'where, where ...' Out of shelling thumps came the noise of animals out there, groaning and hooting and howling. And boots sounding harder, now that he was up and running again, had to get out of here when Aggett burst in. They stared at each other, wincing.

'You okay?'

He couldn't answer but caught Aggett's shoulder, they were back in the sunlight and running. Until both slowed down.

'Where's Eduardo?'

'He's okay. Gone to get the jeep. Nicholas ...' he gathered breath.

'What?'

'Pull up near the road. He'll come down this side.'

'What were you going to say?'

Aggett looked terrible, his face dusty and weak. They heard the jeep coming up. Under the clump, they were shaking and almost laughing at the impact of it.

'I was going to say we mightn't get out of here,' Aggett stumbled. 'And now we might.'

He stood up suddenly. 'The diary . . .'

'What?'

'The diary, I thought . . .'

'What diary?'

'No, no . . .'

'Come on, let Boim have it. Get in.'

Eduardo was at the wheel. He stopped and the soldiers in front scrambled into the rear and they leapt in. Ranse could feel his limbs giving way. 'Sorry,' he muttered.

'We're going out,' Eduardo called. 'Some are caught on the slope. Must go.'

'Yes,' said Aggett.

He could hear shooting now, and turned with difficulty. A man was falling, slumping dead or wounded. Others were running for cover. The jeep slewed into the ditch and stuck for a second, then jumped back on course. Above and in front, Ranse saw all the trees at once – gums, tamarinds, palms tossing – and rocks tumbling into place as they pushed out of Boim.

'Safe,' he asked, 'the road?'

'Not really,' said Eduardo.

The trees were flickering by and he couldn't shake the heat from the transmission off his legs. He was coming back to his senses, to a genuine fear of ambush: in surrounds cut with gullies and caves, with knife-edges around the hills and precipitous slopes, and granite lumps where the dirt wouldn't sit. To lob a grenade: would be nothing, be instant and easy.

His bum was stinging, and beside him was Aggett: tapping out a story in his head.

They cleared the ravine in silence. And suddenly on those flats in the jeep gaining speed, by the parched swamps and abandoned reeds and into the dry landbase, they could all feel Viseu and its hotel racing to greet them. Or was the day itself pulling them forward, dragging them further on? It was an island, he thought, but now it felt like a continent. The interior heat and torture had no channel into the Surrounding Sea: they were sealed quantities and extracted their own, heartless pulse. Out there the waters might toss in the wind, but here the same wind lured the smallest drops of moisture through the toughest surface, and killed it.

They'd come less than six kilometres from Boim, from the abandoned village and the villa that was a retreat, from the curious rain of shells that had struck almost nothing, from the unseen enemy and whoever the Protector was; and a wind had sprung off the island and was tossing the jeep like flotsam on the Sea of Dust, and it was difficult in this strange midday mist to figure out exactly where they were going.

BOOK THREE: REASONS TO SEE

O flogged flesh, the skin has got
accustomed.

THIRTEEN

Looking back – from the shuttered hotel room he imagined, without knowing why – Ranse would convert that single hot, dry November day into a vastness of hours that began in the bellows of his past with Sam Goddard and swelled through the disarray, the sweated bodies, death calls of rocket fire, the clanging of old nerves conscripted to fight, going on not to Goddard's grave but turning back to the broad flat Bras plains loaded with dehydrated grasses that shot from the unseen earth like terrified snakes into the day that wouldn't die, but went on. And drawing him – no reason to exist Nicholas Ranse, not strong enough to resist – back to the fertile coast where the conspiring serpents, having already stung him with some nullifying drug, were coiled and waiting for the kill. What else now but to push his luck? Going there to risk his own existence; to know, to know, to know. He chanted it religiously, evoking a right.

The fires were still burning. But the natives of Maracacume had gone, and taken the gentle columns of greyish smoke with them. As the jeep slithered for an hour – avoiding the village – they could see distress signals coming from the ridges, flames that licked orange and gold. And blobs of spent energy that shot up and cancelled in the sky. And then he could see the solid hump of great Corguinho suddenly, like a gorilla coming down on them. So there it was, in broad daylight. The great uneven shoulders of the monster worn by centuries of lost air – resistance, persistence, the face carved out of decay. The sun's angle

165

hit the pockmarks and Corguinho squinted; and he could see on the missing nose where the cancer had been, and the accumulation of plant life following the hidden water spring like fur down its spine. It was still roaring for him, waiting but Corguinho was no higher than the engulfing war; the question of Goddard's fate would be safely stored there until his own mysteries were solved, and he no longer feared the inevitability of the outcome. *Chaos attended by a hidden order, like layers across a landscape compressed down and down; be they bodies in coffins, or volcanic rocks or trees crushed to coal. Across this burning landscape which wasn't horizontal but vertical were not only layers of historical reckoning but also individual lives as they crossed each other from beginning to end.* He looked up, the fiery mirrors were flashing now in bursts; incendiary sparks were fuelling the Olympian columns. The school was on fire. And higher up, Father Telles' house was insignificant and black in the haze.

'You think he's alive?'

No, not a Portuguese priest when nobody answered. Aggett was right: it was time for settling old scores. But a priest, a schoolteacher . . .

'That's the crime,' said Aggett, 'Just that.'

'Oh god.'

Across the darkened sky, waves of bats were moving out of time and place: the fruit bats of his own youth with their perverted sense of flight, but never in the middle of the day.

Aggett leaned forward: 'Perhaps the driver would like to visit his alma mater, for the last time? To find the Reverend Father floating about. Minus his head or . . .'

'Stop it,' whispered Ranse.

But even now Eduardo was skilfully guiding the jeep through the dust and mist, and wasn't listening. He'd locked the flames out of sight. Was pressing on, was already thirty kilometres down the track.

'It's helped along,' said Aggett, 'by the powers that be. They don't want Vietnam again.'

'But it matters who wins here?'

'Of course.'

The smoke came in waves. Ranse looked at him, equally lost

in paradise. 'You're full of good intentions, aren't you?'

'Perhaps I'm a revolutionary too.'

'Who knows,' he said, coughing.

Aggett folded his arms. 'Before the war they sent me out to a fire. A warehouse packed with cars. Saturday night, hundreds of people around. The fire was belting through two or three floors. And every time one of those Fords or Packards – big things they were – came crashing down, the crowd let out an awful cheer. Revolutionaries at heart, Ranse. We all want to see things burn.'

'But cars aren't people, Aggett.'

A few late flames licked at Maracacume's ruins. In his cold anger Ranse saw the Livres stripping off after a job well done. They were cooling their scorched bodies in the pool, playing mercenary polo with the priest's head. Against a backdrop of Western education going up in smoke. He was trying to be shocked, to shock himself into either fear or sorrow; but his emotions were frozen in the heat and wouldn't budge.

The blank was what he feared most.

At a Fragas camp, they learned that Sergeant e Sousa had been recalled to Viseu military headquarters.

Aggett asked: 'More bullets?'

'He's bringing back regulars,' Eduardo replied, 'to strengthen the Aguema garrison. We can't go that way now.'

And again it was put before them, a choiceless alternative: the roughest track, or nothing.

They sank towards the lower hills, half-way to the coast; the suspension resisted only nominally and the steering made angular thrusts at his senses. The jeep was evenly nursed and abused – their only link with Viseu's relative comforts and safety, but the source of all aches and pains too. Ranse was chained to its groaning personality, when it strained or spluttered his stomach dropped and when it rolled down slopes like a stone, he was massaged by the jolly bumps and sang to it. Because it would eventually stop.

He looked at Aggett, slung between two rice bags in the back – sleeping, resting off past concerns and preparing for new appraisals. Ranse knew if he could eliminate all other sound, the noise trembling in the air would be Aggett's peaceful snore.

He grew even more contemptuous of him, because he, suffering sleepless, was inexplicably waking up as the night was coming down, and could do nothing about it. What was muffled and drowsy by day became wildly accurate to his ears: the birds threw themselves into flight with loud calls, short and long; crickets and other insects filled the air; and over it all the engine belched enough to scare off attackers or alert them in advance. The gears changed up and down, the crudely worn teeth tracing the obstacles in their way.

He was cold, was hot and burning in the rotten jeep; and rising unconsciously were warm thoughts for survival, not just in the immediate future but for always. *We're moving through cyclonic waters, in a dangerous sort of bliss. Beware the calm eye. Because she's sleeping beside me, under hotel sheets so white, and I can taste the slightly impure flavour of alcohol and age. The old Tropicala has a history before us, a life independent of ours: of Ancora and Nicholas on this bed, high off the worn floral carpet. A love-making statement softened in chenille and a place to collapse afterwards with glasses of wine. But where will we go, after this bed? The oak wardrobe is empty; is huge outside and cavernous and has a long mirror, one-sided, through which to observe the changing fashions of love. At the end of the sagging bed, the curtains are faded white blooms on powder grey and maroon. Surely out of print by now. The light's draining from our Number One room and the darkness is being magnified by various mirrors, not all of them visible: the reflectors of our quiet situation, sliding us into the unknown. Ancora holds me tightly about the chest, loses her face in the curve of my neck.* And he sprang up for an explanation. What was going on? A screech of monkeys across the night, the only noise.

The jeep sat there, uncertain of its own behaviour. Eduardo turned the ignition, rolled it over and Ranse could see Aggett rising to a new dilemma. And his own eyes toured the darkness, black spaces could have been anything. A tell-tale clicking.

'Shit,' said Aggett quietly.

Eduardo got out. His skin had lost its copper sheen and turned silver. He was some kind of alien, a moonlit ghost.

'Battery,' he said. 'Could be the starter motor.'

'Or plugs.'

'Yes. Those perhaps too.'

Already the soldiers were under the bonnet, pulling at wires they couldn't see; a toolbox appeared, and they got to work.

'Shouldn't we post some guards?' suggested Aggett.

'It's our territory.'

'Oh.'

'What time is it?' someone asked.

'About eight. I'm starving.'

'How far to Viseu now?'

'Not too far. About twenty.'

'Too bloody far.'

'Get a cab.'

'They'll fix it soon. It's not hard.'

'When you know, eh?'

'Where are we again?'

'Inhumas.'

Silence. 'Wherever that is.' The birds had gone to sleep. Insects gave their position away, without knowing it. The muffled dialect of repairs, under the bonnet. Punctuated by chuckles and giggles. The whole bloody thing is so elemental, he thought. Life, death, and the other thing: whatever it was. He could hear a dog somewhere: they say wild dogs don't bark. Ranse heard it again, and turned to the others:

'Hear that?'

'Something,' said Eduardo.

Aggett hushed, but the soldiers shrugged and went on with their job. The mudguards littered with wires, spark plugs, plumbing, the confused keys of their escape. Viseu would be heaven if they made it. The bits disappeared, one by one. A cough and the jeep was alive, but just as quickly it spluttered and died. They stood there, cheated by unknown forces.

'Um dia horrível,' Eduardo cursed. A terrible day, getting worse. 'Look,' he said.

A light was bouncing and rippling shadows in the dark. The soldiers quickened their pace, but it was hopeless. The trees flashed to full height, a truck bumped around the bend, and headlights caught the jeep.

The occupants emerged. And sure enough, the Minister for Information and Propaganda had come to rescue them; as clearly as da Cunha had trundled up the airstrip on that first day. The dog was growling for effect.

'You,' da Cunha called. 'Come out, it's only us.'

The others came from the shadows with laughter and fear. Ranse had trouble finding any emotion at all.

'It's me,' said da Cunha, unsteady. 'We heard from e Sousa, trouble. But you're not hurt?'

Just terrified and exhausted, he wanted to say.

'The country isn't safe, further up. So I came after you . . .'

'On the way to a village,' Eduardo challenged. 'Saturday night . . .'

'Of course,' replied da Cunha, 'we'll stop at the dance. They've got wonderful food, drinks, coffee. Then back to Viseu, okay?'

The three of them climbed into da Cunha's truck. He turned it around and – ordering the smallest soldier to get in the back, just in case – pushed his foot down and accelerated wildly into dust fused with fog, leaving the jeep more crippled than ever. Ranse saw a clutch of Fragas men and boys, and the engine lid held to the night like a dark mouth about to swallow them all. At the wheel, da Cunha insisted on singing loudly.

On the sleeper, overnight, wrapped in cotton coconut cocoons, k-k-k-katie, sleeping in fits, lying sorely down, sit, roll me over, bang, lie down, rattle, rattle, rot, a thousand diverging dreams all leading up thin city lanes, the country outside thick with green, umbrella leaves and blood mud, life in the land yet, lonely people swagger past, flies drop in for tea, take a leak, boy folding white cotton sheets in the stationary silence, no quits, no butterfly flits, all trapped, locked on the north, Chiang Mai away, the baby kid waves and greets the bleak day, 'Do, do, do, do, do, do . . .' as many times and more, and mother smiles, the Thais a gentle race. And the rest comes.

A village dance: somewhere in the night. A hundred people or more shuffle about an open hall, the music crumbles out of a toyish player. It distorts, in poor taste. (*You shall try strange fruit, the poet said.)* The words and beat spill onto the grass, a setting also for death. At one edge, a blown-up jeep rusts in the damper air. Opposite it, the grave humps. 'From the early fighting,' da Cunha explains. *It's not a cemetery, but a graveyard and that's a hell of a difference; being forced to watch the destructive bits of your own life pass through you.* Sleeping with eyes open, Ranse dazes on the way in. He bends down, finds a typed sheet of paper. It lists the shots in a film sequence, an earlier round in the forgotten war; in the hills and mountains behind Viseu, nobody cares. *Machine gun firing along the bank of Rio Bras, also firing across. Fragas group moves through bushes, too far to see on film. Badly wounded woman on floor of open building, her small child stands nearby. The child runs off, woman hit seconds before by mortar shrapnel. General activity as wounded carried, soldier carries wife, people run. Badly wounded woman being treated; much blood, she dies later. Bloody corpses, some still alive. Relative crying and touching the head of dead woman. Two soldiers seen weeping over body of their friend. Natural sound throughout.* Ranse drops to the ground, can't believe it. Only a film, after all.

Ushered inside, no hero's welcome. They give no chairs to battered Europeans down from higher up, from the mountains. Are self-assured, don't need us, they don't need our distracting presence; the deaths of their own they are feasting here tonight, Eduardo explains. And so transposed by some planetary force from the peeling stucco mansion on a ledge overlooking the Other Sea to this well of fantasia – lights, drinks, laughter, small talk in native terms.

The music plays on, the dancing continues; and rather than strangers they might be friends so old they expect no greeting. One man wears huge bifocals, darkly framed and ponderous on his own slightness; could be an academic, somewhere else. But no animosity here, other than the perceptible feud between Eduardo and da Cunha. That's no business to anyone. The Minister for Information and Propaganda drinks in a cultural vacuum, but happily fills it with inspired wit. Like a child, the children are everywhere tonight. Ranse can't recall seeing children like this anywhere. *Are these the children of chiefs, the new orphans of the king? Where will they end up, now that their school is burning down? And how will these new orphans spend their days, after nights like this?* They are extraordinarily beautiful, swaying under the lanterns that catch the insects; and flutter their limbs just like the wings of trapped moths. The children must dance, must dance.

Propped against the wall, no place in his clouded mind for fear; is losing control of mind, of his body. *The task is to maintain, is to maintain control of your own body. In hunger, muscular exertion, nervous tension, fatigue: how to handle it unless I'm dancing too? Dancing smooths out the effect of weight on the compressed layers of defeat. Only then can the battered mind survive.* Out there a grown man falls about, not drunk perhaps but intoxicated; something to do with tribal death and its dimensions. Only his brothers, uncles, cousins, blood brothers are missing tonight: what's left of his family, is left. Ranse craves sleep, what's left is only a pure desire for sleep. There's a twilight where he knows he will never grow up; and to this problem has always addressed himself, has always been a loner. The children must dance.

Cigarettes, rough; and coffee. The food repeats itself and can't be taken. Ranse is sick, or sick and tired. Would love an aspirin now, or several. From the hands of the orphanic Ancora, whose hands could be felt. And sometimes he feels he could even extract the night from night, given half a chance. In the loins of his imagination going down on her. *And looks around. What am I doing in this beautiful, hungry place? A Saturday night dance, after all I've been through?* The smoke draws itself voluntarily into his lungs, filling the space vacated by heathen calls for sleep. The wall gives way behind, but he leans back and finds it again.

A loud cheer from the crowd, the children run like rabbits through trestles under the food. *God, take me back to Viseu. If I don't reach the Nameless Sea by morning I'll drown, I know. The shock, of veiled ethereal beauties who inhabit this world in times of chaos and war.* One is eating grapes that can't be, but what would a fruit lover know? The girls so young, they wear earrings from the top of their ears to show their perversity – the dark hair tied in buns like some coiled tension, or resentment of my desires. They communicate through waves, smallest vibrations of nose tips, signals to torsos and ears that make no sound. They can extract even more night from night, they can reduce night to the purest knowledge and cannot be touched in either substance or soul; they will dance into eternity. The children must dance, dance the night away.

It is past midnight in a way it's never before been truly past midnight, and two young girls move up past his aching body and do a nice foxtrot around the floor. They are five, or six.

Ranse was quiet, and Aggett had fallen to sleep. The truck crept down to the thick, dark sea; the thick air rose to meet them, and they slowed through Pojuca, the long ago resort. The sprays of bougainvillea bent down and lashed the sides, and tyres rutted in the clay. The feel of Mediterranean night in the abandoned resort, the Portuguese marble street signs. Ranse soaked it up without mystery, the way back now and even the way out. The sea came into being, or was simply there at their left; and on it was a ship somewhere inside a light. And off the dirt, the desperate arc of headlamps bounced into his eyes. He closed them, and slept upright.

A mumble of Portuguese, and he woke to Eduardo and da Cunha talking: the revolutionary bond restored for the moment. The streets of Viseu around them were deserted and absolutely black. Only the flare of oil lamps seen through curtained windows – nobody could be up, surely – and down hallways and lanes. In the official darkness not a single guard, nor a solitary old man whose perfect right it was to defy the curfew. Not a cat or dog anywhere. Only the antiseptic glow of the hospital up there; was Doctor Peyrot in town? And the next ridge above all: where Goddard had put down roots, and for once that house was buried in darkness too. But tomorrow he would see.

And lastly, as the truck found its way through Viseu, evidence of Mrs Mendonça's vigilance signalled at the night's edge. The neon Hotel Tropicala was out, but a flaming kerosene torch burnt like a siren. They pulled up, and went to their rooms in silence.

Pure white cotton sheets. Ranse could have wept, was close enough to it. He stripped off his clothes and stood naked. He could smell them, even on the floor. He was naked and could feel only the darkness and dirt pressing on every inch of his body. He was overwhelmed by tiredness. The door opened behind him, and he turned without surprise.

It was Gecko, his own embarrassment overtaken by concern for Ranse. 'Are you all right, senhor?' He shone a torch into the room.

Ranse was beyond tiredness, but falling off. It must have been four in the morning. Gecko was still in his barman's outfit, after a busy Saturday night.

'Welcome back,' he said. 'There is no water on tap, senhor. They have a power failure at the pumping station. No water for a bath. You okay?'

Ranse choked off tears. 'No choice, hey?' He smiled at Gecko.

'Absolutely, senhor.'

'Well, that's all right. Goodnight.'

'Goodnight to you. Boa noite.'

Filthy days of war, and no water. Ranse crawled between the sheets, felt the starch against his grime. It was a criminal act, but he had no choice. At last he had no choice.

Absolutely, senhor!

FOURTEEN

'Come in,' he called.

But already Aggett was in the room and opening the shutters. It was Sunday morning, he waited for the pealing gongs to summon Viseu to mass. But nothing, only absolute quiet out there.

'What time is it?'

'After midday. Ranse, get up.'

'What's . . .'.

'Eisner's dead.'

'Wh . . .'

'He's dead. Quite.'

'He wasn't that bad, was he?'

'Well he's dead now, old boy. Get up.'

Ranse fumbled with his watch, strapping it on. 'What about his mate?'

'Racovic. He's gone.'

'Gone?'

'Pissed off. The pilots left this morning. Probably on his way to Singers.' He stopped at the window. 'I'm going up to the hospital, Eisner's still there. God knows what they pumped him with.'

'Yes.'

He turned. 'Peyrot's there. You might catch him too.'

'You going now?'

'Five minutes,' said Aggett, tossing Ranse his trousers. 'In the bar.'

The hospital was cradled a mile up from the town: a broad, flat building that had survived twenty or thirty Wet seasons. Nor were the staff likely to wear themselves out. Peyrot was somewhere on his rounds and wouldn't be hard to locate, they were told: *if you want him badly enough, go and find him.* Down the other end.

The ward was cool. Doors and windows were open, but the stench of wounds and stale dressings wouldn't take the hint and leave. The sick helped themselves, hopping across the floor to a large water jug. Others couldn't move. Scars sprang up where missiles had gone in. At one bed a soldier in traction was playing with his nose. It was too big and he played with it a lot, picking it, rubbing it; almost wishing it dead, Ranse thought. The man looked up and smiled, unsure of what any moment would bring.

Aggett was well ahead, striding towards the small European at the far end of the ward. *That was Peyrot, holding dark secrets about life and death?* The doctor's face was moulded in marble, by a competent but hardly exciting sculptor who always stopped for lunch. He looked too boring to be an addict.

'Very disturbing,' he said flatly. 'Only a leg wound, but the infection spreads of course. Not difficult, except I don't have some drugs. Still,' he said, turning to the ward, 'there are worse cases. He was calling out, in a fever. But not so bad, I thought. Then the orderly woke me, and said Eisner is dead. So I came down to the ward. The others knew it – the young American, estrangeiro – some were awake. He was already gone.'

Peyrot gave no sign of lying or telling the truth. He stared into space, giving nothing away.

'Yes,' said Aggett impatiently. He asked to see the body.

'This way,' Peyrot called like a tour guide, ignoring patients to either side. He bumped into one and regained his balance. 'You won't be very impressed. There are no proper facilities, we have to bury them quickly.'

They entered the small room. The body was under a patched sheet on a table. Everything was clean but untidy. The windows had been painted over white, and opened slightly at the top for air. In opposite corners, two ageing fans kept a breeze moving. Ranse had never been in a morgue before, though it was hardly that: a room with a solitary corpse. He could already feel the saliva floating onto his tongue; wanting to spit something out, to expel foreign matter from his own body. Peyrot lifted back the sheet, to observe. It was Eisner all right, looking more alive than he had a couple of days before. Ranse expected to see a human cadaver and had been shown a man asleep. But as he looked for a second longer, the face grew rigid and stony and there was no way its emotions could ever be restored again. He was pronounceably dead.

'You are sure?' the doctor asked. 'We should not stay here too long.'

'Yes,' said Aggett. 'Eisner.'

'He was a reporter too. Are you upset?'

He shook his head. 'Can we go outside? I think Mr Ranse wants to speak to you, about something else. It's a little stuffy in here.'

Aggett pulled the sheet up, covering the face.

On the hospital verandah, they both waited. The doctor patted towards them, but slowed down long before he had to.

'Now,' he said. 'About the professor?'

'Yes,' said Ranse, 'my uncle.' He glanced at Aggett, who'd turned to admire the view. The late sun was stretching under the awning. Peyrot tapped a stethoscope to his own chest.

'You see,' he began, 'Samuel was very troubled. And he had problems, of course.'

'You saw him?'

'We drank sometimes, played chess, discussed things. He then seemed, almost lost.'

'Lost?'

'For purpose, you see. He spoke about his last season. I believe he was schizophrenic.' Peyrot looked away. 'Samuel was *déraciné*, a man not living in his natural time. Or place.'

'Why did he come here then?' It was Aggett's voice, over his shoulder.

'A number of mistakes. It wasn't a good place. Too many tensions here. At first, it was quieter. But he stayed too long. He wasn't comfortable here.'

'Obviously not,' Aggett turned and came to them. 'You

177

signed the certificate,' he said. 'It *was* suicide?'

'Of course.'

'And it's not possible he could have been murdered?'

'Oh no,' said Peyrot. 'He put a gun to his own mouth. I tell you, that's not very pleasant. He was here, in the morgue.'

'And you had him buried?' Aggett pressed.

'In the mountains. He told this to Eduardo, he wanted it. I treated the body. Wrapped it.'

'In a coffin, you mean?'

'Yes. But no, not here. Wrapped in sheets, and like a bundle. To be taken to the military centre. They have coffins there. And up to Father Telles, at Maracacume. He would bury him near the school.'

There was silence, until Peyrot found a new confidence. 'Well,' he said, 'any more?'

Ranse shook his head, but Aggett went on. 'Were there any papers?'

'I have already said. A death certificate was sent to Darwin, the Australian government.'

'And swallowed by the bureaucracy.'

'I suppose. But now we have other problems,' said Peyrot. 'Some people think they're happier, not being alive. Until they know what being dead is like.'

'You know?'

Ranse spoke up: 'I'm sure he wanted to die.'

'Yes.'

Aggett was brushing the floor with his shoe. He looked up. 'I think it's over. Doctor Peyrot has living patients to care for, don't you?'

The doctor half smiled. 'They come, more every day. Not like Zurich.'

'What's the hurry?'

Aggett was stepping out when Ranse caught up and grabbed him. He turned around, slowly.

'I couldn't get a word in. And then we're out of the place.'

'You were tongue-tied, that's all. I asked a few questions. And now that you've got the answers, you can go.'

'He's lying, isn't he?'

'Probably.'

Ranse looked up: 'I'm going up to Goddard's again, maybe I'll spend the night there. What about you?'

'Back to the hotel,' said Aggett. 'I need a drink. You're right, of course. Peyrot's a fraud.' He looked at Ranse carefully. 'Take it easy up there, won't you? There's a war on, Eisner found out. So busy telling us, he forgot to remind himself.'

'Was he really a spy?'

'Eisner?'

'Yes, and Racovic.'

Aggett chewed his lip. 'If he was, the balloon's really gone up. On the Fragas, the whole country.'

'You don't seem too worried.'

He smiled. 'People like me don't have to, we've got no nerves left. Or heart for it.' Aggett traced a rectangle on the dirt, then erased it. 'But you want to leave, and you want to face it. What you're doing here has nothing to do with Goddard. He's dead. You're flirting with something else.'

'What?'

'The kids here. And having none, I guess. If you're not careful it could tear you apart, Ranse.'

He swallowed. 'Don't worry.'

'No. But you'd better.'

'I haven't thought about it.'

'Oh, you have. People like you either try to forget – impossible, of course – or they embrace the whole thing. Like our friend on the table.'

Ranse looked away. 'What about the body?'

'Eduardo's the expert. We'll put him under tomorrow. Here today, gone tomorrow. *A popular journalist on the* Blockhead Courier *– Howard ("Howie") Eisner – has died at 32. His death will come as a shock to nobody, and a pleasant surprise to all. George Aggett writes: I was one of Howie's many colleagues, and always found him underhand and disagreeable. He won't be missed.* Like you,' he said, 'I have to go and pack up a dead man's things. He wanted to be just like me. Ridiculous, isn't it?'

Aggett pushed both hands into his pockets, and tried to give a smile. But it wouldn't come. He turned and set off down the track, and Ranse pushed uphill.

Caught in this odd conflict, going to nowhere, waiting for time to hand down its decision; sucking on ripe fruit. Because after this, the war would surely get worse. The ragtag army of Livres was hacking its way slowly forward, giving nothing away. The Fragas rule was slowed by some kind of half-baked, heart-felt ideology and the Livres relied on a simplicity which the people were quick to understand, even if they didn't agree: fight, or be killed. And it could be enough to win a crazy little war, just as it was still the best way to win an insane big one. Give the people what they fear. He sweated and tacked up, watching birds in the abrupt sky; and unspeaking natives drifting past, a picket line going nowhere. For years he'd let things evolve at their natural pace, and was still waiting for the changes to come. The natives disappeared down the track. The flat sea out there gave no clues. And a warm trickle of water answered only his thirst, briefly.

He settled into Goddard's chair. In this climate of uncertainty, his own body had undergone changes; for a moment it felt like the chair had shrunk, or been remoulded against his frame. He gripped the desk, and saw his forearms swell in the early evening light: the veins thickening under tanned skin, hands roughed to the nails, fine hairs bleached to invisibility. His back was firmer now; and pressing into the chair he could feel strength coming from his shoulder-blades, though he couldn't make it enter his head.

The shelf was empty, the diaries with Teppy Zervos of course. They were on her shelves now and Ranse couldn't bring himself to fight it; to confront her about Goddard while she retained some unexplained feeling for either of them. *She had come here with a gun, and killed his uncle. That was unbelievable. They had shared her as a lover. Just as difficult to believe, but true.* What a life, a hundred lovers and not one had stayed. Only the pilot, the fat Greek: beside her now and dreaming of longer cars and jets. He'd learned to fly before coming to terms with life on earth. From up there, Zervos would surely get big ideas about things: might see whole rivers and valleys, mountains and cities and accept that as the normal scale of human enterprise – of existence even – and not see the details, or the slight differences. And his wife would be needed even less, now that the tourists had gone.

He got up, and wondered if he should pack the books. They'd have to go back to Australia; but it was a plan so devoid of planning that he hadn't taken it up since his arrival here – a week, two weeks ago. What hope did he have of getting three, four hundred precious volumes down to Viseu, over the Restless Sea and safely into the bowels of academia? They would clamour for the hand-tooled spines, but leave them unopened: *the Samuel Goddard Collection, what a once important man had died for.* He held out his finger, and stopped. Unlike everything else on the island, they weren't dusty.

She had been back, he knew. She'd come to Goddard's forbidden study while he'd been in the mountains and cleaned the books, as Goddard himself would have. She was past revenge, had already perpetrated the enormity of killing him; and had wiped clean the offending weapon, so that the blackness of that act would pass. But wouldn't allow herself to forget the subject of it. By cleaning the books, the kitchen floor, the whole rambling edifice, she was keeping Goddard alive, long after she might have left: even in death he held the solution. Or if not Goddard, he thought, the nephew who wouldn't go.

The metamorphosis of insects from grubs into moths and flies is an astonishing process. A hairy caterpillar is transformed into a butterfly. Observe the change. We have four beautiful wings, where there were none before; a tubular proboscis, in the place of a mouth with jaws and teeth; six long legs, instead of fourteen feet. In another case we see a white, smooth, soft worm, turned into a black, hard, crustaceous beetle, with gauze wings. These, as I said, are astonishing processes.

And yet, he wasn't Goddard. He pulled down the blind, shutting out the very thought. She might have found enough in Goddard to rebuild a life on, but Ranse had seen through it all and gone off to fend for himself.

The study had grown darker, and lonely. He could sense dusk coming on. And the insect world that Goddard himself had chosen began to sing: hymns to the passing of heat and to the relief of darkness and night. Ranse stepped out to the hallway, into the half-way house he'd practically grown up in. He couldn't forget – though something not thought of in years – being delivered to Goddard's place on the evening of his mother's death. *And he'd forgotten until tonight how individual death could be, had to be: so that the inevitability of death could be felt, including no doubt his own.* They'd held back the details: now clearly, he saw the face and the high, bold forehead being crushed by metal and glass, and the car buckled under a mistaken truck which wasn't disputed when she was dead and it was too late. Only it hadn't spurred him to sorrow or despair. Goddard had simply entered like a human scoop and saved him from a normal, healthy suffering; and delivered him instead from the humble to the Mighty, or near enough. Confusion of death, of affection and Calvinistic pride were replaced overnight with science.

'This is your room,' said Uncle Sam. 'You'll find it comfortable.'

But hadn't even bothered to remove the half skeleton hanging on the far wall, or the charts of dissected frogs. 'Good-night,' he'd called. And had been too shattered to do anything but nod – not by his mother's death, but by the awesome realisation that Sam Goddard would now take over his life, that all the freedom would come to a halt; would be replaced by discipline, or what Uncle Sam called exploration but was still discipline. *If you keep at it, you'll eventually get there. It's like an escalator, Nicky, powered by clear thinking and hard work. You join at the bottom and eventually you reach the top. But what about the reverse, Uncle Sam, the escalator going down? That can happen too. Oh no, Nicky, the escalators always go up. That's why they're called escalators.* Thereafter, he would always be good at it. And his Uncle Sam would be even better at it. And that, he knew now, had been as deliberate as day following night.

The hallway was interrupted by steps, the ones he knew by heart. Without looking or thinking, he saw the kitchen to his left and went in. It was bathed in that bluish light from the past and the mountains. *And awash with mortar love. The only answer*

182

being that he was shot by Teppy, that Eduardo her friend and lover perhaps and security chief covered it up, and threatened Peyrot to do the same or die. That's all the diary could possibly say, after it stopped. And that was no mystery, it took him no further into his own life. The blue was streaming in now, unsettling his thoughts. His uncle had existed on the same set of tracks – shaky as they were – but always ahead of him, and there was no way of overtaking even if he'd wanted to. *For years reduced to a stick, a rusty machine; a whole lot of eggs in a wound-up leaf, a stone.* And now Goddard was off the rails and the way ahead was open at last. Aggett was right, that's why he was here. But it was frightening, for that.

He felt his way down the hall – two steps with a stumble – and into Goddard's bedroom. She'd cleaned up here too. The traces of their brief history together had been removed. Ranse fell back onto the old mattress, could feel his head striking the feather mass of the pillow. It didn't stop, and sank deeper into the past until dreams were all it could safely hold.

They were about children.

FIFTEEN

It wasn't starched linen, here it never was. But he was a privileged guest in his own house, on his own platform at sea. Only paralysed, he couldn't move. An octopus with only two legs. And try, he couldn't get free. His legs were thrashing but his body was immobile, tense and hard; and then he felt the vibrations and started to boil; and was framing his naked, boiling body over hers; as he screamed, the room spoke to him; and he woke. And she was undressing. He sat up, gathered his legs.

'What are you doing?'

Teppy was shifting about: at the foot of the iron bed, opening the rickety window, moving to the dresser and untying the rope of her hair. The outline was everywhere; and then the navel, the warmth of her dancer's legs as she stood beside him. 'Aren't you pleased to see me?'

'Of course.'

'Wait,' she said, moving away.

'What?'

'Just a minute.'

He watched her go. His own body was cold and confused. Only the bird-calls coming through the window made any sense at all. Ranse got up and wrapped the sheet around his waist. He heard the bathroom door, a rasping tap turned on.

Slowly he was waking up. He staggered around the room, to the window, the dresser, to the wooden chair. Teppy's leather bag sat there with an open zip. And between a towel and a pair of bathers was the closest thing to an answer: the black handle and trigger of a gun. Ranse lifted it slowly. Only slightly bigger than the hand, but a weight of bullets too. The tap shuddered through the walls and he slipped it back.

'What are you doing?' she asked. 'You look like a Roman in your toga.'

'Coming back to life.'

She moved. 'Let's make love.'

'Wait.' He stepped back.

'What on earth for?'

He clutched his arms. 'There's a war going on, that's why.'

'Don't people make love in wars?'

'I don't know,' he said. 'I've never been in one.'

'Well I have, and they do.'

And precise fingers, her hair pressing into his face were achieving what he'd wanted to avoid most of all. He was stroking too, and then throwing the sheet off, lifting her by the waist. They fell onto the bed. The objects of a hundred field trips shook in the morning room, and on her arm Ranse could see the perfect rosette of an innoculation scar. 'Come back,' she whispered, and drew tighter to him. But it was as blatant as granite and distant as the Sea and death, he knew. Ranse closed his eyes. Somewhere he'd read the Moon was a satellite of the Earth, he could remember that clearly. The body was even older, was intense, or vulgar and nothing short of desperate. 'Come back now,' Teppy called, shaking at her loins. Only he could see the truth veiled by another lie – could see it forming, taking shape – and rolled down to the side.

'What?' she demanded quietly. 'Tell me.'

'Nothing.'

They remained silent, until the birds stopped too.

'Goddard?'

'I don't know,' said Ranse.

Teppy sat up. 'Well?'

'I suppose so.'

She lifted her arm to the window, the room.

'Now it's all yours. Well, isn't it?'

Ranse shrugged. 'I've lost something else. Just by coming here.'

She tossed her hair back. 'We can't blame the world,

Nicholas. It's too far away for that. Anyway,' she smiled, 'here we try to help each other out.'

'That's why there are no failures?'

'Oh, come on,' she said grinning. 'I'm taking you for a swim.'

In these last weeks before the Wet, the inhabitants of Novo Viseu gathered at a beach called Luila, in a form of truce.

'I came to get you,' she said in the car. 'Early. You think I really wanted to seduce you?'

Ranse ignored her. 'Who'll be there?'

'I'm not sure. Da Cunha will be, he's always first to arrive. Lives down that end. And your mate Aggett, or Mister Quiet as they call him.'

'Do they?'

She nodded, gliding past the Tropicala and on to the eastern edge of town.

'He's never short of words around me,' said Ranse. 'Who else?'

'The Minister for Finance. Julião Dias. Or Financial Reconstruction to be exact. I think. And his daughter, Ancora.'

Ranse swallowed quietly. 'The President's helper?' he said, and again.

'You know her?'

'No. But I've seen her around.'

'Stunning, isn't she?'

'Oh, ugly . . .'

'Yes,' said Teppy. 'But she might have a beautiful sister.'

Ranse turned. 'That's a funny thing for a woman to say, isn't it?'

'I think we're talking about the same girl,' she said curtly. 'Just watch out, Nicholas. She came down from the mountains.'

'What's that supposed to mean?'

'Nothing. It's where she belongs, that's all.'

'Oh, lovely.'

'Before the troubles she taught at Maracacume, the school. And she'll go back when it's over. Her heart's still there.'

'One of god's innocents, so?'

Teppy looked at him. 'You can't lose it when you've never had any. She might be a virgin – it's strictly politics with Galvão, I'm sure – but she's no innocent. Not here.'

'I saw Telles' school go up in flames,' he said firmly. 'Did they tell you that?'

'Who?'

'Your informants.'

The road turned to dirt, and they veered away from the coastline. It was only five minutes from town when Teppy stopped the car, outside the rusting gates. Behind was a vast concrete slab, then a deserted building. Weeds shot from cracks and walls.

'Prison?' he asked.

'Not quite. Used to be the Viseu public school. My kids went there for a while. Had it now.'

There were no children, only patriot reds and greens oxidising in the sun; and vegetation creeping out to dry. The school holidays were eternal, and unwanted.

'Teppy . . .'

She dug into the bag, between them on the seat and took out the gun. Ranse sat back.

'What's up?' she said, fishing about with her free hand. She looked up.

'This?' she waved it. 'My protective weapon. Zervos got it for me, insists I take it everywhere. I'm quite fond of it, actually.'

'Put it down,' he said.

She dropped it to her lap, and kept searching. 'Here it is. Lucy.'

The girl in the snapshot sat in a bus, with the beach through a window. She was about nine or ten, he thought; but lips curved already into a mouth, and falling across Teppy's back and stroking it. Her mother's child, and almost there.

'The eldest,' she said. 'Last year.'

'What about the boy?'

'He took the photo,' Teppy smiled. 'An idiot. With a hairy chin and spots.'

'Sounds like Zervos,' he said and immediately wished he hadn't. She grabbed the photo.

'Suppose you had kids. What would you do?'

'Send them back, I guess.'

Teppy took the gun, and weighed it in her hand. She was close to crying.

'I know why you're here,' he said.

She lifted her shoulders. 'I can't go without Zervos. He won't go until there's nothing left to save.'

'That's not it.'

She was holding the gun, almost offering it. 'What about you, Nicholas? It's not safe, really.'

'I'll get out, don't worry.'

'Back to Asia?'

His voice stumped. Teppy put the gun back in the bag and started the car.

'Let's go to the beach, all right?'

To their left again, sweeping away none of the tension, the Sea came into view. Could have been the Australian beach, he thought, any one of hundreds except for the hugging slopes here that were dry and bare. Further on, they passed a strange house built half on land and over the water, with a dog tied up and complaining at the back. It was probably da Cunha's place, he thought but didn't want to ask. There was a struggle, always. But she was lying, she *had* killed Goddard, and he'd confront her before the drive was out. She flicked her finger ahead. The others were gathered, a small stranded force waiting down on the beach, and the car slowed into the softer track. He saw a peeling sign in English, could make out 'Flippers, Goggles, Dingies and Liloes' and felt more lost than ever. Higher up were buses, coated with tropical dust in streaks: of doubtful make, via what route of shonky dealers and obsolescence had they come to this final destination? Once chromed, they were rusting now with names like Jesus Christ, Ave Maria and Apollo Six; and had rolled to a stop, as the signs barely indicated, at Luila. A girl's name, perhaps.

She stopped, turned off the ignition and started to undress. 'Changing,' she said.

'Teppy . . .' He looked away.

'What?'

'I need to know . . .'

'What?'

'Did he put the gun to his mouth, or his temple?'

'Oh my god,' she jerked herself into the costume. 'I told you, the temple.'

'Peyrot says the mouth. He ought to know the difference. Even if he's a lousy doctor.'

She looked hard at him. 'Nicholas, I barely want to go over it. But do you honestly think there's much left when a man puts a thirty-eight to his head, and pulls the trigger? I'm trying to spare you the details. You're his flesh and blood after all!'

She sprang out of the car and slammed the door. 'If you want to know,' she yelled, 'half his bloody head evaporated.'

They encountered Aggett first, clad in bathers older than the buses. 'The latest,' he called them. By contrast, his own flesh was shockingly pale. He drew them back to meet the others.

'You don't know Senhor Dias,' he said. 'Mister Ranse, from Australia.' They shook hands with excessive politeness for the beach. Julião Dias was wearing nothing less than a striped business shirt and sunglasses with tortoise-shell frames, perhaps to enhance his rather plain looks. 'My daughter Ancora,' he said with a smile.

She nodded, but said nothing.

'Hello again,' declared Ranse. He'd never heard her voice, even in the President's sanctuary. But as Teppy pressed into the group, Ancora half turned to what could only have been – behind him – the Sea out there.

Ranse smiled uncomfortably, and saw da Cunha coming over with beer in an ice-chest. He was holding it over his head, swaying his hips and raising a laugh among them.

'In Lisboa I studied like a man *possessed*. Everything was *possessed*,' he said, handing the beer around. 'And then I was sent for military training – you can imagine – and it all went to pieces. Luckily my mother died before I came back. It would have killed her to see what a fool I turned into.' He clumsily opened the can.

'You're very clever,' said Teppy, glancing about.

'Not that clever,' claimed Aggett, 'though he bloody well

thinks he is. Listen. If impenetrable means that which can't be penetrated, what does impenetrate mean?'

'What?'

'To penetrate deeply.'

'Oh,' said da Cunha.

'But you'll survive, don't worry.'

Ranse watched Ancora drift away. She made nothing of English word games, of course; and even less perhaps of Teppy's crude attempts to isolate her. He kept watching her. Even from behind, her limbs weren't fulsome but dark and tenacious; and the soft, childish back disappeared into thin legs, leaving almost no buttocks. There was nothing of those purposeful, tanned women he'd grown up with. In an Asian way, he knew what she'd look like unclothed and fully balanced on her feet. He'd never given up that hope. And whatever Teppy said, nor perhaps had the President of the struggling republic.

'There are problems,' boasted da Cunha with a depleted can. 'Even my comrades – some of them – agree that the struggle against colonialism brought on ultra-leftist manifestations that couldn't be contained, and confused the true function of the State in the edification of a socialist society.'

'Perhaps,' said Dias, cautiously.

'You mean they went overboard,' Aggett offered.

'Well, yes. Listen,' he said. 'Can you hear the shells singing?'

They strained their ears. 'No.'

'You're not close enough. Listen again.'

'Nothing.'

'Anyway,' he went on, 'Senhor Dias has promised us the Economic Miracle, sooner or later. We hope sooner, but he warns us not to proceed too fast. Progress goes hand in hand with tradition.'

Dias winced a little and smiled. He was already sweating heavily in his shirt, a handkerchief at his face. 'We will set up a free industry zone, over there.' The driest scrub stared back at them. 'With a minimum of interference,' he added, looking at da Cunha. 'And of course, we would like to encourage oil explorations. At sea, we think.'

'And if everything fails,' said da Cunha, 'there's always the fish.'

'What you really need,' Aggett cut in, 'is more agriculture, not less. Don't they, Ranse?'

But he was distracted. By the sea, or rather the shells. Or lack of them, or lack of noise they apparently made. *Why did Gecko keep a bottle of shells behind the bar?* Or by how little he really knew of this country, or its motley inhabitants. Or by her.

'I think so,' he said. 'Stick with papaws.'

Teppy laughed.

'Very well,' proclaimed da Cunha, 'you can be Minister for Agriculture.'

'Maybe,' he said, but it was a joke he could barely afford. He thought of Galvão's offer, of the model agriculture school and its chalky bones, and the school on fire; and he knew it couldn't work here. For any of them.

'In the meantime,' said Teppy, 'let's bring back the tourists. Which means, of course, some kind of situation where people don't go round killing each other.'

'I'm already working on it. On the brochures now,' said da Cunha. 'In full colour.'

Aggett stepped back: 'They'll have to appeal to very strange travellers.'

They spread themselves across the small beach, an institution upheld by four centuries of Portuguese rule. Not that development had come: the Luila bus stand, the paddle hire, a few concrete structures more like bomb shelters than sun shades. But the beach was another place to go to escape Viseu while not fleeing it entirely. Across the Velvet Sea the town could be seen as a tarnished capsule, caught between the steep Taguas and the ocean. It was still their golden possession.

Off-shore, the native catamarans were rocking against the currents. They were slivers of bark, with outriggers of strapped bamboo poles that plopped up and down, forever suspending the dark occupants on a merry-go-round that went nowhere. There was no hurry: they fished with time, not against it. And were somehow more Arab than Asian in their ways, he thought.

'What do they catch?' he finally asked. To be innocent of

anything more suggestive. But she only smiled, and said nothing. 'Fish?' he asked stupidly. It was useless. There was an increasing chance that she didn't exist. They both gazed at the sea. At least, he thought, she doesn't want to get up and walk away. Ancora cupped her feet into the sand, still the feet of a child. She was set apart, not only from Ranse or by her background or politics. She belonged to no one, not even Galvão, he realised. He looked out to sea; to where turtles, sharks, dolphins, giant jellyfish and sea snakes were cruising. A thousand miles back to Australia, to Asia too and a million between us; and Teppy Zervos only twenty yards away. Was this her revenge for interrogation, to place him close to Ancora Dias and leave him stranded? He looked back. She was playing a ball game with Aggett, both of them pouncing about like children. And so unlike Ancora, the most silent woman he'd met. She was looking at the Sea, the Sea; had looked for so long in silence that she didn't need to question it, or anything else. Least of all, Nicholas Ranse beside her. Beneath his background, his values, his travels and relative good fortune, he could feel a tasteless vanity – was it ego, or lack of love – buried in his every thought and move. It had polluted his every relationship with the world, had brought him unwisely to Viseu, and placed him opposite his uncle's mistakes, and beside Ancora Dias. She would not give him more than an arresting blink; she would not be touched by him. And he was happy for that, at least.

How many beauties are lost in the slums, why shouldn't they emerge like butterflies, silver, all gossamer in beauty and slowly untangling to emerge in triangular beauty, wings in flight, shaking like leaves, away the Thai slum sores and heading in breeze to sunshine, silver glinting in the sun and catching expectant eyes, my eyes wandering for sin, catching beauty in white blouses, soft breasts rising and beware, stripping away my guilt; the beauty of old, aware of something more than struggle, free of mental sores, feeling the gold, happy heart gold and none grow old, love on the mud, on the floor, klongs never die, dry up to dust, all our putrid lust gone in smiling white cotton cloth, under it all, the beauty rising in soft lights, lost in romance, happy hours with Sumalee and Doi, the tall girl with

*the white smile, satin blouse falling, Doi undressing in silk
dreams, in early hours of dusk. A rest again.*

A jeep was stirring from the town. But da Cunha ignored it, for
waves that caressed the rose-gold beaches and fringed the
coral reefs with foam. The sun was bright but didn't burn, the
island was a haven of childhood rediscovered, the pure love of
Paul and Virginie. *How unreal seem smoky, noisy towns here!
How unnatural the hasty snack!* Until the jeep's arrival forced a
halt.

'Eduardo,' he said, and walked across.

'More good news,' said Teppy. 'You can tell by the size of the
dust pall.' There was no response.

'Ranse!'

Da Cunha was waving him over, the comic Portuguese gone
at last. The government minister again.

'You're on,' she said.

'Come with me,' da Cunha called, 'and see a friend.'

Eduardo got out and paused. His eyes stayed on Ranse for
only a second: but the darkest of jet black eyes were protected
by their own curvature, and gave nothing away.

'Let's go,' said da Cunha. 'To the Museum.'

As before, Eduardo stood alone and Teppy Zervos was
stretching her fine hands out and already drawing him back to
the conspiracy, whatever it was. It didn't matter now. Ranse
was being taken away from it, just as dying animals took themselves off at the bitter end. But she moved well, he thought in
the haze.

SIXTEEN

A mess, *confusão*. Once through the double gates, guarded by armed youths, he found himself in a large quadrangle with colonnades on all sides. It was meant to be Roman, and Portuguese by inference. Something like a well sprang at the centre of things: a slimy pool now, being used by female prisoners to wash their clothes in. Mosquitoes hit the air around his ears. 'Alvaro! Alvaro!' a woman called softly, hoping not to be heard. Behind them, in an expanding circle, the children of prisoners were not playing but were somehow active; and further back, under the arches of old, lazed the actual prisoners. Those on the wrong side. One of them repeated the woman's call, but howled it softly. 'Alvaro!' Ranse watched him, at first thinking he was brushing a fly away. The man picked his nose, slapped his forehead and pointed to a precise spot on the ground which he followed with his extended finger until it touched the earth.

They kept walking.

As though proving his innocence or lack of complicity, Sergeant Oscar e Sousa sat alone. Still wearing his slouch hat, minus the feathers, he looked like an actor waiting for his call. When he saw them coming he dusted his boots with the palm of his thick hand. It had started as a private war, and quickly turned into public battle; but in the sergeant Ranse detected the beginnings again of a very private fight. His pride was still intact. E Sousa stood to greet them.

'Boa tarde, to you both,' he called.

They shook hands firmly, and e Sousa sniffed the air. 'Don't worry, you get used to it.' The urine of whole families, turning in the heat.

'Oscar, this is crazy.'

'Just another change,' he replied. 'We fought to gain independence and now fight to save it. The Livres were destroyed and by miracle have come back, the way all rebels do.' He smiled faintly, at the confusion before them: 'And look, we are the authority.'

'We'll try to get you out,' da Cunha said.

'Don't try,' e Sousa stated. 'They will release me before long. Or the Livres will.' He turned. 'How is the President, alive and well?'

'He's working on it.'

'Good'.

'It's these coastal revolutionaries,' da Cunha said mockingly.

'We see how difficult they are. And now Senhor Ranse knows too. But thank you,' he said, 'for bringing him. Could I now speak alone?'

The sergeant waited for da Cunha to go, and Ranse fought the smell. It was strange enough, being locked together even for ten minutes in this place; and still without a reason.

'I wanted to see you at Aguema,' e Sousa said, 'on your way down. Only it did not happen, of course. They sent for me.'

'Yes, I know.'

'But I am not a Livre, so why am I here?' He bent over. 'Because I am not with Fragas either. The army minister is against me.'

'Why is that?'

'He was at Maracacume, a student of Galvão. The school was destroyed, of course.'

Ranse nodded: 'I saw it on fire.'

'The fight, not the fire. He is blaming me,' e Sousa said more loudly. 'But how can I win with boys?'

Ranse looked to the others, saw da Cunha moving through them and talking as he might to friends. Or old enemies, perhaps.

'Galvão's cousin,' said e Sousa. 'It's true. The President's cousin, in jail.' He pointed to the man who was still tracing in the dirt.

'But there is something else,' he said. 'As you know, Senhor Goddard stopped often on his trips. And I know him very well. But your uncle did not commit suicide.'

The urine fumes sank into Ranse's belly, into his own flesh.

'He's not dead?'

'Oh yes, he is quite dead. But did not kill himself. When his body was sent to Telles, they stopped at the garrison. Of course, I looked. He was in a coffin, but inside was wrapped in blankets. I was told...' He lifted a finger to his head.

'And you saw the body?'

He nodded. 'It was wrapped many times. With ropes, and knots. Too tight to open. But I lifted him, and there was nothing from the head.' E Sousa leaned closer. 'He had been shot – a lot of blood – from behind, in the back. I have seen hundreds of deaths, you cannot kill yourself there. With two, three, four bullets. There was blood all over the back. But not from the head. None.'

Ranse had stopped listening. His emotions had given up, he stood as cold as ice in the Museum courtyard with its malodour of human waste. He could smell nothing, or feel nothing. Goddard was actually dead. At last he had a real death to confront, to suffer, to be wounded by. But he felt nothing.

E Sousa went on: 'Because of Fragas, I did not ask questions. I was under their watch for a long time. Perhaps they would try to kill me, whoever did this if they found out. Or maybe nobody cares? But for you to know.'

He could see da Cunha walking back. 'Did they bury him there?'

The sergeant held up his broad hands, asking Ranse to stop. 'At the school,' he whispered.

Da Cunha stood waiting on the next line of conversation, but the air was suddenly flat. 'So,' he said. 'We'll keep trying on your behalf.' He turned to the courtyard, to the shuffling ones. 'I don't envy you here. But no doubt,' he sniffed, 'a fantastic garden some day. Adeus, amigo.'

Ranse didn't shake hands. 'Yes,' he said. 'I hope you get out.'

Again he went on foot, declining da Cunha's offer of a lift. He had nowhere to go in a hurry, no one to see. The remains in question were rusting peacefully under the burning sky of Maracacume, and Teppy was further than ever from the happiness she wanted so badly. If she'd killed Goddard for rejecting her, what could he do about it? And who would punish her here, if not Zervos who knew all – no opportunity missed – and would use it against her to the end? Zervos was probably after e Sousa too, bombing the Aguema water tank. The urine was still there in his nostrils. Or not, was it the smell of floating seaweed? He stood beside the ridiculous Portuguese cannon, pointing not to invaders but to a few native boats still in the water. On the beach, a tangle of nets and fish glinted in the sun. It was grander now than the alleged grandeur of the past, anyway. It was suddenly so simple. As though the view around him had changed: the sea, the hills, faces about him, even his own image wasn't the same. He was here now, with or without a reason to stay.

A truck drove past and in the passenger's seat beside Eduardo sat Aggett, looking paler than ever. And he remembered. They'd been to bury Eisner, the maybe-spy who'd been denied a family funeral. And he knew what they'd done: buried his body on the Livre side of the cemetery, if there was such a thing. For the longest of dumb seconds his eyes met Aggett's and only the movement of the hearse broke the link. The truck would not alter speed; but slowly put space between itself and Ranse at the cannon. His understanding of Aggett shrank with it, and he was more confused than ever.

There was something in the mind that was nameless. That was to say: it not only didn't have a name, it couldn't be named. As soon as you tried to give it a name (easy enough, or not) then of course the nameless object became something else, and you had to start over again. It was tempting to think otherwise, but the problem of the nameless thing was insoluble. Unless it was death, of course.

The hotel sat like a dark, unholy frog: the alerting sign was turned off, and the whole place seemed to be hiding inside itself, tightened up with all its limbs pulled in for protection,

197

windows shut and screens drawn to keep out the awful truth: strangers were coming with guns, and killing desire. For the first time he saw the Tropicala in its entirety, undistracted by lights. A place of no luck, where visitors once came to holiday and left as weary souls; and exiles came to stay. *Was it really like this, even in the good times?* For all its concrete, there was no real strength and no charm despite the ages of wear, but on the contrary: it had gathered up its negatives like bad weather and offered the lot, or nothing. You couldn't break the climate here into constituent parts; and the Tropicala – like the thunder rolling in the hills – had to be suffered as it was, along with its careless guests.

Ranse entered the beer garden, where they'd retired for ports and the wrapping of the day into a smooth end. He'd grown to love and hate this slightest of rituals: the one-eyed stupidity of Louis Culpeper, and Aggett's cynicism and the eternal battle between the inebriated da Cunha and Maria Mendonça, who assumed the head of the table lit by a dozen flickering candles.

DA CUNHA   About twenty minutes. They want to save fuel.

AGGETT   In the meantime, call up the dead. Before we join them. Maybe the Livres have captured the power station, amigo. They're clever like that. Or sabotage. That's my guess.

DA CUNHA   If they were that clever, they'd be running the country.

MRS MENDONÇA   They will be soon. (Slaps a mosquito) Vampire.

DA CUNHA   It's just a power failure, take my word.

AGGETT   Pass the port.

MRS MENDONÇA   If this was a revolution, you would have banned alcohol. (Breaks into a sad, cutting laugh at the thought) Imagine that.

DA CUNHA   But there's a revolution going on in Portugal, they didn't ban it. You didn't know?

MRS MENDONÇA   There are always revolutions going on. It was better when the Portuguese were in charge. Thermudo, there was a spirit here.

DA CUNHA	(Scoffs) Saudade, that's all.
RANSE	What's that?
DA CUNHA	Like nostalgia, being homesick. You still suffer it, Courgette. But the empire's gone.

He looked out to sea; and facing him, Eduardo's eyes blinked into the mountains. They were both quiet, thinking against different backdrops. But tonight Eduardo was more reserved than usual. Ranse recalled the first – no, second – night in Viseu: how the beer garden had danced to the confidence of change. Only a fortnight ago, or less. Aggett, e Sousa, the others. And yes, Teppy too.

MRS MENDONÇA	. . . and was twenty times the size of Portugal itself!
AGGETT	That's why it collapsed. And why it's more lively now than ever. It can breathe again.
DA CUNHA	Right. (Triumphantly) These days we give it life!
MRS MENDONÇA	Oh yes, people like me are to blame. Without this hotel, where would you gather to argue? That's the reason you haven't taken over! It's the saudade for all of you. (Thrusting forward) Go on, turn it into the Karl Marx Home for Cripples. But you wouldn't do that! And the Livres, when they come, will be the same.

Yes, he thought, they're impatient for war to develop; for the rush of violence that will end the suspense of it and plunge them all into darkness beyond this dark, and then light. Only one of them had no concern. No, even Culpeper was worrried: in case his pension cheques would be held up. And where was the President tonight, he wondered? With the enigma of Ancora Dias of course.

DA CUNHA	What date is it?
AGGETT	It's the 28th of November 1975.
DA CUNHA	I thought so. By 455 years to the day that our famous navigator, Ferdinand Magellan, entered the Pacific Ocean out there.
AGGETT	Pass the port, again. What about you, fruit-man? (Waits, no reply) Very quiet tonight. Not worried about getting away, I mean?

RANSE	(Uneasy) To where?
DA CUNHA	Exactly. That's why it's advisable to drink now. Only people like Eduardo – the future President – can worry about such dilemmas. Good to see you here Comrade, but so unhappy. (Aside) He pretends he can't hear, the drunk in me.
EDUARDO	Yes, of course. I hear you. Some of us don't want to lose, and so we won't.
DA CUNHA	Speak up, we are among friends.
EDUARDO	At least Mister Ranse understands that, don't you? He doesn't want the others to win.
RANSE	Not particularly.
AGGETT	That's the spirit.
RANSE	(Quietly) Go take a fucking walk.
AGGETT	Where to, old boy?
RANSE	(Brighter, aloud) Gecko tells me I should shave. Otherwise I'll look like a Portuguese collaborator, he says.
CULPEPER	(Rousing, from slumber) And my wife, my wife . . .
DA CUNHA	What?
CULPEPER	She died of a terrible haemorrhage.
MRS MENDONÇA	(Scoffing) Stupid man.
AGGETT	No, he's getting better with age.
MRS MENDONÇA	He's a pest.

He saw lightning clawing at the night, but it couldn't be. The whole sky above them was detached and surreal, balanced on the edge of bon vivre and doom. They held a collective refusal to die, to survive. The lights flickered briefly, and went out.

AGGETT	Too bad.
DA CUNHA	It reminds me. For years I had an electric lamp at my desk. I switched it on and off several times a day for, say, fifteen years. One day the switch broke. It was metal, snapped off. I called the Viseu electrician, a fool with big eyes. He took one look at my lamp and said, 'Senhor! Do you realise what danger you have placed your life in? These wires are

bare, only a fraction of a hair from the switch you touch every day. Every time you turned the light on and off, you were almost electrocuted. It could have happened at any time!' And before my eyes he touched – to show me – the very wires he condemned. He had forgotten to turn off the power. His body, his eyes, went frozen with burning heat and he collapsed in front of me.

CULPEPER What about the lamp?

DA CUNHA I had it fixed, of course. After fifteen years of living so dangerously I wasn't going to take further risks.

AGGETT Bravo.

Beside him, Maria Mendonça responded with the saddest of sighs: from the bellows not of her massive lungs but of her remote, fractured memory. She had heard it before, from a lover whose possibilities had waned. The eyelashes tonight were laden with pre-war mascara; they looked like dark fossils, as though the magic fluid had congealed over all those confused years. At times she would have found it pleasant to say or apparently think of nothing.

MRS MENDONÇA (Quietly) What a pity.

RANSE What?

MRS MENDONÇA That you're not going tonight.

RANSE Where?

MRS MENDONÇA With Zervos. You really are endangering your life here. That other – American – went down like a fly.

RANSE Zervos, where's he going?

MRS MENDONÇA To Darwin, of course. I have a good suspicion that he's flying out tonight. Never to return, as they say in English. I hope they're right.

RANSE And her, Mrs Zervos?

MRS MENDONÇA She's going to have her baby, no doubt. (Pauses) She's pregnant, Mr Ranse.

RANSE A baby. How do you know?

MRS MENDONÇA (Tightly) A woman knows.

She'd jumped her cue. It was a full hour, though still in darkness, when Ranse and the assembled table heard the low drone of the plane climbing off the Viseu runway and heading towards their small, obscure corner of the world. And then: it wasn't the body of Teppy Zervos that filled his swelling mind, the older body that had carried him to brief pleasure with the unknown foetus of Goddard's making inside; nor the mother of two who'd despatched him to eternity; not the suffering woman who'd engaged the sympathy of Eduardo over there and the hapless Peyrot to cover the damage done; or the cruddy husband who might even forgive these convolutions as the price of tropical enterprise. What he saw in his mind – in the glowing candles, at Pojuca – was the smallest gravestone of all. The one with MENDONÇA on it, because the woman beside him was crying her eyes out. He turned away.

Eduardo searched for lights, but the others considered it unnecessary: it grew louder until they were forced to look up, and they weren't sorry to see the hotel lights come on again.

SEVENTEEN

The pillow was like a board, or a hand pressed into the back of his skull. He listened, no sounds of war. The rest of Viseu was sleeping, sleepwalking, asleep on the run; and the immediate dream came back to him. *He was dancing on tables, the dancer must dance. 'Such a lovely number,' said Teppy too.* Why about celebrating when already the day stank of defeat? He rolled over, tugging the pillow to his face. There was a muffled bell, a thud; or was it Eduardo up early and banging the drum at the airport? He'd turned out to be the security chief, an unlikely role. *The waiter at the party wasn't Gecko, but Benny the monkey: stretched into a six-foot orang-utan, with gloves!* He tossed the pillow to the floor, and flecks of dust rose in the light. The birds squawked, and a monkey chatted, and the lawn was attacked daily with shears – and whole days passed with distant mortars heard and rumours of Livre assaults to come. That was all, at a steady pace.

For the moment, he was alone and felt stronger, and knew why. Out there with Aggett and the others, he was threatening his security and losing his judgement. And at Goddard's house, he was working at Sam's edge of madness and risked going over, the closer he got. But cooped up here in the solitude of his Number One room, he was reassessing the idea of freedom. Just as a prisoner sentenced to life in jail could welcome the finality of the term, he thought. The parameters of restraint having been set, the true freedom might begin.

Zervos was gone, so was Teppy. He knew even as he slipped

in the early light from the hotel and scrambled along the beach, and stealthily – arms parting boughs of hibiscus – into the grounds of the Happy Bay Guest House, and standing then on the empty drive. The whole place was deserted; as though a dry, silent flood had swept by and cleaned out the inhabitants. Already the vegetation was taking over.

Ranse stopped. Scurrying from the back were two locals with kitchenware, gardening tools, clothes. Another was chasing them. He was carrying more loot. Ranse hid against the shrubs and allowed them to go. Without detection, he thought.

Already the rooms were a mess. Zervos had flown deliberately low, alerting Viseu that they wouldn't be back. Help yourselves, the engines and flicking lights had signalled. *On her way to the beach, what had she said? That she felt like she was going in twenty directions at once.* It wasn't a fond farewell, but hurried and messy. Ranse waded from one room to another. Tables were missing chairs, and beds mattresses: and chests stood with their drawers open and empty. From ceilings, the cords dangled; already the cold bulbs were gone, and shades and fittings too. The rooms all ended up looking the same, with the same functions and flesh: rented beds to either sleep in or make love on. To dream plans of escape. She wouldn't be back – and there was no note to signal her intentions, or even doubts – but would remain Mrs Zervos: settled in Darwin with two children she loved, and another to come, and a fat erroneous husband always prepared to forgive. They were inseparable, their deceits woven too tightly now to ever come apart. But what sort of life was that? The difficult pleasures and mysteries that kept her going in Viseu wouldn't survive there.

He shifted inwards, hoping like hell these fringes of doubt would stay behind. Old rattan chairs, card tables, lamps were all knocked about by the same flood. And then the first light struck an abandoned mirror in the bedroom. He went in.

It all seemed so long ago. Ranse could almost see her there – in the morning, coming out of night – dressed in an old robe. *Squeezing the cream from a tube and rubbing it into her face, a scene so utterly sexual and domestic: the hand massaging her own flesh, slightly aged but still fine. She'd looked at* herself, flicking her lashes at Goddard's mirror; had seduced herself with the cream, and her own eyes. And then had taken a tissue, and violently and childishly blown her nose simply because she'd earned the right to. Then she had no need of him, or anyone else. And now, of course, he understood why.

Ranse stepped into a broken pile of books, and brushed them aside. And there they were, the diaries. The one thing she knew he'd come looking for. *Which he had, and hadn't.* Or had she simply fled and left them, knowing this time she would have to erase Goddard completely from her life? She had the child, what use were the diaries to her? Or to him? Ranse bent to touch them, and stopped. He'd just received the purest of information, enough to base a life on. He was no longer Goddard's protégé, or next of kin. Ranse felt a sudden need to relieve himself, and went outside.

The empire of Happy Bay sank behind him, a temple to life's insecurities.

Gecko was cutting the hotel lawn. A lizardy hand flexed the clippers into the grass, which offered the briefest resistance and fell; and his own face was being lulled by the repetitive blows. Already the heat was rising, and sweat was dripping onto clippers and lawn. Benny was climbing the trunk of the mango tree. A century of this had passed when he heard Ranse stepping on the path.

'Ah, ah,' he got to his feet.

Ranse kept moving. 'What is it, Gecko?'

'Mrs Mendonça wants to see you, about Senhor Aggett. He went away.'

'What?'

He stopped, and broke into a run to the hotel office.

'Your friend has disappeared,' said Mrs Mendonça. 'Left nothing but a note.' She was sitting on a stool, and handed Ranse an envelope. His name was scratched on it.

Mrs Mendonça descended from her perch and set about other things. 'You might tell me where he is,' she called as she wandered off. 'I gather there's trouble. He's run up 13 000 escudos.'

The light didn't work, and he opened the shutters. Outside, the same Gecko looked up nervously and smiled. He was still clipping away. The sunlight poured in like silver.

'Ranse,' it began. 'There isn't much time, excuse the scrawl. I tried to find you but guess you're out walking – hardly a bright thing to be doing. When you read this, the Livres will be close to the edge of town. They knocked out a few trucks at Pojuca last night – there's no way Fragas will stop them from there. Got the will of the underdogs, and they're well organised. Also they've learned a few tricks – pulling the best Fragas up to Aguema and Boim, there's a hell of a battle going on. And the Central Committee met early today – they've decided to take Galvão and the leaders back to the hills a few miles. But not Dias or da Cunha, who agreed to stay on. (In case you need help, because you will.) That's how they gained power in the first place, from the mountains. To stay in charge you have to keep vacating office! God knows why they bother, but I've decided anyway to find out – I'm going with them. The future president (you know who, waiting for him now) asked me to keep Fragas in the news, though it won't be easy – they've got a single transmitter, that's all. But you asked what I was doing here – I suppose I've been waiting for something like this. They couldn't run a country without trouble. Of course no glory for an old hack in this – but something I thought I'd lost, or handed over to Eisner the unshakable. It's jumped back at me. Don't know what's waiting up there – all I know is what's back in Malta, a slow death, when I intend to make a show of dying at least. The house will keep rotting, as it has for centuries. Get there and use it one day. Which brings me to this – if the Livres can't be stopped, you'd better get da Cunha or Dias to take you to the hospital. I know it's the wrong side of town but you won't make it otherwise, only at Peyrot's side. He's a snivelling creep but they're going to need him, one way or the other. And he won't stray far from the medicine chest. Sorry I won't see you, unless you turn up soon. Eduardo should be here any minute. He said eight, and it's five to. I'm fishing for things to say, realise. When we first met, I thought you were as weak as two sticks tied with a piece of string – still not sure what's holding you together, though (unwisely) I had a crack at it. It's a mystery, at your age.

And the Goddard business, I hope you've sorted that out – it's not hard to understand, for me. Death is what happens when you can't decide where you want to go – so maybe this is attempted suicide, since I've got no intention of being killed. Just shaking things up a bit. They might say I'm supporting the Fragas, though god knows why – but it's true I admire their crazy belief in themselves. I won't apologise for not saying farewell, in case we meet again. But that could be embarrassing too. There's great activity now, must go.' No signature, but a few more lines: 'Check the top drawer. Teppy gave it to me yesterday, coming back from the beach. Said to give it to you after she'd gone. Sorry I didn't tell you in advance, but I'm as good as my word. I couldn't see Zervos giving you a lift, anyway. But she's right, you might have to use it.' And a postscript, dashed off: 'Eduardo sends his regards. I thought you two didn't get on.' He looked up, and saw Aggett pushing things together again. And pulling them apart. And could only think of Mrs Mendonça's complaint: that for the first time in his well-mannered life, Aggett had rushed off without paying his bill.

He smiled at the handwriting. So it was Aggett who'd written the Mujumna note, from Malta of course. The scrawl was the same, up and down and wasting away; and he'd thrown it to oblivion. Another of those pieces Aggett carried in his wallet, and had given to Teppy one fine day. Had she placed it as a tribute to Goddard, with a yellow flower; or just to throw his nephew Ranse off the scent if things ever got that far. So he'd suspect Aggett, of all people.

Ranse went to the drawer, and opened it. Teppy's gun was lying next to a box of bullets. It was a killing tool, and a statement of fact – that she knew, that Ranse knew what she'd done. She couldn't have risked Customs but could have dropped it overboard and destroyed the evidence for all time. Ranse could never kill anyone, as she already had with this. He closed the drawer, and moved away. On the chair beside the shutters was Goddard's last diary, and he went to it. There was no blood and the pages were white and not Wednesday yellow, but it was still the incomplete diary of his mountain dream. On the bedside table, he found a pencil and began to write.

'And my diary died; lacked food, fuel and idle gossip. Who reads this – Nicholas, I suppose, will come – knows I'm no longer in Viseu. Only a man hanging onto his years knows this fairly simple dilemma, I came to be inspired and stayed far too long. So now it's Europe – after an insufferable flight, I'll be lost to Inhumas forever. With a ladybird crawling inside the sealed window at my elbow, trying to avoid the tropical sun. I'll always wonder how it got there in the first place . . .'

Ranse stopped, and looked at her. She'd either grown or the stool had shrunk. 'I don't normally ask,' said Mrs Mendonça. 'But your friend . . .'

'Aggett's gone to the mountains,' he said quickly. 'He'll be back in a couple of days.'

She nodded, seemed afraid to say more. And he saw it wasn't greed or even curiosity in her eyes.

'Don't worry,' she said. 'You can stay here. You should have gone back with Zervos, of course. But you didn't know.'

She paused, waiting for an answer. Ranse said nothing.

'Excuse me,' she began to rise. 'I must start preparing for the lunch.'

'I'll be back,' he said.

As he walked around the side of the hotel, Ranse looked into the dining room and there was Julião Dias. With his daughter. They were seated at the window, but paid no attention to him. Ancora was crying. The tears were streaming down her face, and he wondered if she'd stayed deliberately?

Ranse hurried past, his pulse leading him on.

In the streets, things seemed normal enough: as though the intensity of whatever struggle was coming would be restricted to those directly involved in it, and the lives of those below or to one side would remain intact, or at worst shaken loosely. But as he got closer, it changed. The footpath sellers tried feebly to grab his attention, and Chinese traders were taking stock down from their shelves. A small boy stood watching, folding his hands behind his back like an inspector.

He stopped at the gym, and went inside. At one end was da Cunha's movie screen, but there was no projector. The cupboards were dark, and Culpeper's rusty dumbells and bars hung off the walls. And leather straps for skipping. There was something else, under a loose cover. Da Cunha's printery. The decrepit machine that stamped out the *Imagem* was having a rest. Ranse put the sheet back, and left. On the footpath a man came up and tipped out what looked like a bag of pearls; but they were only mock, cheap ones. Ranse looked back: the man was popping them into his mouth, like pills. A food stall fire glowed. He could see activity, but the scale of everything seemed reduced. The everyday people of Viseu were backing off, just in case.

The Museum was deserted.

When he got there, the gates were bent: one sloping inwards, the other out. There was nobody in sight. Ranse stepped into the foul courtyard, where entire families had managed to cook, eat, wash, defecate, urinate and possibly make love. The gates were broken and the captives had dissolved back into Viseu. The guards were needed elsewhere, to fight. And wherever he'd gone, Oscar e Sousa was not here. Clutching his nose, Ranse turned and walked out. His one thought had been to free the sergeant.

The lanes outside were grubby too, but the activity that soiled them had stopped – only the odd person shuffled by. Perhaps it was the invisible smoke he could smell. Of the unknown, advancing enemy: and who would survive the phalanx of retributions, and flying shells? He thought again of Ancora Dias; and how to break through the silence that had brought them strangely together and kept them apart. He wanted to see things as they were; but things kept changing. And the people of Inhumas tumbled on their own happy way to ruin.

As he left the backstreets and the water came into view, Ranse saw a crowd gathered on the beach. And further out, past the breakwater, a white yacht: with crinkled sails flopping at the mast. He could just make out a single figure on deck.

He didn't hurry. An unexpected visitor had arrived, and could afford to be kept waiting in the order of things as they were. He was still a long way off.

Gradually then, Ranse worked his own way through the heart

of Viseu, past the abandoned ice-cream stall, down by the ancient cannon and towards the beach-front; catching sight of the lone yacht, then a native boat moving like a waterbird towards it to investigate, then the linking of the two craft, docking sideways to converse; then a gap, widening into isolation and Ranse – starting to move quickly, breaking into a run – could see the sails rising up the mast, being pulled by the lone sailor and the yacht turning briefly into shore and then in a broad sweep back out to Sea and sailing off. Away from this place, and war.

He was moving at speed. But it was a curve he surrendered to and then was only jogging and fell back to a walk. The yacht was leaving faster than it had come, going anywhere but here. It was useless.

Da Cunha hurried to meet him, breaking the caked sand with urgency. He'd never seen the Minister for Information and Propaganda move so quickly, and Ranse almost laughed at him. Da Cunha stopped with straining lungs, clutching a bottle of whisky and a carton of cigarettes. The colourful shirt was sprayed from the canoe ride to the yacht. He looked at Ranse carefully, and regretfully.

'Australian,' he said. 'He wanted fuel, and water. I told him, impossible. About the fighting. You've heard?'

'Yes.'

'He hadn't, of course. Crazy, eh?'

'Did he say anything?'

'He looked over here, the town. I don't think he believed me. But something must have, troubled him. He started to lift the sails. I told him about you.'

'What did he say?'

'He said he couldn't wait. Take these.'

Ranse watched the yacht floating on the infinite space of sea; the Sea was lifeless and it was taking ages. He didn't want to know who he was, what he looked like, where exactly he was going. It would have been just another swing, back to uncertainty.

'Thanks.'

'I told him you didn't smoke.'

'But I drink.'

'Yes. Are you mad?' asked da Cunha. 'I sent him away. I didn't try to stop him.'

Ranse looked out. 'He must have been pretty stupid, coming here in the first place. Australian, you sure?'

'Oh yes.'

'And he didn't know about the trouble?'

'No.'

'Going back to Darwin?'

'Yes.'

'Good. He'll probably never go sailing again.'

'Maybe not.' Da Cunha had lost the point.

'You want a drop?' said Ranse, turning the damp bottle in his hand. 'It's much better than port.'

'Better than getting out?'

But already da Cunha was acting; knew that he'd thrown off all visions of escape and saw the lone sailor as a fool, or worse: a pathological killer who couldn't have been trusted.

'Yes, it is.'

'But they've all gone to the mountains, the others. Aggett too.'

'They'll be back.'

Da Cunha frowned. 'You must be crazy. The Livres are almost here.'

'It helps to be a little crazy,' said Ranse.

'Good,' da Cunha replied, and smiled out to sea. 'When our Queen Maria was fleeing Napoleon's force – in 1807 – do you know what she told the admirals?'

'What?'

'Don't go so fast, she said. People will think we're running away.'

Ranse wanted to smile and tried to, but first he needed a drink. 'Come on,' he said.

Sergeant e Sousa lit a cigarette, and puffed at it several times; and passed it on to the man beside him. From the boiling hillside, he watched. The military headquarters was ablaze: either the Livres had already come and gone, or the remaining Fragas had set fire to the place and left. The small guard hut was engulfed. The barracks behind it were smoking; not on fire everywhere, but smouldering through wooden pores. And on the rise behind the drill ground, the rest of the compound was already in ruins: the skeleton of black uprights and galvanised roofs had collapsed inwards. *They'd done it themselves, perhaps.* He could feel his heart and lungs thumping against what it meant, colliding with it. *On whose side this time? Soldiering was work, he'd told the boys. Sometimes it was political – generals became ministers, and presidents even – but in the end the soldiers had to fight with the same unfortunate zeal that priests had to pray. And no use making feeble excuses about defence. To survive from one war to the next, you have to kill.* Behind him, the scrub rustled and e Sousa felt his finger tense on the trigger. It was only his scout and they were good friends. *Sometimes you had to kill your friends, that was part of soldiering too. And even though it happened rarely, when it did it wasn't possible to understand what you were doing or why. It was a mystery to a soldier, a survivor.* The black smoke was curling now from the barracks – the rows of cramped bunks, going up inside – and he could smell his own body, his bare arm stinking in the sun. It must have been close to midday, or even past it. Sergeant e Sousa signalled to his small band of followers on the hillside and set off down to Viseu proper, without a sound. *We are very mobile, he thought, very mobile.*

They returned to da Cunha's house over the water, on stilts. It wasn't the Happy Bay Guest House and it wasn't Goddard's house on the hill, but the sea swam almost at their feet. Half house, half boat.

'He didn't know what he wanted.'

'Goddard wanted to die, that's the main thing isn't it?'

'In suicide perhaps,' said da Cunha, already flopped in a chair.

Ranse turned back from the sea, and frowned: 'Da Cunha . . .'

'What?'

'You set up the meeting with e Sousa, at the Museum. Didn't you?'

Da Cunha sat forward: 'He wanted to see you.'

'And you knew why.'

He shrugged, and slumped back. 'In Viseu, we have a saying. People in trouble always have sayings. Here we say a fly doesn't sit on a man's cheek in a cyclone.'

'Meaning?'

'When something's wrong it doesn't make sense.'

'So you know, about Teppy?'

Da Cunha swirled the whisky, and gulped it down. 'I know about death, that's all. He wanted to die, you're right. He came here looking for peace, and all he got was war. Which drives us all crazy in the end.' He was gazing out. 'Look at Eduardo, they were such happy children. Now the brother's dead and also the sister, and he hardly talks to us. And running to the mountains again, to find what he's looking for. And you, the fighting has upset your life. It's too late for revenge, as always. Are you looking for justice? Or solutions, in Viseu? We don't even have a government today.' He paused, and looked up. 'Your uncle was wise because he got in early. Before the rush.'

The needle clunked down, and out of the spitting disc came a male voice. Light and pure, a piano too. Da Cunha grinned, 'Stardust.' It was Hoagy Carmichael and he hummed the tune. *We are attempting to survive our time so we may live into yours, thought Ranse.* An odd record to play in the burning heat of November, in the middle of the day.

'Won't they get you, da Cunha?'

'The chief poet of the revolution?' he asked. 'In Russia you know, poets are considered dangerous. They even kill them. But not here.'

'Aggett said we should go, to the hospital. It's safer there.'

'No, no,' said da Cunha. 'For you, the Tropicala is the best place of all. Maria's the one. She'll give you food and drink, and a bed. A psychic healer, that woman. And she's right – the battles always end at hotels, where the revolutions begin. It comes from Portugal, I think. Once in sixteen years they had forty-four governments and twenty-five uprisings, and three dictatorships. War's a habit, so is drinking. They won't touch the hotel, but I have reasons for staying here. Too many projects. And besides, it's peaceful.'

'But safe, really?'

He poured a ridiculous whisky, and held it towards a pile of writing. 'Peace and safety are not always the same thing. Maybe not a true poet,' said da Cunha, 'so they'll put me under arrest. But I can get on with my history. With the past.'

'Is it worth it?'

'Who knows?' He stood, returning the needle to the start. 'A man's real history is unknown to him, like all history is. Otherwise it wouldn't make sense. And besides, what could I do in the mountains?'

'Fight . . .'

Thermudo da Cunha lifted his arm to Ranse's shoulder and rested it there. 'No,' he smiled, 'it's past that now. Sometimes you think a war's over and you move on to the next, but the first one isn't really over at all. And then you're fighting two wars at once. That's what's happening here. We're caught between wars, and myths. There's no use fighting with guns. Whoever comes up with the right set of myths, they win. And that,' he whispered, 'is the true pattern of colonialism. It never leaves us. Cyclones and earthquakes can't blow it away. Also my dog is missing.'

He stood with the bottle, waiting for his thoughts to catch up. There were a couple of bad decades to contend with; and a few ratty tears were forming. Ranse looked away.

'I saw a very old grave – very small, a baby's – at Pojuca.'

Da Cunha walked unsteadily to the desk. 'That's quite possible.' He smiled and held up a glass bowl with tropical fish in it. 'My early warning system. Do you know what a tsunami is?'

'A tidal wave,' said Ranse.

'Japanese.'

He put down the bowl and picked up the whisky, and poured again. There wasn't much left. 'All of Viseu will be struck by a tsunami, within a year or two. The fish will panic when they hear it. So there's no point in heading for the mountains, or anywhere else, is there?'

Da Cunha held up his drink. 'To my colleague, the new Minister for Agriculture. Oh well, very briefly. But in the hotel, you'll be saved.'

Ranse took a final glimpse at the sea, as calm as treachery; with a curve on it so large you could set out and never come back. But really, where would you go? He thought of the lone sailor again, wondering what fears were ploughing through his confused mind. *In no danger out there: no wild storms or cyclones, none of that; but hell, he must have been wondering.* Ranse looked across at da Cunha, playing with his fish; smiling with all the quietness in the world.

'Though I dream in vain,' he mimed, confusing part of his own youth with da Cunha's decadent record on the player.

But the justice of dreams is all.

EIGHTEEN

Ranse spun in the sand, no shadows. And his balance had gone, falling sideways and over; into the soft, hard shore of Viseu and thumping his head so firmly that he sobered and woke up, and stood up in the same instant. He shook and rinsed his face at the water's edge. Around him was the sheer beauty of the island: where had he been for the last two weeks if not here? In the heroic past, of course.

He tried to smile: a perspective has no power against your on-the-spot reactions, at least that's worth considering. And out there – as distant as survival itself – not the lonely yacht but a huge white tanker buried on the horizon: the bulk hidden below, just the superstructure and steel rigging of a ghost ship moving on. *To China perhaps. Or Japan. The perspective, on this quiet lunch-time in Viseu. Capital of nowhere.* And seeing in his mind again, the yachtsman: now safely at sea and already concocting tales for his Darwin clubmates, of how he actually helped to decide the outcome. *Or his role in Dance's downfall, funny I thought.* Or maybe he'd shut up, freeze and not be able to tell a soul.

That would be his price for not staying, just as Ranse knew it would be his price for not going.

Before reaching the door, he could see Julião Dias at the far table. He was unserved, gazing through an empty window into the deserted beer garden. His hand stroked a clean knife against the cloth, and tiny marbles of sweat formed at his temples and down his arms. Which didn't run, but sat there growing patiently under the silent blades of the fan. He looked malarial, not afraid of dying because he might have been anyway. Ancora wasn't with him. Ranse had never seen Dias without her. *Or with the mother, except once in a dream: as the cart carried a humble coffin into the orange grove. It must have been Portugal, or Spain. 'Be careful!' the old woman wept, as he'd emerged from the half-lit shadows. 'Better a dirty joke than be careful,' he replied.* At all costs she had to be kept from the Livres.

There was only one other guest, Louis Culpeper. He was embattled more than seated just inside the doorway. Ranse couldn't decide if the old bugger was the guardian of the entire room, or simply positioned for a quick exit. It was too late now for gossip.

He was about to sit, bending with hands on the tablecloth when Culpeper scowled. 'Go away!' He held a fork with a large piece of fish on it and shook the lot in Ranse's face. 'Get lowst!'

Across the room Dias gave a sympathetic nod but when Ranse responded with raised eyebrows, the Minister turned away.

'What's wrong with you?'

Culpeper lifted his chin. 'Something about *you*. To do with all this, I can tell. Otherwise you wouldn't be here.'

'You're here, aren't you?'

'I *live* here, dammit!'

'Well, perhaps I do too.'

'Get out!' the old man growled, fish going into his mouth. 'Gwet lowst.'

Ranse wouldn't go far. He sat at the adjoining table. Aggett had been right: the old coot was a nitpicker who'd come here to live in savage retirement when he should have been playing bowls. And could only see half of Viseu anyway, peering out of that patchless eye. He was a total fraud.

'Pah,' he said, and went back to eating.

A clipping reply, it was Gecko attacking the lawn. Comforting everyone's nerves. And then Mrs Mendonça appeared, moving in white like a swan. She was insisting still on starched cloths, and heavy silver for clinking against the Tropicala china in times of stress. They'd almost run out of edibles.

'Fish, scrambled eggs and coffee,' she said. 'And fruit, same as before.'

'Thanks,' he said, taking it.

She stood there, like some immortal statue. The name of Mendonça could never be defeated, he thought, in argument or battle. But she could be, of course. She turned to go, then stopped.

'Will you be staying?'

'For a while. I'll see what happens.' He looked up, and nodded across the room. 'Where's the girl?'

'She's gone to wash her face, and eyes. It's better . . .'

Mrs Mendonça wanted to say more, or perhaps nothing at all.

'Why are they all like this?' he said.

'I don't know. I wasn't born here.'

She nodded with slight formality, and moved off gracefully through the tables.

Ranse looked at the fish, pulled from the sea across the road. He'd tried it grilled, poached, battered, beaten, without lemons. And now he chewed for bones, without the luxury of bread. They'd run out of flour too. Perhaps old Culpeper would choke to death, he thought with half a smile.

'Lucky you,' Aggett would have jibed in a week's time. 'What did you order?'

'*Camaroes com vinho do porto.*'

'Which is . . .' Culpeper asked.

'Prawns with white wine.'

Aggett grinned. 'I'm afraid I'll have to call you a bloody liar, Ranse. You wouldn't know one end of a camaro from the other.'

'But you forget,' he interrupted, 'I graduated in science. Once there was a naturalist who dined happily on crocodiles and rodents.'

'The quacks collect in little circles, eh?'

'I normally dine alone,' said Culpeper.

Ranse ate all before him – an act of tidying, more than hunger – then took time over coffee. The dark liquid sat smooth in the cup, the fumes rising to his nostrils. The quiet was making him tense. He looked at Culpeper; at his age and dogged persistence, born from lifting weights and putting them down again. He clearly had nowhere to go, nothing to do. A man like that couldn't be threatened by death, thought Ranse. He lived alone with one eye and waiting for a pension cheque, in a dream world which he had every intention of continuing after his earthly departure: so that his harmless rumours and lies would live forever, and when challenged wouldn't be defended with a gun, but with another scowl and a smile.

But the other: Julião Dias. He was a curious study in fear. The others had gone, successfully fled the coming attack or coup or whatever they faced in the day. He waited on, sweating like a well-groomed pig in a fazed hotel. And his daughter, Ancora had gone where? She couldn't be safe alone up there, not safer than here: inside Maria Mendonça's crumbling walls and even that would push her luck to the edge. But at the Livres' hands, she'd be raped, murdered, finished off and dumped into the sea for sharks. There was almost no choice, to hide in the hills of course.

Ranse was facing that eternal fade without her. An awful vacuum sat there: opposite the Finance Minister, who wasn't worried by that. But by something else. Wearing the knife out with worry, rubbing it anxiously one minute and absently the next. His face was now a bath of sweat. It sat there, for Ranse to see. Dias made no effort to hide his fear, or his illness. And then Ranse, from out of nowhere, thought of the lone sailor as murderer; and suddenly saw Dias for what he really was. And saw Ancora leaving her father in tears to catch up with the Fragas in the foothills. Yes, that was it. Dias was a traitor. He had every reason to be here, waiting for them to come. And she had none, or worse.

Staring into his coffee: at the final, comsuming lie. As though by one of da Cunha's tremors, he'd been shifted over the wasted years from his own reality to one side. He had been taken away, or had taken himself away from the centre of it. He'd been tripped, and tricked; fooled by misplaced events and rash influences: and now the price was falling from the sky – well past Goddard's house on the hill – and was right on target.

Ranse gulped his coffee, and Culpeper looked up as he quickly left the room.

'I thought that's what you'd do.'

He ran onto the lawn. A green plateau of blades, and Gecko was standing at the other end. He was calling Ranse with a childish wave. 'What?' he asked, but turned and saw clearly. Down the beach, a fire was burning in the early afternoon sky: the heat was intense, shaking the blueness around it and above. At the base of the spiralling flames was da Cunha's stilt house. Already pieces had fallen away, to a sizzling end in the sea; like a burning pier at the beach, on a sunny day. And the monkey jumped in glee, or awe.

'Senhor Ranse, see!'

It couldn't be. 'The Livres?'

'Yes, yes. Oh terrible, it's . . .' Gecko leapt up and down, looking in all directions and lost for words.

But it was too soon for that. And they would come, were coming anyway from the other side. Ranse watched the flames gushing deliberately into the Viseu sky: strange it should end, how much he had enjoyed it, how totally his own life was being changed. The house on stilts was burning, was already under thick black smoke and da Cunha was somewhere inside.

'The Livres, senhor! You must go!'

For the first time Gecko touched Ranse: it was like being touched by an alien, a friendly one. 'You go now.'

He looked at Gecko, and stopped.

'No, no,' the old man said, 'they don't hurt us. But you go, Senhor Ranse. Yes.' He brushed his chin. 'And shave. Beard no good. And go . . .'

Ranse was already there. He took Gecko's hand by the wrist, and pushed his wallet into it. 'Tell them in Darwin what I've done,' he said. 'Okay?'

Gecko nodded, with a shaky smile. They turned and saw the remains of da Cunha's island house crumbling into the sea. 'No,' said Ranse suddenly.

He spoke carefully to Gecko, who was trembling: 'Tell them Mister Ranse died in the fire. You understand? Burned to death.'

The old man looked at him – absurdly – and there was no

point in explaining. Or time to waste. He couldn't imagine Gecko surviving the onslaught, with nothing to protect and nothing to hide.

And then the old gardener fumbled in his pocket and dug out a shell, and gave it to him. For luck, of course.

He sprinted through the hotel, pushed open the door and spun around the room. The sun was belting in, Ranse pulled the screens and turned on the light. It didn't work. Could see enough, had to keep moving. Couldn't stop. He ducked to the basin: for soap, towel, razor. Shit! Must shave, no time now. Four bars of it, important to keep clean. Just like Goddard, he grubbed. Same, same; but different this time. After a certain point, no need to go forward or back. He was rising to freedom, embracing it, bypassing that death palace on the hill. Could do better than that, the books could rot. And landed next to the dresser, pulled the drawer open: the gun. He stopped, and looked at it. There was no point, in that; or perhaps now more than ever? He shut the drawer. Opened the others: underwear, shirts, jeans, socks, pulling them to the floor. The boots. Shined by Gecko, with love. A notebook, pens; some batteries might be handy. For the first time, planted at the centre of his own life. And what of Aggett, and Eduardo: would they wait for him, would they embrace his new spirit? And the others, the children most of all. To find out what Goddard hadn't bothered to, never taught him to. Ranse saw the diary on the bedside table. And wouldn't be needing it. Everything was fresh, from now on. With the others, and her too. Not lumped together with those stupid or brave enough to stay. And cold up there, grab a coat. He crossed the room, and opened the wardrobe.

The face came forward. From the shadow of jackets and he imagined a smile, of recognition alone. He didn't see the knife, the blade in the darkness as another might have; in fear. It was Ancora Dias, hiding from the Livres in his Number One room. In all of his thirty years he'd never seen a face like hers, coming towards his with a smile that held neither love nor kindness nor humour: it wore determination. As much as his eyes tried to engage hers, as fast as his brain could bring itself to identify her intentions and engage her eyes to divert the smile into love or fear, she could not be stopped. And beneath the clothes he imagined too that she was naked, and as the second passed his whole life didn't flash past but her body did: her lower lip the fuller, the chin that couldn't stop coming forward as though tumbling from a cliff edge, and her perfectly conical breasts, dark in the darkness and still dark as they emerged from the clothes that wrapped her body and were his own. They were for the hills, the mountains, for all the years to come. And in front of all – one ahead of that silver glint of light, the other pushing it – the two arms of Ancora Dias said more about her at that moment than all the words he wanted to put in her mouth. *There is love in Inhumas.* The arms above the elbows, where woman is defined: the flesh was suspended not from the bone, but in air like two javelins from the warm shoulders and the heart. It was a body in full flight, like an arrow classical and native at once; and it swelled from the shadows, and her teeth like marble shone in the blade. They suggested freedom, honesty, no doubts. At any moment her smile would change, and her eyes would acknowledge his in the time it took to blink; and they would both flare their eyelids for another moment and then squeeze them tightly together. And then they would go to the mountains. But there was room for one brief memory: being whipped about the legs as a boy, by a man with bull-rushes. He'd been late for supper, and Goddard was angry.